Discovery Guide to West Africa

The Niger and Gambia River Route

by Kim Naylor

999 January 5, 1990

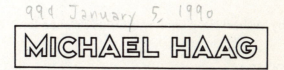

If I was a cassowary,
On the plain of Timbuktu,
I would eat a missionary,
Skin and bones and hymn book too.
          —with thanks to Uncle Peter

Michael Haag also publishes guides to East Africa, Zimbabwe, Egypt, Cairo, Alexandria, Rajasthan, Eastern Turkey, Aegean and Mediterranean Turkey, Greece, etc.

Please send for our complete list:
Michael Haag Limited
PO Box 369
London NW3 4ER
England

Discovery Guide to West Africa, second edition
Text and photographs © 1989 by Kim Naylor

Cover design by Colin Elgie, cover photograph by Kim Naylor

Printed in Great Britain by litho at the Bath Press, Lower Bristol Road, Bath BA2 3BL

Published by Michael Haag Limited, PO Box 369, London NW3 4ER, England

ISBN 0 902743 67 8

CONTENTS

ABOUT THIS GUIDE

The Sahel is a belt of semi-arid land stretching the width of Africa and sandwiched between the Sahara to the north and the tropical forest of black Africa to the south. This Guide is about the Sahel region of West Africa.

For centuries the curiosity of Europeans was excited by this mysterious and impenetrable quarter of the Dark Continent. It was rumoured that its soil was rich with gold, that the kings lived in unimaginable opulence, that Timbuktu — referred to as the Capital of the Interior — was a dazzling spectacle in the heart of the desert and that a great river cut through these lands and served as a highway for boats carrying extremely profitable merchandise.

In the 18th and 19th C explorers were sent out to search for the elusive great river (the River Niger) and legendary Timbuktu. Their adventures are tales of courage, heroism and determination and their accounts of places show that surprisingly little has changed in this part of the world since they first ventured there. For these reasons the book includes many of the descriptions recorded by such great explorers as Mungo Park, Gordon Laing, Rene Caillie and Heinrich Barth.

But though the book does provide stories of discovery and a historical background to the western Sahel, its main purpose is as a practical guide for travellers wishing to visit this wonderful part of Africa that includes present-day northern Nigeria, Niger, Mali, Senegal and Gambia.

The route outlined starts at Kano — or Agadez or Zinder for those who have crossed the Sahara and do not want to go as far south as Kano. Roads lead west from these three ancient caravan towns to Niamey on the banks of the majestic River Niger. From here the huge arc of the river is followed northwest, passing by Timbuktu — a place still synonymous with remoteness — and then southwest to Bamako. West of here are Senegal and Gambia which are on the Atlantic Ocean.

Much of this route is the one more or less taken by Mungo Park on his second African journey in 1805 (though both his expeditions began in Gambia — thus

he travelled from west to east — and his second one ended with his death at Bussa which is downstream of Niamey). A summary of his travels and those of the other renowned explorers of this region have been included as an appendix at the end of the book.

This Guide begins with a *Background* chapter which helps prepare you for the journey. Each subsequent chapter then marks a stage along your way and is usually followed by a *Practical Information* section with advice on where to stay and eat and how to continue along the route. Because of inflation, devaluations, the replacing of old currencies by new, etc, it is impossible to give reliably detailed costs for hotels, bush taxis and steamers along the way. Instead, as the Guide takes you from one country into another you will find on the first page for that country some general information about costs, as well as much basic information about population, language, the political system and so on.

To help with the next edition, the reader is asked to send information and comments to the *General Editor, Discovery Guide to West Africa, Michael Haag Limited, PO Box 369, London NW3 4ER, England*. Thank you.

PRACTICAL BACKGROUND

Geography

Nearly all of the area of West Africa covered in this book lies between the latitudes of 12 degrees and 18 degrees. Altitude is under 500 metres, except for a few hilly outcrops such as the Bandiagara Escarpement, Hombori Hills and Manding Highlands of Mali which rise to between 500 and 1000 metres, and the Aïr Plateau in Niger where several mountains are between 1500 and 2000 metres.

The divide between desert and savannah

Draw a line from east to west through Timbuktu and generally speaking there is desert to the north of this line, though in Niger the desert reaches further south. Below the 'Timbuktu line' is semi-arid savannah grassland which becomes less barren the further south one progresses. Parts of western Mali, Senegal and Gambia are in fact luxuriant. The annual flooding of the Inland Delta of the River Niger results in extensive marshland.

Climate

The best time to visit the part of West Africa documented in this book is between October/November and February/March. This period is relatively cool and dry (see the temperature chart) and as it follows the wet weather (most of the rain falls in July, August and September) the land is at its lushest. Also this is when the River Niger steamers are in operation.

The steamer season

From March the weather grows uncomfortably hot and as the rainy season draws near the sandstorms gradually become stronger and more frequent. May/June heralds the first light showers. At the height of the rains the humidity is high: in Mali for example it averages 80 percent in August.

The harmattan, a dry northeasterly wind, blows during the winter months. At times it is unpleasant as it stirs up the dust and leaves the sky hazy.

The motoring season

Many of the roads are seasonal and some may well continue to be impassable during the months succeeding the rains. Most notable are those in the Inland Delta region between Timbuktu and Mopti in Mali. Seek up-to-date and on-the-spot information whenever possible. Avoid the Sahara between June and mid-September/October as this is when the heat and the sandstorms are at their worst.

The River Niger

The source of the River Niger is in the Fouta Djalon Highlands of Guinea, near the eastern border of Sierra Leone. From here, only 240 kms from the Atlantic, it pushes northeast to the southern limits of the Sahara before turning east then southeast to the Gulf of Guinea where it discharges its waters into the ocean through the numerous streams of the Niger Delta. Thus the course of the River Niger forms a huge arc. From source to mouth it measures 4160 kms, which makes it Africa's third longest river after the Nile and the Zaire (Congo).

For many centuries the Niger has been the great highway of the Sahel and West Africa. For the medieval kingdoms of Mali and Songhai it provided all-important trading links. In the 18th and 19th C European explorers were sent in search of the **West African lifeline** mysterious Niger, the course and location of which baffled contemporary geographers. Today the Niger continues to be the lifeline and means of communication for millions of people.

In the latter half of the Tertiary Period the Upper Niger, known as the Joliba, was linked to the River Senegal. A dry period followed which resulted in a barrier of sand forming between the two rivers. Consequently the Upper Niger changed its course and flowed northeast into Lake Arouane, the southern part of which used to extend to the area now covered by Mali's Inland Delta region. During the Quarternary Period the climate became wetter. To the east fast flowing streams cut their paths southwards from the Adrar des Iforas and Aïr regions of the Sahara and joined up as one big river near present day Gao. From here the Lower Niger, as it is known, headed south towards the sea. During the same wet period Lake Arouane overflowed and a river channelled its way east and met up with the Lower Niger at Gao. Thus the link between the Upper and Lower Nigers was created and the course of the River Niger as we know it was formed. Another dry period followed: the original headwaters of the Lower Niger dried up, as did Lake Arouane — though Lake Debo and the Inland Delta (the region from Segu to just east

TEMPERATURE CHART

	Jan	Feb	Mar	Apr	May	Jun	Jul	Aug	Sep	Oct	Nov	Dec
Kano	36 9	38 11	41 14	42 19	41 21	38 19	34 19	33 18	34 19	35 16	37 13	35 11
Agadez	29 10	33 13	38 17	41 21	44 25	43 24	41 24	38 23	40 23	39 20	35 15	32 12
Niamey	34 16	36 18	39 22	41 26	41 27	38 25	34 24	32 22	34 23	36 23	37 19	34 15
Gao	30 14	33 18	37 21	40 25	43 28	41 27	38 25	35 24	38 24	39 22	37 20	32 16
Timbuktu	31 13	34 15	38 19	41 22	43 26	42 27	38 25	34 24	38 24	40 24	38 18	32 14
Mopti	30 15	32 16	37 19	40 22	41 25	38 25	35 23	31 23	33 24	34 24	34 19	32 16
Bamako	33 17	36 20	39 24	39 26	39 26	35 27	31 23	30 23	32 22	34 22	35 19	33 18
Kayes	38 12	42 15	45 18	46 21	46 22	43 20	38 19	35 20	37 20	39 19	40 16	39 13
Banjul	32 15	32 16	35 17	33 18	32 19	32 22	30 23	29 22	30 22	32 22	32 18	32 16

The above chart shows the average monthly maximum and minimum Celsius temperatures of towns along the route. To convert Celsius into Fahrenheit multiply the Celsius by 9, then divide by 5, then add 32. To convert Fahrenheit into Celsius, subtract 32, then multiply by 5, then divide by 9.

of Timbuktu) are relics of this once huge Saharan lake.

Nowadays the annual rains cause the River Niger to flood the Inland Delta and the area affected by this inundation is the size of England and Wales.

Navigating the Niger

The Niger is navigable over three sections, though only the first two can take larger vessels. Moving west to east, first there is the stretch between Kouroussa in Guinea to Bamako in Mali. A boat goes from Kankan on the Milo tributary to Bamako between the months of July and October/November. Second there is the 1500-km long section from Koulikoro, 57 kms north of Bamako, to Ansongo, 95 kms south of Gao (the Sotuba rapids just below Bamako prevent navigation direct from the Malian capital). A steamer service operates between Koulikoro and Gao during the full-flood months and between Mopti and Gao during the semi-flood period. The Labbezenga rapids below Ansongo interrupt navigation. Third is the stretch from Niamey, capital of Niger, to Gaya on the Niger-Benin border. It may be possible to go all the way from Gaya to Port Harcourt on the Niger delta, but this would depend on border formalities and the situation at Kainji Dam in Nigeria.

A source of food

Apart from being an avenue of communication, the Niger is also a source of food. The river is richest in fish in the Inland Delta/lacustrine region. In a good year in Mali alone nearly 200 million kilos of fish are landed from the River Niger and its biggest tributary the Bani. But in recent years the catches have been lean and the Bozo, the tribe traditionally associated with fishing, are now more dependant on the land than normal.

It is estimated that there are 200 species of fish in the Niger. The Nile perch (lates niloticus), nicknamed Le Capitaine, is the largest and most delicious fish; lung fish (protopterus annectens) and alestes (alestes macrolepidotus) also figure importantly in diets. Some 70 percent of fish landed are dried or smoked and in many of the villages along the banks there are small earth ovens where you can see the process in action.

Health

This section offers some helpful information, but you

should consult your doctor for further details before your departure. Relevant books include *The Traveller's Health Guide* by A C Turner, *Stay Alive in the Desert* by K E M Melville and *Preservation of Personal Health in Warm Climates* issued by the Ross Institute, Keppel Street, London (Tel: 01-636 8636). To be in good health is a great advantage when travelling in Africa. Not only are you better conditioned to cope with rough travel, but also you are less susceptible to disease and sickness.

Vaccinations, etc

Vaccinations, inoculations or tablets are officially recommended to help prevent travellers to Gambia, Mali, Niger, Nigeria and Senegal contracting cholera, malaria, typhoid, polio and yellow fever. In some cases courses of vaccination, etc, are ideally started at least two months before departure. In other cases all you will need is a booster to regain protection if you have been vaccinated in recent years. So it is best to see your doctor at an early stage.

Cholera is contracted through contaminated food and water. Prevention consists of either one injection or two taken about two weeks apart. It is effective for six months, though there is no certainty of complete protection.

Malaria is transmitted by a bite from an infected mosquito. It is strongly recommended that anti-malaria tablets are taken (either daily or weekly, depending on the type of prophylaxis). Start the dosage just before entering an infected area and continue the course of tablets for 28 days after leaving it. Your doctor will advise you on the most suitable brand of malaria tablets.

Polio is usually contracted from an already infected person but also from contaminated food and water. Prevention is in the form of three doses of drops, normally administered on sugar lumps, taken four to six weeks apart. It is effective for ten years.

Typhoid is caught from contaminated food, water and milk. Prevention is achieved by two injections taken four to six weeks apart (though the period can be reduced to ten days). It is effective for three years.

Yellow fever is caught from the bite of a contaminated mosquito. One injection should be administered at least ten days before arriving in a risk area. It is effective for ten years. The vaccination is given at certain clinics only; the ones in central London are mentioned below. Some doctors advise a period of several weeks in between the taking of gamma globulin (see hepatitis) and vaccinations for yellow fever.

The World Health Organisation has declared that *smallpox* has been eradicated worldwide.

Infectious hepatitis is caught from contaminated water, food or even from people (for example the disease can be contracted from an infected colleague if you share a common spoon, glass, cigarette, etc). When in places which appear unhygienic make sure that raw vegetables and unpeeled fruits have been washed in purified water and do not drink untreated water. Gamma globulin is the vaccination against hepatitis, though its effectiveness is not total. Seek advice from your doctor.

Rabies is the result of a bite or scratch from an infected animal (avoid familiarity with animals, however innocuous they may seem). There are injections which provide some protection against the disease. Consult your doctor for further details.

Tetanus is contracted from contaminated soil, manure, dirty (eg rusty) objects and finds entry into the body through a wound. Two injections six weeks apart allows one year's protection; a booster six to 12 months after the initial course gives a ten-year immunity.

The following clinics in London give yellow fever vaccinations, etc. Doctors at these centres can advise you on how to look after your health in Africa. If possible go to National Health surgeries as they are cheaper.

British Airways
Immunisation Centres:
Heathrow Airport.
Tel: 01-750 5453
74 Regent Street, London W1
Tel: 01-439 9584

Medical Department
Unilever House
Blackfriars
London EC4
Tel: 01-822 6017

Hospital for Tropical Diseases
4 St Pancras Way
London NW1
Tel: 01-387 4411

Vaccination Service
53 Great Cumberland Place
London W1
Tel: 01-262 6456

Other precautions

Food: Avoid raw vegetables and unpeeled fruits unless you know that they have been washed properly. Be

11

careful of salads if the restaurant has poor hygienic standards. Uncooked, cold or reheated food is susceptible to contamination, so try and eat freshly cooked food.

Water: Tap water in the main towns is usually safe to drink. If you have doubts anywhere about the cleanliness of the drinking water then boil it or add purifying tablets (an essential in your medical kit). Diseases can be caught from cutlery or glasses washed in unclean water. Also be wary of ice cream and the ice used to cool your drink. To be on the safe side it is often worth paying a little for a cup of tea or a bottled drink; the cost of treating an illness will work out a lot more expensively.

Cuts: Wash and treat all cuts and grazes immediately. An antiseptic solution like TCP should be carried in addition to antiseptic cream (the latter is greasy and attracts dirt, but is useful at times). Some doctors recommend applying stronger antibiotic powder to wounds. Cover the cut to avoid exposure to dirt.

Sun: Protection against the sun like a hat, a good pair of sunglasses (preferably polarised) and a lotion which acts as a barrier against ultraviolet light is strongly recommended. If there is the chance that you will suffer badly under the sun (eg sunburn) then ask your doctor for the necessary medicaments before your departure. Be sensible about exposing your body to the sun and do so in gradual stages if you are not used to it. During the winter months the heat is by no means unbearable.

Bites: Insect repellant cream helps ward off mosquitoes. Mosquito nets are useful, but some people feel that they are an unnecessary burden, especially during the winter months when the mosquitoes are not so prevalant. Scorpion and snake bites are less common than most people fear and a nip from such creatures are rarely fatal; all the same, if you are bitten see a doctor immediately. Consult your doctor at home for advice on what to do if you are travelling off the beaten track and have to administer your own treatment. There is a black stone, Pierre Noire, which can be bought in West Africa; soaked in milk and strapped to the affected area it apparently draws out the snake bite venom. Shake your shoes in the morning to make sure scorpions, etc, have not been harbouring in them.

Diarrhoea: The most effective way to cure diarrhoea is to eat as little as possible and drink lots of fluid. A recommended concoction is a glass of fruit juice with a pinch of salt and a teaspoonful of sugar. Drink tea if you have no alternative and if you have doubts about the purity of the water. Doctors will advise you on the medicines which prevent and cure diarrhoea. Also ask your doctor how to distinguish diarrhoea from dysentery and how to treat the different types of the latter disease. Fresh onions and lemons can be recommended as a specific against stomach upsets.

Bilharzia: This is contracted from fluke parasites which infest ponds, lakes and slow-flowing rivers. Avoid swimming in such places.

Medical insurance (and insurance for personal belongings) is highly recommended. Thomas Cook (policies can be drawn out at any of their travel agencies) and Endsleigh Insurance Services Limited, Cranfield House, 97–107 Southampton Row, London WC1; Tel: 01-580 4311 (head London branch), are two companies experienced in travel insurance.

What to Wear

A great advantage of travelling in hot countries is that there is no need for the heavy and sometimes specialised clothing that is required for cold climates. Thus weight and initial expenditure should be minimal.

Cotton is best
A few changes of light cotton clothing is all that is required, though surplus T-shirts and jeans can be exchanged or given as presents along the way. If necessary additional clothes, including Western-style garments, can easily be bought in towns throughout West Africa. A pair of jeans, though heavy, should be packed as they can withstand rough travel; they also provide a warm layer during the cold nights. A long-sleeved shirt is protection against mosquitoes.

Officials and others may well behave more favourably towards Westerners with a reasonably smart appearence rather than to those with a 'scruffy hippy look'. Of course it is not necessary to be completely clean-cut or have fancy clothing, but it is worth men considering an everpressed (seersucker or similar) jacket and trousers as part of their luggage.

A Westerner dressed entirely in 'native' garb may be a subject for mild ridicule.

For travelling track/gym shoes and flip flops (as they are rubber they can easily be washed) are suggested footwear. A variety of leather sandals — unique to this part of Africa — can be bought at places along the route. Shake closed shoes before putting them on in case any undesirable creatures like scorpions are inside.

Conservative dress

The countries in this area are predominantly Moslem, consequently scantily-clad Westerners, particularly women, cause offence and could be the butt of a few jokes. It is polite as well as advisable to dress conservatively in public places: women should be prepared to wear below-the-knee dresses.

Sunglasses and a hat offer protection against the sun and some travellers wear the local *cheches* and *tagoulmousts*, lengths of material wrapped around the head, to shield them from sandstorms in the Sahara.

Nights can be cold during the winter months, particularly in the desert, and some form of covering other than ordinary clothes is needed if you are sleeping in the open. If you have a good compact sleeping bag then take it, otherwise consider buying a locally handmade blanket which, besides providing sufficient warmth at night, is a lovely present or souvenir from West Africa.

Money

It is advisable to carry the bulk of your money in travellers' cheques; if they are lost or stolen they can least be refunded (how quickly depends on the place, the circumstances and luck). It is best to buy cheques from a well-known organisation like American Express as they are most recognised by the banks, better hotels, etc, throughout West Africa. All local banks accept sterling and dollar travellers' cheques.

Banks are to be found only in the larger towns, so make sure you have sufficient local currency funds to keep you going while travelling around.

There are several reasons why it is worth carrying some hard currency cash, eg pounds, dollars, French francs. Cash is far easier to exchange than cheques when banking facilities are unavailable. In Nigeria cash can be exchanged on the street at a much better rate than in the bank (this is also true, but to a lesser extent, in Gambia); similar transactions with cheques are less usual. But note that black market deals like

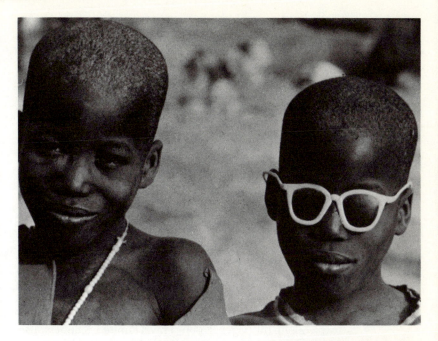

Sunglasses offer protection against glare

this are illegal. It is not a bad idea to have some French francs, because if you are off the beaten track in a Francophone country without any local currency there is a greater chance that someone will change French money rather than pounds or dollars. Carry a few low denomination notes and travellers' cheques as there are times when you do not want to change large quantities of money (for example if you are about to leave the country) and be stuck with an excess of that currency; also if the exchange rate offered is poor you only want to change the minimum amount necessary. A hard currency note tip is greatly appreciated, particularly in Nigeria. It can be difficult to change local currency back into foreign money (for example in Nigeria) except at a poor rate on the street.

If you are short of funds then your bank can send you money. It is best to establish the procedure with them before you leave home and with which West African banks they have an agreement. The Union Bank in Nigeria and the Standard Bank in Gambia have close ties with British banks; in Francophone countries Banque Internationale pour l'Afrique

Occidentale (BIAO) has links with Banque Nationale de Paris (BNP). American Express specialises in sending money around the world, though they charge a high commission for their services.

Visas

It is best to obtain all visas before leaving home as when you get to West Africa the local authorities may for no logical reason decide not to give you entry permits. Details of visa requirements will be found at the beginning of each country section in this Guide.

Tourism

The tourist industry is still small in West Africa. Gambia and Senegal attract the greatest number of holidaymakers, many of whom are on short package trips. Both these countries have first class hotels situated on fine sandy beaches and there are enough things to do to keep the average visitor occupied during a two week stay. They also make comfortable places at which to end up after an extended journey along the Niger. Kuoni Travel Limited, Kuoni House, Dorking, Surrey are experienced in holidays to Gambia, while PLM Hotels, 62 Avenue des Champs-Elysees, 75008 Paris are specialists in Francophone West Africa generally.

Package holidays
The limited number of tourists who go to Mali and Niger are usually on some sort of adventure package trip (most often organised by a French company). Some, especially those passing through Nigeria, are individual overland travellers. Several British companies (they advertise in travel magazines) take bus- or truck-loads of people across the Sahara and through West Africa.

There are Western businessmen and aid workers all over West Africa. In former British colonies they are more than likely to be British, and French in former French colonies. American aid workers are everywhere and they are probably the only people in Mali and Niger whom you will come across who speak English.

Travel Around West Africa

Road transport. A tremendous network of road transport scurries around West Africa. The vehicles most commonly used by the public are the fast

Taxis and pick-up vans

Peugeot 504s — cinq zero quatres as they are often called — which have been converted into eight- to nine-passenger taxis. A bit cheaper than the 504s are the *baches* which are converted Toyota — or similar — pick-up vans capable of carrying around 15 people squashed in the back.

Buses

Even cheaper are the country buses which cover certain routes; these tend to be cranky old machines, invariably crammed beyond credibility with locals and their assorted accessories. The journeys are long, laborious and uncomfortable; however, some will argue with possible justification that you have not experienced the country until you have undergone the torture of this type of travel. In Niger the government-run SNTN long-distance bus service has a designated departure time and is relatively efficient.

The vehicles mentioned above are often known collectively as *taxis brousse* — literally bush taxis. They leave from the town's gare routiere/parc autocar and their fares are usually fixed, though you may have to pay a supplement if you have any large pieces of

The locals find tourists interesting

17

luggage. Taxis brousse do not have a set time of departure, but they leave when they have a full complement of passengers.

Hitching

An alternative is to hitch a ride on a truck, but this would probably involve some kind of payment. Hitchhiking in our sense of the term is rarely practiced.

Sometimes you do not have any option as to your means of transport but if you do then the cinq zero quatre is the quickest and most comfortable way to travel.

The quality of the road surfaces vary from good new tarmac to poor potholed tarmac through to rough dirt tracks. Some of those in the latter category are impassible during the rains or when the waters of the River Niger are high.

River Transport. The River Niger is the main highway in the Sahel belt and riverboats are often the most practical means of getting around this region.

The pirogue

Pirogues, the traditional canoes, are an indispensable form of transport for riverside dwellers. Their design has not changed for hundreds of years; Mungo Park noted in the 18th C: 'The canoes are of a singular construction, each of them being formed of the trunks of two large trees, rendered concave, and joined together, not side by side, but end ways; the junction being exactly the middle of the canoe; they are therefore very long and disproportionately narrow, and have neither decks nor masts; they are, however, very roomy; for I observed in one of them four horses and several people crossing over the river'.

The pinasse

Large pirogues, often motorised and capable of taking 100 passengers, are known as pinasses.

Steamers

Besides these local crafts there are steamers along the River Niger from Gao (Mali) to Koulikoro (Mali), 57 kms north of Bamako; from Bamako you can travel by boat into Guinea. (Note that these are seasonal services only: see *The River Niger Journey* chapter.) A steamer service also operates along most of the River Gambia.

Trains. The only train service in this region runs from Koulikoro via Bamako (both in Mali) to Dakar (Senegal), a total of 1287 kms.

Flights. A reasonable number of local flights operate within this area, but it is advisable to book a seat as far in advance as possible. There are international flights from the capitals to other African destinations as well as to Europe. The only direct flights from London are to Kano (Nigeria Airways and British Caledonian) and Banjul (British Caledonian and various charter flights).

Consider indirect flights from London, eg Air France via Paris to Dakar, which is 'just up the road' from Banjul; or Air Algerie between London and Niamey via Algiers, as well as within the Sahel.

Doing the Route. From Kano there is no shortage of road transport to Niamey via either Zinder or Maradi. For those approaching West Africa from the Sahara (the In Salah-Tamanrasset route) there are taxi brousse from Agadez south to Zinder and Kano and southwest to Niamey.

From Niamey vehicles go west to Ouagadougou, the capital of Burkina Fasso, and then on to Mopti and Bamako in Mali. The route covered in this book between Niamey and Bamako, the capitals of Niger and Mali respectively, follows the course of the River Niger. From Niamey a taxi brousse has to be taken to Gao, the main town in eastern Mali.

Gao is Mali's downstream terminus for river transport and from here steamers travel via Timbuktu and Mopti to Koulikoro (57 kms north of Bamako) between the high water months of July/August and December; the boat continues to operate from Gao to Mopti in December and January (note that the high water season varies with rainfall). Many roads in the vicinity of the River Niger, especially in the Inland Delta region between Timbuktu and Mopti and also the north bank Gao-Bourem-Timbuktu road, are impassable in August and the succeeding months. There is a fairly rough road from Gao west direct to Mopti which cuts out Timbuktu and the bend of the Niger.

A road east from Mopti goes to Bandiagara and Dogon Country, and Djenne, to the south of Mopti, can be reached by small boat or by car. An all-weather road connects Mopti to Segu and Bamako which lie to its southwest.

Trains run northwest from Bamako to Kayes —

the road is too poor for most vehicles, though there is a better road north from Bamako to Nioro du Sahel and then southwest from there to Kayes. From Kayes you can continue by train to Tambacounda or Dakar (there is a twice-weekly express service from Bamako direct to Dakar) and from either of these two places — or from anywhere else in Senegal — there are road links to Banjul, the capital of Gambia.

Accommodation

Hotels... High standard hotels along this route are found only at Kano, Niamey, Timbuktu, Mopti, Segu, Bamako, Tambacounda, Dakar and Banjul. In addition there are a few lodges used by tourists at the game parks.

Other than a handful of places at these centres, accommodation is quite basic. Campements — government-run hotels — are in many of the provincial towns; they tend to be, in the case of Mali, rather dated, colonial-style, shabby and provide little more than the bare essentials.

Cheaper than the campements is the pension-style lodging which can be found in some of the towns; this type of accommodation ranges from simple and fairly clean to distinctly unrecommendable. If there are no rooms then ask a local or the police. In the small villages ask the alkali (the headman) if you can stay in the village; he will invariably arrange for a hut or **and huts** space in a courtyard to be prepared. In these cases the question of payment may never be raised, but all the same be prepared to contribute something to your host.

HISTORICAL BACKGROUND

Sudan and Sahel

Land of the Blacks

The Arabs called the land south of the Sahara *Bilad al-Sudan*, the Land of the Blacks. But the meaning of the word Sudan has shifted with history. With 19th C European colonisation the French called a part of their West African territories the French Sudan, while to the east the British together with the Egyptians ruled the Anglo-Egyptian Sudan. On independence the French Sudan took the name Mali and the Anglo-Egyptian Sudan called itself Sudan.

Today the geographical term Sudan can include everything between the Sahara and the equator or it is limited to that semi-arid belt stretching from the Atlantic to the Red Sea with the Sahara lying to its north and the tropical forests to its south. This latter definition is synonymous with the Sahel. It is through the Sahel that this route leads.

Arab Writers and European Explorers

Europe had little or no knowledge of Africa except north of the Sahara until after the arrival of the Arabs in the Maghreb (the west) of North Africa in the 8th C. Over the following centuries a handful of travellers crossed the Sahara with the trading caravans and wandered around the Sudan. It was from these itinerant geographers — men like Ibn Haukal (10th C), El Edrisi (1099–1180), Ibn Battuta (1304–1378), Ibn Khaldun (1332–1406), Leo Africanus (1493–1560), El Sadi (1596–1655), as well as El Bekri (1028–1094), an armchair traveller who never actually visited West Sudan — that the first accounts of the region were obtained.

Fabulous tales

They wrote of abundant gold supplies (like those at Bumbeck, Bure and Akan) deep in the tropical forests of the Sudan, extremely active trade links with the black states (Ghana, Mali, Songhai) across the Sahara, magnificent market cities (like Gao, Djenne, Timbuktu) and fabulously opulent kings (like Mansa Musa and Askia Mohammed). These stories of untold wealth in the heart of this mysterious continent slowly filtered through to Europe and naturally excited all those who heard them.

It was not until the 18th C however that European

explorers were commissioned to find out about the riches of darkest Africa. But even at this late stage very little was known about this land, as Dean Swift indicated:

Geographers, on Afric maps
With savage drawings fill their gaps,
And o'er unhabitable downs
Draw elephants for want of towns.

Intrepid adventurers like Mungo Park, Gordon Laing, Rene Caillie and Heinrich Barth were the European pioneers of West African exploration. They travelled extensively in the Sahara and the Sudan and made important discoveries, but by and large they found that the supposed golden cities were a gross disappointment. Had Europe been deceived? Not really. The accounts of the Arab writers are evidence that trade had been practiced on a large scale over long distances and that great quantities of gold, the main exchange commodity, had been bartered at thriving markets. What happened was that the Moroccans ransacked West Sudan at the end of the 16th C and destroyed much of the prosperity of the area; at the same time trade connections with the Europeans along the Guinea coast stole business from the trans-Saharan merchants. Consequently caravan routes across the desert became redundant and market towns like Timbuktu fell into decay.

So by the time the explorers arrived the golden age of Sudan was something of the past. The fabulous wealth had eluded them. But they achieved personal fame — which was probably their greatest wish anyway.

Early Trans-Saharan Trade

At the time of Christ, much the same as today, the Sahara was a vast, hot, virtually waterless expanse, bordered to the north by what is now known as the Maghreb and to the south by the Sahel. First reports of the camel in the Sahara date from this period.

From about the 4th C AD Berbers from the Maghreb were crossing the desert on camels and gradually trade developed with the sedentary black settlements in the northern part of the Sudan. (Incidentaly, *sahel* means shore in Arabic; quite an

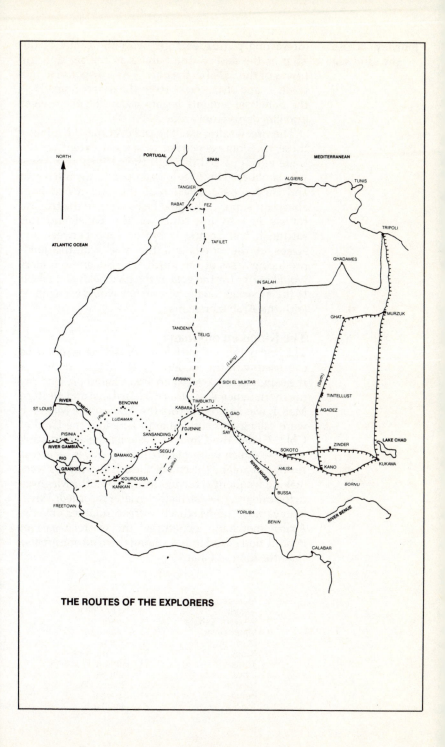

THE ROUTES OF THE EXPLORERS

23

interesting picture emerges with the camel as the 'ship of the desert', the Sahara as the sea and the towns of the Sahel as the ports.) As a response to this trade — and also attacks from the desert nomads — the Sahel settlements began organising themselves into kingdoms from around 500 AD.

The rise, wealth, stability and eventual downfall of these kingdoms depended to a great extent on the trade which passed through their lands. The Arabs who conquered the Maghreb desperately wanted gold and they soon realised that the Sudan had it in abundant supply. The gold fields were in the tropical forests just to the south of the Sahel and this savannah belt became a buffer zone between the Arabs in the north and the blacks in the gold-producing areas of the south. The Sudanese traders would barter for the gold at the gold fields and take it to their market towns, where they would exchange it with the Arab merchants.

The Kingdom of Ghana

The first of the Sudanese kingdoms, Ghana (not to be confused with the modern West African country of the same name) covered an area around present-day northern Senegal, southern Mauritania and western Mali. It was not long before the Arabs of the Maghreb were calling this sub-Saharan kingdom the Land of Gold. Under the Omayyad caliphs the Arabs sunk wells — which were maintained by slaves — across the desert and by the end of the 8th C caravans were making frequent return journeys from the Maghreb to the Sudan. An Arab historian later recorded: 'When Ifriqiya and the Maghreb were conquered [by the Arabs] merchants penetrated the western part of Bilad al-Sudan and found among them no one greater than the king of Ghana'.

1	Morocco	12	Ghana
2	Algeria	13	Ivory Coast
3	Western Sahara	14	Chad
4	Mauritainia	15	Cameroon
5	Mali	16	Liberia
6	Niger	17	Sierra Leone
7	Tunisia	18	Burkina Fasso
8	Libya	19	Guinea
9	Nigeria	20	Guinea Bissau
10	Benin	21	Senegal
11	Togo	22	Gambia

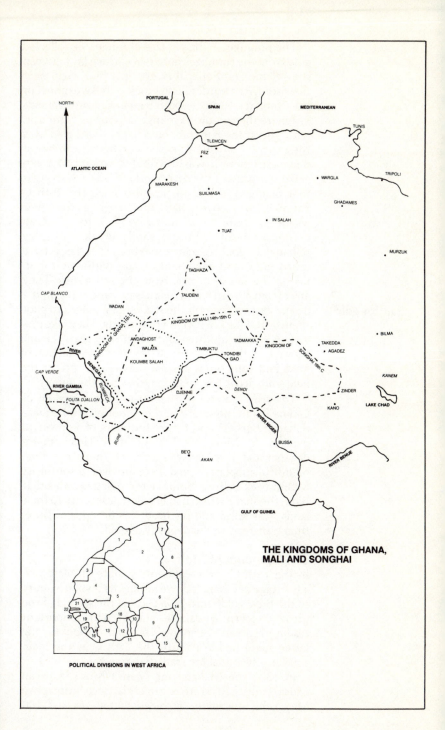

THE KINGDOMS OF GHANA,
MALI AND SONGHAI

POLITICAL DIVISIONS IN WEST AFRICA

The Soninke — the peoples of Ghana — collected gold from the Bumbeck goldfields, which lay between the Faleme and Senegal rivers (just by Kayes) near their southern border. They took it to Awdaghost or their capital Koumbi — both Sahelian trade terminals — where they would exchange it, principally for salt, with the trans-Saharan merchants. The gold was then carried by camel to the northern terminal of Sijilmasa where it was distributed around Morocco and other parts of the Arab world. Trade was so great that Sijilmasa is said to have provided the 10th C Fatimids with over half the revenue for their Maghreb state. An anonymous 12th C Arab chronicler wrote: 'In the sands of that country [Ghana] is gold, treasure inexpressible. They have much gold, and merchants trade with salt for it, taking the salt in camels from the salt mines. They start from a town called Sijilmasa ... and travel in the desert as it were upon the sea, having guides to pilot them by the stars or rocks in the deserts. They take provisions for six months, and when they reach Ghana they weigh their salt and sell it against a certain unit of gold, and sometimes against double or more of the gold unit, according to the market and the supply'.

Salt for gold

Towards the end of the 11th C the Kingdom of Ghana fell to the sword of the Almoravids who were Saharan Berbers and future founders of a powerful dynasty in Morocco. The great Sudanic empire degenerated into petty states; at the same time bountiful supplies of gold were discovered southeast of Bumbeck at Bure. Soninke mythology relates that Bidu, the snake which had brought prosperity to their lands, was killed and his head was dropped in Bure, thus transferring the deposits of gold.

The Kingdom of Mali
In the 13th C the neighbouring state of Mali took advantage of Ghana's downfall and its own proximity to the Bure goldfields. Mali became the second of the great western Sudanese states, with important trading centres at Djenne, Gao and Timbuktu; the latter succeeded Walata in the 14th C as the main southern terminal for trans-Saharan trade.

In 1324 the Malian king Mansa Musa (Kankan Musa) embarked on an extremely lavish pilgrimage to Mecca; his entourage included 500 slaves and 100 camels laden with gold. Along the way he took all opportunities to show off his opulence, and while in Cairo he was so generous with his gifts of gold that its price fell in the markets. This verified the rumours of his and his country's wealth to such an extent that the 14th C *Catalan Atlas* of Charles V pictures Mansa Musa sitting on his throne in the Sahara holding a golden sceptre and nugget. The caption reads: 'The Negro lord is called Musa Mali, Lord of the Negroes of Guinea. So abundant is the gold which is found in his country that he is the richest and most noble king in all the land'. It was not only Mansa Musa's fame which travelled far: it is estimated that two-thirds of the gold for the European and Arab mints in the early 14th C came from the Sudan.

Mali was one of the greatest kingdoms in the history of black Africa. But it weakened, largely due to internal disputes, and it was Songhai, Mali's eastern province, which rose up and eventually established itself as the dominant kingdom after Mansa Musa's death in 1332.

The Songhai Empire and the Collapse of the Sudan

Empire of the river

The Songhai controlled the River Niger from the Bussa rapids in the east to just north of Bamako in the west. The river was the key to their development as a great West African state and under them Timbuktu, Djenne and their capital Gao — all entrepots significantly located and connected with each other by the Niger waterway system — prospered as trade centres. Songhai, like Ghana and Mali, thrived because it was the middleman between the trans-Saharan merchants and the gold mining communities in the southern forest areas. Towards the end of the 16th C the Moroccans, under Sultan Ahmed el Mansur, wanted to cut out the Songhai link and have direct access to the gold mines. This resulted in the battle of Tondibi near Gao in 1591, where the Songhai were heavily defeated and consequently their kingdom collapsed.

The Moroccans took control of Timbuktu, Djenne and Gao and for a while they managed to export a reasonable amount of gold across the desert — enough anyway for el Mansur to be nicknamed *el Dzehebi*, the Golden.

But the invasion was expensive in both lives and money and largely because the Moroccans never really gained control of the mines the amount of gold crossing the Sahara did not justify these losses. Thus early in the 17th C the Sultans in Morocco lost interest in the Sudan. In passing they had destroyed the highly organised and successful Songhai state system and left behind little more than anarchy. Caravans continued to cross the desert, but the golden era of Saharan trade was now in decline.

Caravan Routes Across the Sahara

Sijilmasa, south of Fez, was Morocco's major caravan terminus until it declined in the 17th C. At first the principal route ran down to Wadan and Awdaghost; in the 13th C the route lay more to the east, through Taghaza to Walata; and in the 14th C it lay more easterly still, through Taghaza to Timbuktu. Other important routes linked Timbuktu and Gao with Tunis via Tuat and Wagla; and there were east-west routes to Egypt — one of these, the pilgrim route, passed through Murzuk, Siwa and Cairo from where the faithful continued on to Mecca.

The desert crossing was extremely arduous. The routes followed by the caravans were no more than a series of oases five to ten days distance from each other. Although the journey was made during the mild season, the heat was still intense and there was **Tempting death** no guarantee of finding provisions enroute. A merchant would only make a single crossing in any one year; each trip he was tempting death and five trans-Saharan voyages was considered enough for any man in his lifetime.

The journey from Sijilmasa to Taghaza took three to four weeks and from there it was another two months to the southern terminals of Walata or Timbuktu. The most treacherous part of the journey was south of Taghaza. The only water between these salt mines and Walata was at Bir al Ksaib, ten days out of Taghaza. The caravans could not carry enough water from here to Walata, so guides were sent ahead of the main party to collect water from Walata; they would then double back, about four days' journey, to meet the caravan. This task was made particularly difficult because of the notorious shifting sand dunes in this region and failure to meet led to certain death

A camel-borne Tuareg near Timbuktu

for the main party. In 1805 a complete caravan of 2000 men and 1800 camels perished because they ran out of supplies while on their way to Timbuktu.

Some of the best guides were blind; by feeling and smelling the sand they managed to find their way across the desert.

Cannibalism

There are many dramatic stories of how death was staved off in the desert: Heinrich Barth, the 19th C German explorer, slit his wrist and drank his own blood; more common was the drinking of camels' urine or killing the animal to get at the water in its stomach or bladder. Around 1815 a shipwrecked American, Captain James Riley, was captured with several fellow sailors and taken in a caravan across a section of the desert. 'Hunger, that had preyed upon my companions to such a degree as to cause them to bite off the flesh from their arms, had not the same effect on me. I was forced in one instance to tie the arms of one of my men behind him in order to prevent his gnawing his own flesh; and in another instance, two having caught one of the boys, a lad about four years old, out of sight of the tents, were about dashing his brains out with a stone, for the purpose of devouring his flesh.'

Merchants had to contend with more than just the severe elements. During the more recent centuries in particular, there was a constant fear of being attacked by Tuareg or Berber desert bandits who were in search of booty. Consequently large detours often had to be made to avoid the areas where they were rumoured to be lying in wait.

The Luxury of Salt

By far the most important product the northern traders brought with them was salt, which they collected at the Taghaza mines and carried in block form on their camels to the Sudan.

The Sudan had a very limited quantity of salt at Dendi (around the Benin-Niger-Nigeria border) and the transporting of small quantities of sea salt from the Senegal coast did not prove viable. The traditional alternative was to sift ash or scrape millet stalks.

Salt was in such demand that the Sudanese merchants would often exchange it for an equal weight of gold. In the 18th C Mungo Park stressed its value: 'In the interior countries, the greatest of luxuries is salt. It would appear strange to a European to see a child suck a piece of rock-salt as if it were sugar. This, however, I have frequently seen; although, in the inland parts, the poorer class of inhabitants are so very rarely indulged with this precious article, that to say a man eats salt with his victuals is the same as saying he is a rich man. I have myself suffered great inconvenience from the scarcity of this article. The long use of vegetable food creates so painful a longing for salt, that no words can sufficiently describe it'.

Houses and mosques of salt

Taghaza, the important mine between the 11th and 16th C, was a desolate hell on earth. Ibn Battuta wrote about it: '... an unattractive village, with the curious feature that its houses and mosques are built of salt, roofed with camel skins. There are no trees there, nothing but sand. In the sand is the salt mine'. The black slaves who cut blocks of salt 4 metres underground throughout the year were the only inhabitants. These men were expected to live only two years under these conditions. The mine depended totally on passing caravans for its food: dates from the north and millet from the south. If a caravan failed to arrive then the workers perished.

The salt was cut into slabs of around 100 centimetres by 30 centimetres; those which were streaked with red and grey veins in a similar way to marble commanded a lower price than the pure white blocks. Merchants in Timbuktu would buy 500 slabs at a time and sell them for double the price at Djenne.

Taghaza closed down for good after the Moroccan invasion in the second half of the 16th C. New and larger deposits were found 190 kms further south at Taudeni (700 kms north of Timbuktu). Conditions here were equally horrific and as recently as 1910 56 workers died because the supply caravans failed to come. Today the Taudeni mines are worked by convicts and produce over 3.5 million kilos of salt a year.

The Secret Source of Gold

Timbuktu succeeded Awdaghost and Walata as the main southern trade terminal and under the Songhai it reached its peak. It is situated about 9 kms north of the port of Kabara which is at the point where the river is most accessible to the Maghreb and the Tuat crossroads. By not being directly on the riverbank Timbuktu avoided the annual floods and consequently it had contact with caravans all the year round. But the great advantage it had over Awdaghost and Walata was its access to the River Niger. Thus Timbuktu was linked by land and water to Gao — which had important trade routes to Wargla and Tunisia and also to Egypt. More importantly the Niger water network connected Timbuktu with Djenne, 250 miles to its south.

Djenne, on the River Bani, is an island for part of the year and during the floods is only accessible to Timbuktu by water. Being surrounded by fertile land it provided crops for Timbuktu on the edge of the desert. But like Timbuktu and Gao it was essentially an entrepot for merchants who brought goods from the north or south. Pirogues provided the transport for salt from Timbuktu to Djenne and gold travelling in the opposite direction.

The Sudanese merchants from the time of the kingdom of Ghana had a peculiar way of trading with the blacks from the gold-producing forests to their south. A special class of merchants evolved known as dyulas. From Djenne, for example, dyulas would enlist up to 200 slaves to carry blocks of salt to outposts like Be'o which were in reach of the gold fields of the Akan forest. The salt and any other goods would be left at a predetermined spot and the dyulas would then retreat. The forest dwellers would appear and put quantities of gold next to each item and then return to the forest. If the dyulas were satisfied with the amount, they would collect it, leave their goods and the transaction would be finished; if not they waited until the locals offered more gold. This went on until agreement was tacitly reached. This method of exchanging was known as 'silent trading'.

Over the centuries the dyulas built up a complex network of trade routes deep into the forest belt. Because of their trustworthiness the gold collectors would deal only with them; the dyulas cleverly kept sources a secret. It was largely because foreigners were prevented from learning the whereabouts of the gold fields that the western Sudanese states prospered for such a long time.

Djenne was the greatest Sudanese gold market, yet it was Timbuktu to which mystery and stories of

A Fulani woman, near Mopti, with huge gold earrings

fabulous wealth attached so that it became the goal for explorers and a household name in Europe. Today not many people outside West Africa have heard of Djenne. Felix Dubois, a Frenchman who visited Mali at the end of the last century, suggested that Djenne remained little known because the trans-Saharan merchants were not encouraged to visit the city. In fact earlier travellers mentioned that the merchants of Timbuktu were Berbers while those in Djenne were Sudanese blacks. This was in keeping with the method of trading in the Sudan: the Sahel served as a buffer preventing the North African Arabs from establishing direct contact with the sources of gold.

The Slave Trade

Hundreds of thousands of blacks were taken across the desert to North Africa and many more were exported from the West African coast to the European colonies. Slaves were often obtained as a result of local wars; captives were sold by the victorious king to Arab merchants. Or they were captured as a result of direct raids — known as *razzias* which literally means 'attacks against infidels' — led by either Arab or black Moslems.

The price of slaves varied with demand, but generally the price was low. Leo Africanus, who travelled in Sudan in the 16th C, recorded a list of prices; it is interesting as it shows the comparative values of the merchandise:

skin of the addax gazelle	8 ducats
slave	20 ducats
eunuch	40 ducats
camel	50 ducats
civet cat	200 ducats

Eunuchs were used by the Arabs as harem attendants. The healthiest young slaves were selected, but only one in ten of them survived the crude and brutal operation.

The main trans-Saharan slave route was not in west Sudan, but further to the east running from Kanem (Lake Chad area) north through Murzuk in the Fezzan and on to Tripoli. Five hundred to 1000 slaves per caravan was probably quite normal. In the 19th C there were reports of men being walked across

Across the Sahara in leg irons

34

the desert chained by the neck and in leg irons; traders showed no compassion and slaves who weakened under the conditions were left by the wayside to die. However, it was obviously in the merchants' interest to avoid loss of life; on arrival in the north the skeletal figures of the slaves would be fattened up and sold for up to 500 percent profit in Tripoli. Most of these slaves were distributed around the Arab world, though some ended up in the northern Mediterranean countries.

Horrified 19th C European explorers — many of whom travelled with slave-trading caravans as they were often the only means of getting round — returned with alarming stories: James Richardson, when he was in Zinder, saw men being bought for less than £1; and Captain F G Lyon wrote: 'None of the slave owners ever marched without their whips, which were in constant use. One was so frequently flogging his poor slaves that I was frequently obliged to disarm him'.

Slave-trading was very much a way of life in the Sahara. A mother offered Laing her child as a slave for 30 shillings and when he declined the offer the woman accused him of hindering the economy of the country. It is interesting that in central Sudan, where slavery was rife, the economy survived on razzias and skirmishes, but in western Sudan a peaceful, organised and centralised state system had — up to the 17th C — helped to confine trading to gold.

Explorers may well have been appalled by the atrocious slave trade which they encountered, but their own countries had been committed to slavery from the 16th C up until the early part of the 19th C.

Slaves for the New World

In 1510 the first shipload of slaves sailed from West Africa to the Spanish gold fields of Hispaniola. Demand for labour in the plantations and mines of the New World intensified. In 1562 the first slave ship under an English captain, John Hawkins, left for the West Indies. Sources differ on the statistics of the trade, but all agree that huge numbers of West African blacks were exported to the Caribbean islands and the Americas.

Official reports record that 300,000 African slaves were transported to the British colonies in the last 20 years of the 17th C. Between 1700 and 1786 over 600,000 slaves were shipped to Jamaica alone. From that first shipment in 1510 to 1865, when the United States abolished slavery, it is estimated that at least 12 million Africans were taken from their native shores as slaves. The vast majority of these slaves were captured in the interior and taken to the ports for shipment. Dr Livingstone claimed that ten Africans died for every one who reached the coast. The number of Africans lost to their continent through slavery is staggering.

The Decline of the Trans-Saharan Caravan Routes

At the end of the 16th C the Moroccans defeated the Songhai; by killing the goose which laid the golden egg the Moroccans destroyed the symbiotic relationship the Maghreb had enjoyed with the western Sudanese states for many centuries. About the same time Europeans traders appeared along the coast of West Africa. African traders turned their sights away from the Sahara and set them in the direction of the sea ports. The Saharan highways were used less and less. The oases and their small cultivated patches required very careful attention, but many became neglected and the desert swept over them in a short time.

Also the abolition of slavery by the Western nations in the 19th C gradually restricted the flow of slaves cross the desert. Not only did the Saharan merchants lose one of their most profitable merchandises, but also they had depended on slaves to look after the oases.

Despite this decline there were many accounts of large Saharan caravans in the last century. Rene Caillie travelled in 1828 with a party comprising 1400 camels; earlier this century the annual azali caravan left Agadez for Bilma with 20,000 camels. Even today some merchants cross the desert with their hardy beasts of burden.

The twentieth century

The European powers carved up Africa at the end of the last century and the beginning of this. Roads and railways were built from the coast into the interior for the purposes of trading and exploitation of natural resources. These, along with the sea routes, the trans-Saharan road capable of taking motor vehicles and the airplane have stolen the trade from the desert caravans.

NIGERIA

Basic Facts

Total area: 923,773 sq kms.

Neighbours: Niger lies to the north, Chad to the northeast, Cameroon to the east, Benin to the west and the Gulf of Guinea to the south.

Population: 95.2 million nationwide. Lagos: 6 million; Ibadan: 3 million; Kano: 450,000; Abeokuta: 290,000; Port Harcourt: 280,000; Kaduna: 225,000. All figures are 1985 estimates.

Capital: Lagos.

Official language: English.

Religion: Moslem 44 percent; Christian 22 percent; traditional beliefs 34 percent.

Independence: 1960. Formerly a British colony, declared a republic within the Commonwealth in 1963.

Economy: Nigeria has huge reserves of oil, natural gas and coal. Oil accounts for 90 percent of foreign exchange revenues and over 70 percent of the government's total revenue. Dependency on one resource obviously has its drawbacks: if the oil market is weak then the balance of payments will suffer, as Nigeria has experienced over the last few years. Also the population began to rely too heavily on their strong oil economy; in the late 1970s and early 1980s people drifted to the cities and neglected the fields which have a tremendous agricultural potential; now imported products account for over 10 percent of their food bill. As a response to this over-reliance on oil, the government is now broadening its economy by investing in manufacturing industries and in addition it is going to great efforts to improve its agricultural output.

Per capita GNP: US $870 (1981).

President: Major General Ibrahim Babangida, commander of the armed forces, came to power after a bloodless coup in August 1985.

Electricity: 230v.

Time: GMT +1.

Currency: The unit of currency is the Naira (N). 100 Kobo = 1 Naira. Coins: 1, 5, 10 and 25 Kobo. Notes: 50 Kobo, 1, 5, 10 and 20 Naira.

£1 = N4.75; $1 = N3. Approximate 1988 rates.

In Nigeria a currency declaration form has to be filled in on arrival and will be inspected against bank receipts and cash on departure. What money you decide not to declare can be converted on the black market, though this is of course illegal. Street dealers will exchange your surplus Naira into CFA at the Niger border (and also at towns like Zinder and Maradi), though their rates are not that good. It is therefore advisable to use up all your local currency before leaving the country.

Visas: Essential for entry into Nigeria. They are not available at borders or at airports; in Britain visas are obtainable in London (see below), Liverpool (Tel: 051-227 4921) and Edinburgh (Tel: 031-557 0275).

Applications for visas should be made as far in advance as possible. Most foreigners who go to Nigeria are businessmen and they are usually required to show a letter of invitation from a company in Nigeria and a ticket out of the country before they are granted a visa. The relatively few 'tourists' who visit Nigeria are normally asked to follow a similar procedure; seek advice on this matter from the Tourist Department, Nigeria High Commission, Nigeria House, 9 Northumberland Avenue, London WC2. Tel: 01-839 1244.

If you are coming overland from the north then Nigerian visas may be available from their consulate in Niamey. Confirm this before leaving home.

Nigerian visas last several weeks and you can get extensions in the main towns.

The Nigerian Consular Section in London: 56–57 Fleet Street, London EC4. Tel: 01-353 3776/7/8/9/0.

Accommodation: In Kano expect to pay around $15 to $20 for a cheap room (dormitory accommodation will be less expensive), at least $30 at a reasonable mid-range hotel and in the region of $100 for a double at an expensive hotel.

Transport: Kano to Zinder will cost in the region of $20 by local public transport. The longer journey via Maradi via Katsina may well come to $25. Budget $40 to $50 for travelling expenses from Kano to Niamey.

Tourist office: Nigerian Tourist Board, POB 2944, Tafawa Balewa Square Complex, Lagos. Tel: 630 247.

High Commissions and Embassies: British, 11 Eleke Crescent, Victoria Island, PMB 12136, Lagos. Tel: 611 551; telex: 21247. USA, 2 Eleke Crescent, Victoria Island, Lagos. Tel: 610 097.

KANO

'Arrayed in naval uniform, I made myself as smart as circumstances would permit ... At eleven o'clock we entered Kano, the great emporium of the kingdom of Haussa; but I had no sooner passed the gates, than I felt grievously disappointed; for from the flourishing description of it given by the Arabs, I expected to see a city of surprising grandeur: I found, on the contrary, the houses nearly a quarter of a mile from the walls, and in many parts scattered into detached groups, between large stagnant pools of water. I might have spared all the pains I had taken with my toilet; for not an individual turned his head round to gaze at me, but all, intent on their own business, allowed me to pass by without notice or remark.'

— Hugh Clapperton, the first European to reach Kano, January 1824

Kurmi Market in Kano's Old City

39

Kano, the most important city of northern Nigeria, has grown rapidly and has become increasingly Westernised over the last ten years. Perhaps this has happened too quickly for its own good, as today it is a frenetic, hectic, volatile and crowded city. This may seem an overstatement if you compare it to Lagos and other major Third World cities, but next to the towns along the route followed in this book, Kano is the epitome of urban chaos.

Kano was founded around AD 1000 and for centuries has been one of West Africa's greatest market towns; even today it remains to some extent a place where trans-Saharan merchants meet with black traders and craftsmen. In the 19th C, when European explorers were channelling all their efforts into reaching Timbuktu, it was Kano (its population of 30,000 would double during the trading season) and not Timbuktu which was the most significant commercial centre in the Sahel.

Unlike many of the other Sahelian towns, Kano was more than just an entrepot: it is surrounded by agricultural land and produced goods on a large scale, as the German explorer Heinrich Barth commented halfway through the last century: 'The great feature which distinguishes the market of Timbuktu from that of Kano is the fact that Timbuktu is not at all a manufacturing town, while the emporium of Hausa fully deserves to be classed as such'.

Kano no longer has the Arabian Nights atmosphere you may have hoped to find here; maybe it never existed, as Clapperton's description of the town would suggest. But this was his initial reaction, and like Barth and many present-day visitors, when he wandered round the market he realised that cosmopolitan Kano was teeming with highly skilled and industrious craftsmen, whose goods, in particular dyed cloths, metal and leather crafts, were in demand throughout Africa and even in Europe.

Points of Interest in Kano

The **Old City** lies within the splendid city **walls** which measure 17 kms in circumference and were built by slaves almost a thousand years ago. Of the 16 gates (*kofars*) — three of which are not original — **Sabuwar Kofar** and **Dan Agundi Kofar** are the most interesting. This part of Kano is renowned for its intricate network of winding narrow lanes, Sudanic architecture and traditional bustling urban life.

At the heart of the Old City is the vibrant **Kurmi Market**. Covering 16 hectares, the market — with its crowded, almost claustrophobic layout — was, and to an extent still is, the pulse and hive of Kano. It was here that the trans-Saharan caravans and the merchants from the south would trade their wares. Though motor vehicles are now the main means of transport, traders from Niger, Mali and even further north still arrive at Kano market with their laden camels.

The heart of the city

A great variety of goods can be bought here, including tie-dye cloth, leatherwork, local crafts and fabrics, gold, bronze, silver, domestic paraphenalia, livestock and a wide range of food and spices. Guides may approach you and insist on escorting you through the labyrinth of alleys. They can be helpful, but expect to pay them. Always be prepared to bargain the price when buying things or when accepting somebody's services.

Until recently it was possible to climb one of the 30-metre high minarets of the **central mosque**, but now you are forbidden to enter the building. The Friday prayer meeting is colourful and spectacular, even those glimpses of it you get from outside.

Just south of the mosque is the **Emir's Palace**.

The traditional ways of dyeing material are still practiced in Kano. Indigo is the most important dye and you can buy freshly coloured deep blue lengths of cloth from the **dye pits** at Kofar Mata. The indigo comes from the seeds and leaves of the Nila plant.

Sabon Gari means 'new town' or, more colloquially, 'foreigner's quarter'. It is here that most of Kano's non-Hausa population (Yoruba from southern Nigeria being the majority) live. This distinctive district has a large market just to its south. Local traders boast, 'If it can be found in Nigeria then it can be bought in Sabon Gari'. Inexpensive and moderately-priced hotels and cheap restaurants are located here and during the evenings the street-life remains alive and interesting. There are also several Western-style shops and supermarkets near here, and department stores such as Chellerhams on Bello Road, and Levantis and Kingsway, both on Murtala Mohammed Way.

The attractively laid out 8-hectare **Kano Zoo** is just

off the Zaria Road. It has numerous birds and over 50 species of animals including giraffes, rhinos and cheetahs.

Diminishing layers of neatly stacked groundnut sacks rise to form the **groundnut pyramids** south of Kofar Nassaraw and west of the Zaria Road. Each pyramid weighs around 650,000 kilos.

PRACTICAL INFORMATION

ACCOMMODATION

Kano has a reasonable range of hotels, but they tend to be expensive for the standard they provide.

The top two hotels, the Central and the Daula, have air-conditioned rooms with private bathrooms, and mainly cater for visiting businessmen. Reservations should be made well in advance.

Central Hotel, Bompai Road, PO Box 3023. Tel: (064) 5141/9. Telex: 77151.

Daula Hotel, 150 Murtala Mohammed Way, PM Bag 3228. Tel: (064) 5311/3. Telex: 77241.

Middle range hotels – for example the **Mileka Hotel** on Church Road, and the **International Hotel** on Enugu Road – and still cheaper accommodation can be found in the Sabon Gari area.

The recently established **Kano Tourist Camp** behind the Central Hotel has the cheapest and best value accommodation in town; dormitory beds and private rooms are available. It is centrally located and the majority of the clientele are trans-Saharan travellers. An alternative to the Tourist Camp is the **SIM Mission**, Tafawa Balewa Road, east of Sabon Gari and the stadium.

FOOD

There are restaurants in most hotels, their standard and price usually relative to the class of hotel.

The best restaurant is the **Magnum Water** on Audu Bako Way. Other central restaurants include the **Great Wall** (Chinese), the **Fellowship**, the **Brick Castle** and the **Lebanese Patisserie**, all of which are popular and reasonably priced.

There are many cheap eating places serving local dishes in the Sabon Gari area.

Roadside vendors throughout Kano sell local foods (eg pounded yams, rice dishes, garri, stews, kebabs) as well as fruits and vegetables. Street stalls and supermarkets stock tinned foods.

ENTERTAINMENT AND RECREATION

There are several **cinemas**. Popular **discos** include the Moulin Rouge and Campari; and some of the hotels and bars have dancing at night. The Central Hotel and the Kano Club are popular and reasonably pleasant evening rendezvous. The lively Sabon Gari district has many small restaurants and bars. But note that it is not wise to walk around certain parts of Kano alone after dark.

For a small charge you can become a day member at the **Central Hotel** and use their swimming pool and other facilities. The **Kano Club** is a popular expatriates meeting place where temporary membership entitles you to make use of their swimming pool, tennis court and other facilities.

GETTING AROUND TOWN

The places of interest within Kano are quite spread out. It is, for example, a long walk from the Central Hotel to the Old City.

Taxis are generally shared: just hail one going in your direction. The set fare is low and tips are not expected within the city. Private taxis are a lot more expensive; negotiate the fare before embarking on a trip.

USEFUL INFORMATION

Office hours: 8am to noon and 2 to 5pm.
Government offices: 7.30am to 2.30pm,

Monday to Thursday; 7.30am to 12.30pm Friday and Saturday.

Banks: 8am to 3pm Monday; 8am to 1pm Tuesday to Friday.

There are over a dozen banks in Kano, most of them clustered around the downtown area of Niger Road, Bank Road and Lagos Road. The **Union Bank of Nigeria** (Barclays Bank) is in Bank Road; there is a **Chase Manhattan Bank** in Murtala Mohammed Way and a **Societe General Bank** in Club Road. Locals exchange hard currency at a better rate than the banks, though transactions of this sort are illegal.

Ministry of Home Affairs and Information, Tourism Division, New Secretariat, Zaria Road, PMB 3088. There is also a **Tourist Information Centre** at the airport. The concierge at the Tourist Camp in Club Road is helpful and informative.

Post Office: Lagos Road. It has a poste restante service.

Airlines: Kano is linked to cities in Africa, the Middle East and Europe by several airlines. **Nigeria Airways** and **British Caledonian** have daily flights to London; both have offices in the Central Hotel. Nigeria Airways has flights from Kano to Lagos, the capital of Nigeria, and to Niamey, the capital of Niger. The **airport** is 6½ kms north of the city on Airport Road.

Consulates: There is a **British Liaison Officer** at 64 Murtala Mohammed Way, at the junction of Tafawa Balewa Road, open from 8am to noon, Monday to Friday. There is also a **Deputy High Commission** at 2A Lamido Road, Kaduna. Tel: 212178. The **British Council** is at Kofar Nassarw, near the Emir's Palace.

The **Niger Consulate** is on Alu Avenue, just south of the racecourse.

The **Immigration Office** is on Murtala Mohammed Way.

ROUTES TO NIGER

There are two direct bitumen roads from Kano to the Republic of Niger: northwest via Katsina to Maradi or directly north to Zinder. The routes are the same until the road divides 14 kms northwest of Kano. While there is frequent transport from Kano's several lorry parks to all parts of Nigeria and neighbouring countries (for details go to the Tourist Camp or the Tourist Office), transport for both Maradi and Zinder leave from the **Motorpark** by the

army barracks on the Katsina Road, a 10- to 15 minute taxi ride from the town centre.

Whichever route you opt for, it is more than likely that you will have to change taxis at least once at the border towns. This can be laborious and time-consuming because you pass through a string of immigration, customs and police posts, which usually means continually opening your bags for inspection and showing your passport. On leaving Nigeria you will be asked for your currency declaration form. Money dealers are found at the border posts.

The Road to Zinder

North of Kano on the road to Zinder there are a few interesting places at which to pause. One of the largest cattle markets in northern Nigeria is held on Sundays at **Danbata** (56 kms from Kano), where also a wide variety of crafts and other goods are sold. **Kazaure** (85 kms from Kano) is a scenic spot by a lake; it is possible to fish here if you have permission from the local Agricultural Officer. The townsfolk of **Daura** (137 kms from Kano) celebrate the Prophet's birthday (*Moulid el Beni*) in style. The Emir's Palace is worth seeing, and there is the Baya Jiddah well which figures in local myths.

At 150 kms is the Nigerian border post at Kongolam; at 185 kms is the Niger border post at Matameye. Thereafter the route passes through Takieta (213 kms) to Zinder which is 265 kms from Kano.

The Road to Maradi

The route passes through Bichi (40 kms from Kano), Yashi (92 kms) and Kankiya (113 kms), before reaching Katsina, 174 kms from Kano.

Katsina in an interesting 12th C town which is particularly well-known for its spectacular festivities at the time of Sallah at the end of Ramadan. Landmarks of Katsina include the Emir's Garden and the Gobir Minaret, from the top of which Mecca was supposedly once sighted by a holy man.

The Nigerian border post is at Jibya (219 kms from Kano) which has a large Sunday market. The border post for Niger is at Dan Issa (229 kms), and the route passes through Madarounfa (255 kms) before reaching Maradi, 314 kms from Kano. (For a description of Maradi, see the route from Zinder to Niamey in the Niger section).

NIGER

Basic Facts

Total Area: 1,267,000 sq kms.

Neighbours: Niger is a landlocked country. Algeria and Libya lie to the north, Chad to the east, Nigeria and Benin to the south and Burkina Fasso and Mali to the west.

Population: 4,727,000 (1976), 5,686,000 (1981 estimate), nationwide. Niamey: 225,314; Zinder: 58,436; Maradi: 45,852; Tahoua: 31,265; Agadez: 20,475 (1977 figures). 15 percent of the population is urban and 20 percent is nomadic.

Ethnic groups: Hausa, 2,279,000; Djerma-Songhai: 1,000,000; Fulani (Peul): 450,000; Tuareg: 127,000; Beriberi-Manga: 386,000.

Capital: Niamey.

Official language: French.

Religion: Moslem: 85 percent; traditional beliefs and Christian: 15 percent.

Independence: 1960. Formerly a French colony.

Economy: Over 80 percent of the workforce is involved in agriculture, though only 10 percent of the land is cultivable. Principal crops are millet, sorghum and cassava. As of 1988, Niger was self-sufficient in staple food grains. But in the 1970s and mid-1980s Niger was severely hit by droughts; stock rearing — traditionally an important source of revenue — was badly affected as large numbers of cattle died or had to be taken south to grazing lands. The drought has been one reason for the increased migration of people from the countryside to the towns. In 1966 uranium was discovered at Arlit; in 1980 Niger was the fifth largest producer of uranium in the non-communist world and the mineral accounted for 75 percent of the country's exports. However a drop in the world price of uranium has checked Niger's new found prosperity. Deposits of cassiterite and phosphates are also mined.

Per capita GNP: US $250 (1983–85).

President: President of the Supreme Military Council is Colonel Ali Seybou. There is no official political party.

Electricity: 220v.

Time: GMT +1.

Currency: The unit of currency is the franc CFA. 100 centimes = 1 CFA. Coins: 1, 2, 5, 10, 25, 50 and 100 franc CFA. Notes: 50, 100, 500, 1000, 5000 and 10,000 franc CFA.

£1 = 500 CFA, US $1 = 300 CFA. Approximate 1988 rates.

CFA stands for Communaute Financiere Africaine (originally Colonies Francaises d'Afrique until 1962) and is the currency used by Benin, Burkina Fasso, Cameroon, Central African Republic, Chad, Comoros Archipelago, Congo, Gabon, Mali, Niger, Senegal and Togo. The CFA is pegged to the French franc and is interchangeable within these countries.

Visas: British citizens do not need a visa to enter Niger. Niger does not have a representative in Britain but does have an embassy in Paris: Embassy Nigerienne, 154 Rue de Longchamps, 57016 Paris. Tel: 504 8060.

Accommodation: If you ask around in the provincial towns you may well find somewhere to sleep for a few dollars a night. The cheaper hotels should have rooms for under $10 and the more expensive hotels, such as the better ones in Zinder, offer rooms for around $20. In Niamey there are only a few cheap places to stay (for under $10 a room). Expect to pay from $25 for a double room with bath in the moderate/ mid-range hotels and between $50 and $75 in a top hotel.

Transport: Road is the means of transport within Niger. Prices — as well as comfort and speed — depend on what means of public transport one takes (SNTN, ordinary bus, etc) and also the standard of road on which one is travelling. Of Niger's 19,000 kms of classified road and track some 18 percent is tarmacked; the main roads are the 900-km route between Niamey and Zinder and the 700-km 'Uranium Highway' between Arlit and Tahoua. As a rough guide expect the fare between Zinder and Niamey to be $20 to $25 and from Niamey to Gao about $15. Niger has no railway. 300 kms of the River Niger is navigable within Niger and there is a river route to the sea, from Gaya to Port Harcourt, between September and March.

Tourist office: Office du Tourisme du Niger, Ave. du President H Luebke, BP 612, Niamey. Tel: 73 23 87; telex: 5467.

Embassies: USA, BP 11201, Niamey; Tel: 72 26 61. There is no British embassy in Niger.

ZINDER

'It is exceedingly painful to live in a place like Zinder, where almost every householder has a chained slave. The poor fellows (men and boys) cannot walk, from the manner in which the irons are put on, and when they move they are obliged to do so in little jumps. These slaves are ironed, that they may not run away ... It must be confessed, that if there were no white men from the north or south to purchase the supply of slaves required out of Africa, slavery would still flourish, though it might be often in a mitigated form; and this brings me to the reiteration of my opinion that only foreign conquest by a power like Great Britain or France can really extirpate slavery from Africa.'

— James Richardson, 1851

Zinder's past

Zinder, the historical capital of the powerful 19th C Damagaram Sultanate, was Niger's only significant city in the pre-colonial era. At this time it was an important southern terminus for the trans-Saharan caravans and over 3000 slaves a year were sent north to Fezzan in exchange for guns and other European goods. But this was just a fraction of the trade; by this stage the majority of the business was conducted with the merchants who were dealing with the white men along the coast.

With French rule established at the beginning of this century, Zinder was the capital of Niger from 1911 until 1926 when that status was transferred to Niamey. James Richardson wrote: 'Zinder is a most unlovely place; by no means desirable for a stranger to live in ... Verily the Zinder people have a stranger love of dust, dirt and bare mud walls'. But despite Richardson's comments, Zinder today has some of the desert town charm you may have been disappointed not to have found in Kano.

James Richardson in Zinder

Richardson's second trip to Africa was in 1850–51 with Heinrich Barth and Adolf Overweg. Part of the purpose of the mission was to study slavery at its grassroots and it was Richardson, a devout Christian

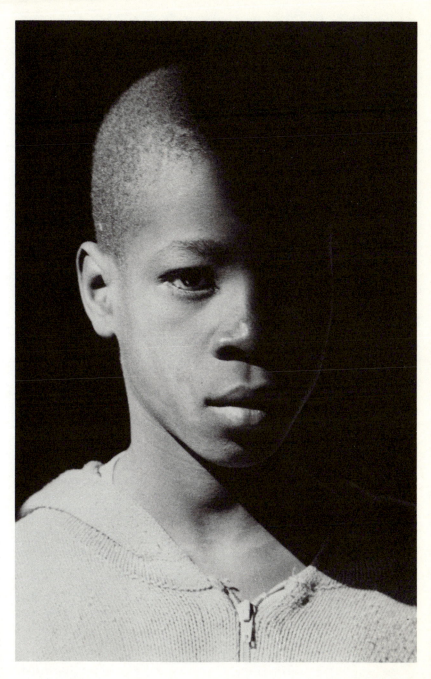

A Malian boy

and moralist, who was particularly concerned about the abominations of this trade and other unethical practices.

He spent some time in Zinder and his account of the city – in those days it was a busy market town with a population of 20,000 people – gives an interesting insight into life at that time. Much of Richardson's writings concentrate on the Sultan's treatment of the people, which was probably not untypical of rulers in the central Sudan.

The Slave Trade

Richardson recorded: 'I have obtained some information on the slave trade, which I here give its crude shape. Slaves are classed as follows:

Males

1st. Garzab: those who have a beard.
2nd. Morhag: those with a beard beginning.
3rd. Sabaai: those without a beard.
4th. Sadasi: grown children.
5th. Hlamasi, or children.

Females

Ajonza, old women, not classified.
1st. Shamalia: those with breasts hanging down.
2nd. Dabukia: those with the breasts plump.
3rd. Farkhah: those with little breasts.
4th. Sadasia: girls smaller.
5th. Hlamasiah, or children.

'The best of the slaves now go to Niffee, to be there shipped for America; they are mostly males, of the class 2nd, 3rd, 4th, and are minutely examined before departure. From all reports, there is an immense traffic of slaves that way exchanged against American goods, which are driving out of the markets all the merchandise of the north.'

The price of slaves

He went on to compare the prices of slaves at the various markets, thus revealing the profits of the trade:

A good male is sold at:

Kano/Zinder	10 or 12 dollars
Tripoli	60 to 65 dollars
Constantinople	90 to 100 dollars

A good female is sold at:

Kano/Zinder	32 dollars
Tripoli	100 dollars
Constantinople	130 dollars

Sultans and chiefs would capture their slaves by raiding villages whenever it suited them. These attacks were known as 'razzias'. Originally Moslems would only herd up pagans as they felt there was nothing wrong in abusing the lives of those who did not believe in Allah. But this was only a passing justification: by the mid-19th C many natives had adopted Islam, but the Sultan of Zinder was quite prepared to enslave people of his own religion and country.

While Richardson was in Zinder, the Sultan was preparing a razzia against some of his own villages. The Englishman sought the opinion of some of the locals about this practice: 'My informants observed merely, "Oh, he must have slaves to pay his debts; and as the largest fish eat the little fish, so the great people eat the small people". Thus the protection of Islamism is now come to nothing and the cry is – "To the razzia!" without mentioning even the name of Kafar (infidel) or Kardi. In the end this will retard the progress of Mohammedanism, for the blacks see that it is now no protection for them against their more powerful neighbours and their periodical razzias.'

A few days later Richardson was in the market. 'In the souk today, it was proved beyond all doubt that the Zinder people sell themselves into foreign slavery. Many of the slaves for sale had the Zinder sacrificed marks on their faces ... Indeed it now appears that all this part of Africa is put under contribution to supply the South American market with slaves.' Richardson was repulsed by traders who would come to Zinder and 'drawse away the period of their residence in this sleepy city. They sell their goods in a lump, on trust, to the Serkeen, and then compose themselves to slumber whilst he goes forth on a razzia, and brings them slaves in payment'. Sometimes the chief would trump up a petty quarrel, so that he would have an excuse to attack. Richardson gave an example: 'A boy steals some trifling articles – a few needles; he is forthwith sold in the souk, and not only he, but "if the Sarkee wants money" his father and mother, brothers and sisters: and "if the Sarkee is very much pressed for money", his familiars search for the brothers of the brothers of the father and all their relations'.

But pretexts were not really necessary. The Sultan with an army of possibly 2000 horsemen and 10,000 infantry would swoop down on villages – the Daura region was particularly popular – and employ siege and burn tactics. Resistance was usually offered but the Sultan's forces were superior and nearly all the villagers would end up in captivity or dead. The Sultan would often leave a handful of people alive so that they would breed and thus replenish the supplies for a future razzia.

The fruits of a razzia

Richardson mentioned the elation of the townsfolk in Zinder when a razzia returned, and then described the pathetic scene as the expedition entered the town: 'A cry was raised early this morning, "The Sarkee is coming!" Every one went out eagerly to learn the truth. It turned out that a string of captives, fruits of the razzia, was coming in. There cannot be in the world – there cannot be in the whole world – a more appalling spectacle than this. My head swam as I gazed. A single horseman rode first, showing the way, and the wretched captives followed him as if they had been used to this condition all their lives. Here were naked little boys running alone, perhaps thinking themselves upon a holiday; near at hand dragged mothers with babes at their breasts; girls of various ages, some almost ripened into womanhood, others still infantine in form and appearance; old men bent two-double with age, their trembling chins verging towards the ground, their poor old heads covered with white wool; aged women tottering along, leaning upon long staffs, mere living skeletons; – such was the miscellaneous crowd that came first; and then followed the stout young men, ironed neck to neck! This was the first instalment of the black bullion of Central Africa; and as the wretched procession huddled through the gateways into the town the creditors of the Sarkee looked gloatingly on through their lazy eyes, and calculated on speedy payment.'

Most of the slaves were taken to Kano and from there they would go to the coast.

The Tree of Death

Gruesome tortures and capital punishment were also intrinsic acts in the Sultan's inhuman repertoire. 'I am told his highness is much feared by all the people of the provinces,' Richardson wrote. 'He has the character of being impartial. But the way in which he carries out capital punishment is truly terrible, and beyond conception barbarous. He neither hangs nor beheads. This mode of punishment is too mild for him. No: he actually cuts open the chests and rips out the heart! or else hangs people up by the heels, and so inflicts upon them a lingering death.'

One afternoon Richardson was taken to an execution spot. The place was covered with human bones which had been licked clean by hyenas. He walked a little further on: 'I came to the Tree of Death! a lonely tree springing out of the rocks, some forty or fifty feet in height, and of the species called here kanisa'. The area under the tree (which was not the only tree of death) was swept daily by the executioner and anybody who dared venture here was put to death. 'I certainly began to feel sick myself at the recital of the various horrors perpetrated at this place by the executioner. Never in my life did I feel so sick at heart — so revolted at man's crimes and cruelties. The tree itself was a true picture of death — a tree of dark, impenetrable foliage, with a great head, the upper part larger than the lower one, and this head crowned with fifty filthy vultures, the ministers of the executioner, which eat the bodies of the criminals! The number of executions here performed is very great — some two or three hundred in a year.' There was carrion in plenty for the vultures which pecked by day and the hyenas which prowled the streets by night.

'Fifty filthy vultures'

Strenuous Idleness

'His highness the Sarkee of Zinder is a prince of true African and Asiatic calibre. He has three hundred wives, one hundred sons, and fifty daughters; but his women are not prisoners of the harem ... His wives and daughters are seen about the streets walking alone, and the daughters are given in marriage to the grandees of the court ... His wives are likewise often found with paramours outside the palace.'

Life in the harem

Richardson also described the scene inside the harem of an official. 'The harem was full of fine, handsome Hausa slaves, attending on his four wives; they were all polished, and apparently clean, lying about on the floors of the huts, and in the courtyards, in the most strenuous idleness — one cleaning, polishing and decorating another.'

Points of Interest in Zinder

Zengou, the old town, was originally outside the city walls and was the stopping point for the merchants' caravans. Today it is the commercial centre and site of Zinder's famous colourful **market** — one of the largest in Niger — which is held every Thursday.

About one kilometre southeast of the Zengou area is the walled district of **Birni**, the oldest part of Zinder. Several tombs of former sultans are in the grounds of the **old palace**.

The area between Zengou and Birni — both were sites of large slave markets during the 19th C — is the **modern part of town**; here you find the police, cinemas, hotels, the bank, post office and super-market. The wide avenues are uncluttered and the buildings have a distinct colonial desert style. The **military camp** overlooking the town was formerly known as Camp Cazemajou, after a French officer who was assassinated in Zinder in 1898. A force was sent out to avenge his death which led to the French occupation of this region in 1899. After independence the camp was renamed Tanimoun in honour of the influential 19th C Sultan of Damagaram.

A feel of the desert

Everything in town is within walking distance.

Ten kilometres to the west of Zinder is the village of **Tirmini**, where the French-commanded Senegalese troops defeated the Damagaram army in 1899 and thus took Zinder.

PRACTICAL INFORMATION

ACCOMMODATION AND FOOD

The **Central** and the **Damagaram** are two well-established **hotels** with pleasant gardens and a friendly atmosphere. Both are centrally located, opposite each other on the Avenue de la Republic, both have air conditioning and baths with rooms, and both are on the expensive side. Though they are deteriorating, they still have charm and style. You feel that places like these, often found in outposts of former colonies, must have had an interesting clientele and a colourful past. The Damagaram is the more expensive of the two, while the Central is a particularly popular rendezvous in the evenings.

The **Hotel Kourandaga** may now be open; its rates and standard were not known when I was in Zinder.

You can find cheaper places to stay if you ask around at the Gare Routiere or the African Restaurant.

There are **restaurants** at the Central and Damagaram hotels, and many cheap restaurants and street stalls around town.

TRAVEL

The Gare Routiere for **taxis brousse**, and the **SNTN bus** stop are in the centre of town. From here you can find transport to Kano, Niamey, Agadez and Nguigmi on Lake Chad.

There is an **airport** handling domestic flights to Niamey, and sometimes to other destinations such as Agadez and Maradi.

ONWARD ROUTES
Zinder to Niamey
A surfaced road covers the 909-km distance:

Takieta	52 kms
Tessaoua	114 kms
Gazaoua	145 kms
Maradi	237 kms
Madaoua	397 kms
(junction)	451 kms (road north to Tahoua and Agadez)
Birni N'Konni	487 kms (border town with Nigeria)
Dogondoutchi	632 kms
Dosso	769 kms (junction with road north to Filingué and south to Nigeria and Benin)
Birni Ngaouré	802 kms (junction with road north to Filingué; also see below)
Niamey	909 kms

There are at least 5 fast SNTN buses along this route a week, and cheaper, slower local buses. Expect the journey to take around 24 hours.

Maradi (237 kms from Zinder) was a provincial town of Katsina (Nigeria) when in the 19th C they were both conquered by the Fulani. Hausa refugees from Katsina built up their strength and overthrew the Fulani in Maradi and then settled here. For many years the two towns, under their foreign occupants, fought one another. Maradi vies with Zinder for being Niger's second largest town (population around 40,000 in 1976) after Niamey, and it is known as the peanut capital because its hinterland produces 50% of the country's groundnuts. It is also near the border on the busy direct Lagos-Kano-Niamey route, which is an important lifeline for land-locked Niger.

Birini N'Konni is a centre for the Hausa animists known as Azna, who are non-Moslems.

Zinder to Agadez
Tarmacking is in progress, however sections of the 471-km road remain rough and unsurfaced and can be impassable during the July through September rains:

Sabonkafi	115 kms
Tanout	160 kms
Aderbissinat	310 kms
Agadez	471 kms

The journey will take from 12 to 24 hours, depending on the means of transport and whether you stop at night. Trucks and buses cover this route, though many drivers prefer to travel to Agadez along the better though longer road via Birni N'Konni and Tahoua.

AGADEZ

'At length the day arrived when I was to set out on my long wished for excursion to Agadez ... For what can be more interesting than a considerable town, said to have been once as large as Tunis, situated in the midst of lawless tribes, on the border of the desert and of the fertile tracts of an almost unknown continent, established there from ancient times, and protected as a place of rendezvous and commerce between nations of the most different character, and having the most various wants? It is by mere accident that this town has not attracted as much interest in Europe as her sister town Timbuktu.'

But by now the age of magnificence was over for Agadez. Here, like elsewhere in the Sudan, Barth was disappointed when he entered the town:

'The streets and the market-place were still empty when we went through them, which left upon me the impression of a deserted place of by-gone times; for even in the most important and central quarters of the town most of the dwelling houses were in ruins. Some meat was lying ready for sale, and a bullock was tied to the stake, while a number of large vultures, distinguished by their long naked necks of reddish colour and their dirty greyish plumage, were sitting on the pinnacles of the crumbling walls, ready to pounce upon any kind of offal ... Agadez is in no respect a place of resort for wealthy merchants, not even Arabs, while with regard to Europe its important-ance consists in its lying on the most direct road to Sokoto and that part of Sudan.'

Fluctuating populations of the Sahel towns

So wrote Heinrich Barth in 1850, but what he observed was just one phase in the changing fortunes of Agadez, and typical of a Saharan town whose main reason for existing, at least until recently; was as an entrepot.

The Azali

The Taureg town of Agadez, founded in the 15th C, grew up at the crossroads of four main trading routes: to the east, Bilma, Tibesti and Kufra; to the south, Zinder and Kano; to the west, In-Gall, Gao and Timbuktu; and to the north, Tamanrasset, Tuat and Tripoli. In the 16th C, while under the influence of the

Songhai kingdom, Agadez reached its zenith as a gold market for merchants travelling between Gao and Tripoli. Its population stood at 30,000. When the Moroccans ransacked west Sudan this trade, and along with it Agadez' prosperity; declined.

However, the town was able to survive through its involvement in the salt trade. Parts of Aïr were fortunate in having extensive pastures capable of feeding large numbers of camels, and this enabled huge caravans to be assembled by the merchants. In pre-colonial times the *azali* (as the caravans were known — a similar azali also used to bring salt from Taudeni to Timbuktu) averaged 10,000 camels stretching 25 kms in length, and in 1906 the azali was comprised of a staggering 20,000 camels. Each October they would meet north of Agadez at Tabello and then travel east to collect salt from the Bilma mines. Here the merchants would exchange corn and cloth from Hausa for salt and then return via the same route to Aïr. The round trip would take three weeks. From Agadez a large part of the caravan would head south to Kano to barter the salt for material and other Hausa products.

More camels than people

But though the caravans mustered were large, and the town persevered, its population continued to fall, so that when Barth arrived in 1850 its inhabitants numbered no more than 7000. The main trade route across the Sahara passed through Iferouane to the north, bypassing Agadez by 310 kms. In the first quarter of this century there were only 3000 people in the town. Today the azali has declined and trucks take care of most of the trade.

Nevertheless, the population of Agadez has recently rocketed, first with the discovery of uranium in the region and then again dramatically to over 100,000 in and around the town when the nomads migrated here during the Sahel drought of the mid-1970s. Many of these subsequently returned to the desert and Agadez settled down to a population of around 20,000; renewed drought in the mid-1980s has seen yet another increase. At any rate, as Agadez is now the first main town reached after crossing the new Trans Saharan highway, it should be guaranteed a certain level of population.

Drought and migration

Local Hero

A folk hero here is Koacen Ag Mohammed who in 1916 attacked Agadez in a bid to oust the French. After a three-month siege the colonial power sent for reinforcements from Zinder and so managed to suppress the Koacen revolt. As the uprising was religiously inspired, the French retaliated by killing well over 100 marabouts (holy men) in Agadez and In-Gall.

Points of Interest in Agadez

The **Great Mosque** (Messallaje) was originally built in the 16th C, but was reconstructed in 1844. It has a square base, 9 metres each side; the 27-metre spikey clay minaret with the characteristic wooden beam supports gradually tapers to a diameter of 2.5 metres at the top. Part of its function was as a watchtower and you should climb the minaret, particularly at sunset, for a good view of the town and the surrounding landscape.

The large colourful **central market** sells a variety of foods, handicrafts and general paraphernalia. There are many artisans in Agadez. The town is renowned for its silversmiths and the cross of Agadez (each Taureg district has its own design of cross) is particularly famous. These silver crosses and the Taureg leatherwork are popular souvenirs with passing tourists and are, along with other objets d'art in Agadez, often relatively expensive.

There is a **camel market** on the western edge of town and also a small **zoo** next to the tourist office, which is up the main street from the mosque.

The **architecture** of Agadez is generally traditional and like Zinder there is the sensation of being in a historic Saharan/Sahelian town.

The Moslem New Year and the Prophet's Birthday are celebrated in style in Agadez.

PRACTICAL INFORMATION

ACCOMMODATION AND FOOD

Some modestly priced **hotels**, with air conditioning and shower, include:
Hotel de l'Aïr, formerly the Sultan's palace until it was confiscated after the Taureg uprising in 1916; it is opposite the Grand Mosque.
Family House, a popular place, is opposite Ruetsch in the Place des Boulangers.
Hotel Atlantide is on the western side of

town in the direction of the Niamey Road. **Hotel Sahara**, opposite the central market, is the least expensive of the hotels mentioned.

You may find somewhere cheaper to stay if you ask around at the Gare Routiere.

There are two camping sites in the vicinity of Agadez: **Camping Escale** and **Camping de l'Oasis** (Chez Joyce), 3 and 8 kms out of town respectively. Most overland travellers with their own vehicles stay here.

In addition to those at the hotels, there are small **restaurants** such as Le Sengalais, Big Boy, Le Restaurant Populaire and Bar l'Ombre du Plaisirs.

TRAVEL
For the taxi brousse and the SNTN **bus**, ask for the Gare Routiere.

Agadez has a domestic **airport**. There are at least 2 flights a week to Niamey; other destinations are Arlit, Tahoua and Zinder.

ONWARD ROUTES
Agadez to Niamey
The route via Birni N'Konni is 1023 kms. The road between Agadez and Tahoua is surfaced; the Tahoua-Niamey route via Filingue is an unsurfaced track, thus the southern route via Birni N'Konni is preferred because it is surfaced and quicker. An SNTN bus covers the full distance in about 16 hours.

Assaouas	68 kms
	(junction for road to
	Tamanrasset)
In-Gall	127 kms
In-Waggeur	214 kms
Tagamanir	276 kms
Abalak	338 kms
Tahoua	449 kms
Badeguisheri	498 kms

Birni N'Konni	601 kms
	(see Zinder to
	Niamey route)
Dogondoutchi	746 kms
Dosso	883 kms
Birni Ngaoure	916 kms
Niamey	1023 kms

In-Gall (127 kms from Agadez) was founded by Songhai soldiers from Askia Mohammed's army and grew up as a small oasis caravan stop. Many of In-Gall's small population work seasonally in the Teguidda salt mines.

Tahoua is Niger's fourth largest town and an important market centre.

Other Routes
The Tourist Office, locals or other travellers will give you information about how to visit the picturesque **Aïr Plateau** (Aïr ou Azbine); there are several routes around this spectacular area, some of them impassable during the rainy season.

The Agadez to **Bilma** (610 kms east) route passes through the Tenere desert and is notoriously difficult. Just under halfway to Bilma is a sculpture commemorating the Tree of Tenere (see Niamey museum). Bilma is the small desolate salt producing town which the azali visits annually.

There is transport, including SNTN buses, to **Arlit** (240 kms north), the main uranium town, established in the 1960s to provide services for the mines and their workers. You should find transport going along the route to **Iferouane** (313 kms) in the heart of the Aïr ou Azbine most times of the year (especially between November and May).

The Agadez to **Tamanrasset** (859 kms northwest) and trans-desert routes should be avoided between June and October because of the severe heat and sandstorms.

NIAMEY

There are several stories about how Niamey gained its name. The one most favoured relates how a local chief, Koiri Mali, brought his people, the Niammane, to settle at this spot. The name Niammane became Niame and finally Niamey.

From the time it was founded Niamey was never anything greater than a small, unimportant fishing village; even the diligent 19th C explorers seem to have overlooked this insignificant settlement. However, in 1926 the French transferred the capital of Niger from Zinder to Niamey.

Like Bamako, the capital of Mali, Niamey's population has grown rapidly in recent years. In the early 1930s it had only 1750 inhabitants; by independence (1960) the population had swelled to 31,000 and 12 years later Niamey had three times that number of people. In 1977 the population was 225,000.

But like Bamako it is still a small capital. For most Westerners it is more akin to a mid-sized town rather than a major city. However the aid workers such as the American Peace Corps volunteers who spend months on end out in the bush will testify that Niamey is the only 'bright lights' for hundreds of miles around, and that a visit here for a bush volunteer is more exciting than a trip to New York is for a rural Midwesterner.

Bright lights amidst the bush

Many of Niamey's roads are dust and the majority of the houses are mudbrick and single-storeyed. But a lot of money is being poured into the capital, construction is underway on a large scale, and new Western-designed buildings such as banks, hotels, the post office, office blocks and the Kennedy Bridge are becoming very obvious landmarks.

When the French came here they developed a European quarter on the plateau where now the President's Palace, ministries and embassies are situated in elegant tree-lined avenues. To the east of this, on the other side of what was then a park and is now the National Museum was the African quarter. Today these quarters have conurbated.

The majestic Niger

Niamey sprawls along 7 kms of the River Niger's east bank (since the construction of the Kennedy Bridge in 1970 it has begun to develop on the west

The National Museum at Niamey

bank too). Much of the city is elevated and from places like the Grand Hotel there are picturesque views over the wide majestic river.

Niamey is pleasant. It is still not too hectic, congested or developed. At present it is a city in its infancy, but if it continues to grow at a fast rate it is likely that Niamey will end up in urban chaos.

Points of Interest in Niamey

The very impressive **Musée National du Niger** covers 24 hectares of gardens in the middle of town; it was set up by IFAN (Institute Francais d'Afrique Noire) and opened in December 1959. The whole concept of the museum is refreshingly original. Within the prettily laid-out gardens are a series of attractive pavilions based on traditional architectural styles. The pavilions — each one houses a different theme of display — exhibit costumes, jewellery, weapons, handicrafts and other artefacts and arts from around the country. Part of the grounds are occupied by artisans (there is a section for disabled craftsmen) who produce excellent work and sell it at competitive (sometimes fixed) prices; you can place personal orders. Another section has traditionally-built huts suggesting the village life of the main ethnic groups in Niger.

Dotted around the gardens are cages with a small selection of animals which include lions, chimps, hyenas, also ponds for hippos, crocodiles and tortoises, a reptile house and a small aviary. There are also palaeontological and botanical displays, which include the well-known Tree of Tenere. It is said that the tree had 45-metre roots where it stood alone in the harsh Tenere desert; it used to landmark a small oasis three days east of Agadez. The tree was knocked down by a vehicle and brought to the museum; the spot where it originally stood is now marked by a sculpture.

The Tree of Tenere

The museum, between the Petit Marche and the River Niger, has no entrance fee and is open from 9am

LEGEND

1	Grand Hotel	8	Hotel Domino	15	Tourist Office
2	Hotel Rivoli	9	Musée National du Niger	16	Post Office
3	Hotel Gaweye	10	Petit Marche	17	Sureté
4	Hotel Tenare	11	SNTN Terminal	18	Banque PIAO
5	Hotel Sahel	12	American Cultural Centre	19	Banque BDRN
6	Hotel Terminus	13	Stadium	20	Banque BCEAO
7	Hotel Maourey	14	American Recreation Centre		

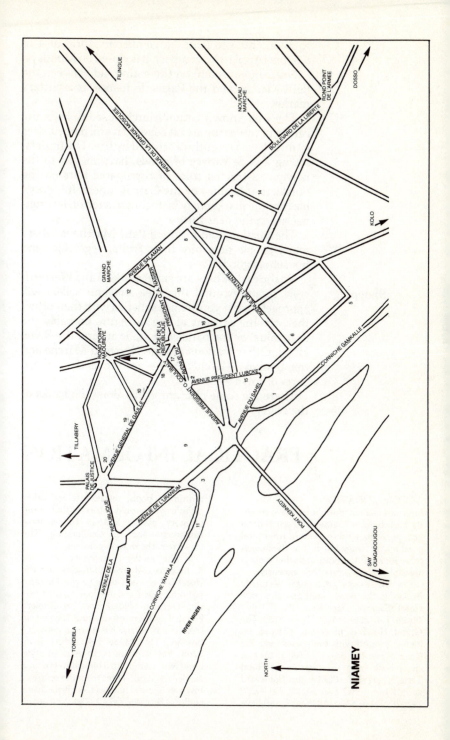

FILINGUE

NOUVEAU MARCHE

ROND POINT DE L'ARMEE

DOSSO

BOULEVARD DE LA LIBERTE

AVENUE DE LA GRANDE MOSQUEE

4

14

KOLO

GRAND MARCHE

AVENUE SALAMAN

8

AVENUE PRESIDENT G. A. NASSER

12

13

AVENUE DU SAHEL

5

16

6

ROND POINT YOUREYE

PLACE DE LA REPUBLIQUE

AVENUE DU

7

17

15

AVENUE PRESIDENT LUBCKE

CORNICHE GAMKALLE

18

2

1

10

AVENUE PRESIDENT KENNEDY

AVENUE DU SAHEL

19

AVENUE GENERAL DE GAULLE

TILLABERY

20

9

PALAIS DE JUSTICE

3

AVENUE DE LA REPUBLIQUE

AVENUE DE L'URANIUM

PONT KENNEDY

SAY OUAGADOUGOU

11

PLATEAU

CORNICHE YANTALA

TONDIBLA

RIVER NIGER

NORTH

NIAMEY

to noon and 3 to 6pm (November to April) or 4 to 6.30pm (April to November). It is closed on Mondays.

Near the museum, on the main road between the Petit Marche and the Palais de Justice, is a **pottery market**.

The well-known **Grand Marche** used to be in the centre of town (the area it covered is still named after it) until it was recently destroyed by fire. The traders, selling a wide variety of goods, have moved to the newly-constructed rows of corrugated huts on the outskirts of Niamey by the Gare Routiere. It is possible that the market may be reconstructed on its original site in the near future.

The bustling and intimate **Petit Marche** is where many people now buy their fruits, vegetables and household goods.

Shopping

To the east of here are supermarkets and Western-style shops. Around this area souvenir sellers will approach you; if you are not satisfied with their offers then try the artisans at the museum, probably the best value, or the handicraft stalls around the Rivoli Hotel. Other markets are the Nouveau Marche and the Boukoki Marche in the eastern and northern parts of town.

There are some pleasant walks along the **banks of the Niger**.

PRACTICAL INFORMATION

ACCOMMODATION
International-standard hotels have recently been built in Niamey by French hotel groups. To back these up there are several good middle range hotels. But the budget traveller has little choice and what there is available to him is relatively expensive.

On the river's edge, near Kennedy Bridge, is the newly built and first rate **Hotel Gaweye**, Place Kennedy, PO Box 11008. Tel: (227) 723400. Telex: 8237. The **Grand Hotel** is pleasantly situated on higher ground with fine views over the River Niger: PO Box 471; Tel: 732641. A short walk from the river is the **Hotel Tenere**, part of the PLM group: Boulevard de la Liberte, PO Box 10734. Tel: (227) 732020. Telex: 5330. All these hotels have

swimming pools, restaurants and other facilities you would expect to find in top category places, and all rooms have bathrooms and air conditioning. The Gaweye is the most expensive.

In the moderate category, all with bathrooms and air conditioning, are the **Hotel Sahel**, next door to the Olympic swimming pool and overlooking the river; the Terminus Hotel; and Les Roniers Hotel. The **Terminus** is about 250 metres from the river and has its own pool: PO Box 882; Tel: 225236; Telex: HOTEBAT 5268. **Les Roniers** is an African-style hotel with cone-roofed bungalows set in a small park about 4 kms from the centre of town along the Tondibla road; it also has a pool: PO Box 795; Tel: 723138. A bit out of the town centre is the **Sabka Lahiya**, a hotel with a high standard and a good reputation, though not much used by Western visitors; it has a pool.

The hotels **Rivoli** and **Maourey** are only slightly cheaper than the above group but they are of a lower standard. Both are central and have rooms with air conditioning and private bathrooms. The Rivoli's bar and restaurant is a popular rendezvous for overland travellers.

The cheap **Mission Catholique** and **Maison des Jeunes**, near the cathedral and stadium respectively, may have reopened their doors to provide accommodation. The unsalubrious **Moustache** (though it may have been cleaned up) is fairly inexpensive and frequented by Western travellers, but being on Rue de l'Islam it is not centrally located. Or there is the **Hotel D** which has been mentioned a few times in travellers' despatches recently. The **Domino** restaurant may also have a few cheap rooms.

The **Yantale campsite**, 4 kms out of Niamey on the N1 west road, is cheap and provides basic facilities.

FOOD
The main hotels have their own restaurants which tend to be expensive. Other up-market restaurants popular with Western visitors are: **Chez Nous** (various cuisines) in the El Nasr Building opposite the Rivoli Hotel; **Cascade** (French) in the Petit Marche vicinity; **Diamangou** boat restaurant (various cuisines) a few hundred metres downstream of the Sahel Hotel; the **Vietnam** and **Lotus Blue** (oriental cuisines), both near the Hotel Terminus; **Flotille** (Russian) near the SNTN bus terminal; and the **Oriental** (Lebanese) on the road to Tillabery.

There are many fairly cheap popular restaurants; most are outdoors, have bars, serve steak and chips as their main course, and have a lively, friendly atmosphere. The following are recommended: **Marrakesh, Marlkatoum, Epi d'Or, Bamboo, Ibis Noir, Saigon** and **Croisette**. All these are in the area just to the east of the Petit Marche. The very popular **Marhaba** is a few streets behind the American Cultural Centre. The **Islam** (no alcohol) is a bit out of the centre; **La Capitaine** (specialty is fish) is near the Hotel Moustache; **L'Ermitage** is along from the Hotel Tenere in

the direction of the airport; **Lalle Lalley** is near L'Ermitage; the **Baobab** (African dishes) and **Domino** are near the stadium; and the **Nigerienne** (cheapest in town, no alcohol) is near the Hotel Terminus.

In addition you can buy a variety of snacks such as beignets, brochettes, fruits, nuts and millet dishes from roadside vendors.

The **Karami**, almost opposite the Hotel Tenere, is a popular and cheap bar.

ENTERTAINMENT
The **outdoor restaurants** mentioned above are pleasant and popular places to spend the evening. There are a few **cinemas** (though films are rarely in English). Organised entertainment and discos are found at the **top hotels** or at independent discos like the **Hi-Fi** and the **Satellite**.

The **American Recreation Centre** near the Hotel Tenere is a good place to meet English-speaking people.

GETTING AROUND TOWN
In the very centre of town the easiest way of getting around is on foot. But Niamey is a sprawling city and many of the places frequented by visitors are spread out. **Taxis** cruise the streets; they are shared and quite cheap (set fare) — just hail them from the roadside. Street names are almost superfluous: most drivers will know your destination (hotel, restaurant, embassy, etc) by name rather than by address. Alternatively, rent a bike from the Petit Marche area.

USEFUL INFORMATION
Tourist Office, Avenue President Lubcke, near the Grand Hotel. Detailed city maps can be bought here. Office hours are 7.30am to 12.30pm and 3.30 to 5.30pm, Monday to Friday. Tel: 73 23 87.
Post offices are found near the Place de la Republic (new post office) and opposite the Palais de Justice (old post office). Check at both for poste restante mail. The philately bureau is at the new post office. Hours are 7.30am to 12.30pm and 3.30 to 5.30pm, Monday to Friday.
Banks: 8 to 11am, Monday to Friday. The 3 main banks are all on Avenue du General de Gaulle: BIAO, BDRN and BCEAO. BIAO is the most convenient for changing foreign currency and travellers cheques.

Ministry of the Interior: on the 'Plateau', near the elegant President's Palace. The required photo permits are issued here, though not necessarily on the spot.

Surete Nationale, Place de la Republic. It is advisable to have your passport stamped by the police at the Surete on arrival at Niamey. An exit stamp is necessary when leaving Niger; it is suggested that you get this in Niamey, even if you intend to travel overland for several days before reaching the next country.

Embassies: **Algeria** (PO Box 142) and **Nigeria** (PO Box 617) both have their embassies in Avenue President Lubcke, next to the Tourist Office. **Mali** (a Malian representative is here only to issue visas) is in a small street on the northwest side of the former Grand Marche. **Benin** (PO Box 944) is on the Plateau Ministere. Ask the Tourist Office about the **Togo** representative. tive.

There is no British Embassy in Niamey. If you have a problem consult the **American Embassy** (PO Box 11201) through the American Cultural Centre. There may be a Briton working in Niamey who has been appointed honorary consul; the American Embassy or the Tourist Office should know.

Airlines: Most, eg Air Afrique, UTA, Air Algiers and Nigeria Airways, have offices around the Rivoli Hotel. Air Algiers has the cheapest flights for those under 29 flying to Europe and certain West African destinations.

TRAVEL OUT OF NIAMEY
Taxis brousse and **trucks** travel from the Gare Routieres (Parc Autocar) in the eastern outskirts of the city to destinations around Niger and West Africa (eg Lagos, Kano, Lome, Ouagadougou). Fares by taxi brousse are rougly a third less than SNTN bus fares.

SNTN (Societe Nationale des Transports Nigeriens) are modern, efficiently run coaches which travel between the main towns of Niger and a few places further afield. They leave according to a timetable rather than waiting until they are crammed full. Seats are bookable and only one person per seat is allowed. Compared to the average taxi brousse, this is ordered and comfortable travel.

SNTN buses leave from the depot on the east bank of the River Niger about 10 minutes' walk upstream of the Gaweye Hotel. The reservation office is also here and seats should be booked in advance.

From Niamey buses go to destinations such as Agadez, Tahoua, Zinder, Maradi, Gao, Ayorou, Tillabery, Ouagadougou and Mellanville (on the Benin frontier from where it is possible to get transport to Cocontou and then to Lome in Togo).

For travelling within Niger by **air**, Air Niger is the only domestic airline: it flies at least once a week from Niamey to Tahoua, Agadez, Arlit, Maradi and Zinder. In conjunction with the Tourist Office, Air Niger also provides excursion flights to various places around the country. There are international flights from Niamey to Bamako, Abidjan, Kano (erratic), Dakar, Ouagadougou, Algiers, Marseilles, Bordeaux and Paris.

ONWARD ROUTES
Niamey to Ouagadougou
Ouagadougou, the capital of Burkina Fasso, is 520 kms west by road. The entire length of the route is now said to be surfaced, hence the journey, which used to take some 20 hours, should be considerably quicker. But tiresome checks by the customs at the frontier can last hours, making it impossible to predict the duration of the journey. SNTN buses operate on Mondays, Wednesdays and Fridays (there may be more services by now), and there is a reasonable flow of taxi brousses between the two capitals.

Torodi	70 kms (border post for leaving Niger)
Kantchari	147 kms (border post for entering Burkina Fasso; also junction for road south to Parc d'Arly and Benin)
Matiakoali	204 kms
Fada N'Gourma	297 kms (junction for road south to Benin)
Koupela	385 kms (junction for road south to Togo)
Zorgo	419 kms
Ouagadougou	520 kms

Niamey-Ayorou-Gao

The road to Gao via Ayorou follows the River Niger northwest for 443 kms. To Tillabery, and possibly as far as Ayorou by now, it has been surfaced. From Ayorou to Gao the road is unsurfaced and there are stretches which are in poor condition. The journey takes about 12 hours by bus (4 hours to Ayorou), operating Mondays and Thursdays.

Boubon	25 kms
Farie	62 kms
Tillabery	120 kms
Ayorou	208 kms
	(border post for leaving Niger; also see later chapter)
Labbezenga	255 kms (border post for entering Mali)
Ansongo	348 kms
Gao	443 kms (downstream terminal for the River Niger steamer)

Tillabery has a big market on Sundays and another one on Wednesdays.

ALONG THE NIGER NEAR NIAMEY

An enjoyable way to spend your time in Niamey is on the river. There are pleasant walks on both banks, or you can hire a pirogue from the boatmen at Pont Kennedy and travel for several hours or several days along the magnificent Niger.

Mentioned below are a few of the villages on the river which are within reasonable distance of the capital. It is more practical to get to some of them by road rather than by pirogue, and it is certainly worth consulting the Tourist Office for further details — such as the best means of transport, accommodation, price and duration of the trip — before embarking on a journey. They will also tell you the places to see wildlife such as hippos and crocodiles.

Upriver

North of Niamey at 25 kms is **Boubon**. The village is a few kilometres off the main road on the east bank of the Niger and is also a popular daytrip for foreign visitors as it gives a glimpse of the rural way of life. There is a market every Wednesday at which pottery is a major feature. You can take a pirogue across the river to the island of Boubon. Here there is a small, simple camp with a swimming pool, bar and restaurant. It is tastefully laid out in a clearing in the thick vegetation, and accommodation is in mock traditional huts. At weekends the camp is frequented by expatriates living in Niamey, but for the rest of the time, unless there is a special group, it is fairly empty. Lodging here is no more expensive than at hotels in Niamey and if you want to be a cut away, but still within striking distance of the city, then this is an ideal place to stay. Local transport leaves for Boubon from the Petit Marche in Niamey; the road is surfaced and so the journey does not take long.

Back to nature (with bar and swimming pool)

A further 5 kms north of Boubon is the village of **Karma** which has a market on Mondays.

Namaro, 50 kms north of Niamey on the west bank, also has a tourist camp.

Downriver

A short drive south of Niamey on the east bank are the villages of **Saga** and **Kolo**. The former is known

Pirogues awaiting the end of market at Ayorou

Fulani village   for its pottery and its rice mill, while the latter is a typical traditional Fulani village. Both are put on the daytripper's itinerary by tourist agents. Kolo holds a market on Fridays.

On the way to Parc du W is the village of **Say**, 50 kms south of Niamey on the west bank. This is where Heinrich Barth first saw the River Niger. There is basic accommodation here and a colourful market is held every Friday.

A boat trip to **Gaya**, Niger's southernmost town, and on the Niger-Nigeria-Benin border, takes around three days. If you have a visa you can go from Gaya into Benin; there is a bridge and a road here.

Parc National du W

Parc W covers an area of 630,500 hectares around the point where, Niger, Burkina Fasso and Benin meet. It owes its name to the W-shaped meander of the River Niger which forms part of its northern border.

The park is a popular tourist attraction and best visited between November and February (it is closed

Elephants and monkeys

during the rains). The 40 different species of wildlife here includes lions, elephants, buffalos, cheetahs, crocodiles and many types of monkey. It also has scenic parkland with small rivers, gorges and areas of luxuriant vegetation. There is an entrance fee; a guide is an extra expense but he may be necessary. Campement accommodation is at Tapoa.

Tapoa, 160 kms south of Niamey on the west bank, is the main entrance to Parc W. From the capital it can be reached by road via Diapaga, or by boat to Boumba and then the last 15 kms by road to Tapoa. There is also a tourist plane during the height of the season.

The tourist agency Transcap at the Gaweya Hotel in Niamey organises trips to **Parc de l'Arly** which is about 300 kms southwest of Niamey in Burkina Fasso.

AYOROU

One of the liveliest markets in the Sahel

Ayorou is a small market town on the east bank of the River Niger, 208 kms north of Niamey and just south of the Mali frontier. For six days of the week the town is quiet and fairly deserted, but on Sunday the whole place bursts into life.

Ayorou holds one of the largest and most colourful markets in Niger and Mali. On Sunday mornings locals from neighbouring homesteads, nomads (most noticeably the Tuaregs), and even people from Mali, Burkina Fasso and as far afield as Nigeria, seem to appear from nowhere, on foot, on donkeys or on camels, or in buses, trucks or pirogues. A recent addition to this Sunday congregation are tourists either on a day-excursion from Niamey or passing through on their way to or from Mali.

By mid-afternoon the large main square — about the size of two football pitches — is packed with camels and cattle, but the blaze of colour is quickly muted by the dense cloud of dust, resembling a thick fog, kicked up by the animals. In another area the Tuareg Bella women tend clusters of donkeys, patiently awaiting buyers. Locals will also bring goats, chickens, fruits, vegetables — quantity and quality depend on the season — and spices. Traders, some of them Moors from Mauritania, have their own shops or temporary stalls and depend on the Sunday market to sell their wide range of domestic goods, cloth and tinned foods.

The mooring point on the river is a continual bustle of activity. Pirogues come and go, friends exchange greetings and catch up on the week's news.

As evening draws near people start to make their way home. Many, it seems, have neither bought nor sold anything, but most are content to have enjoyed the atmosphere of this weekly rendezvous. By Monday the square is deserted and the market stalls empty; life is back to normal.

Except at a handful of places, notably the Amenokal Hotel, there is neither electricity nor pumped water in Ayorou.

PRACTICAL INFORMATION

ACCOMMODATION AND FOOD

The only hotel in Ayorou — quite incongruous to the town — is the French PLM group's 4-star **Amenokal.** (It is addressed via Niamey: Amenokal Hotel, PO Box 10224, Niamey.) Situated on the east bank of the River Niger, it has a pleasant garden, and a swimming pool, bar and restaurant. there are 25 rooms, all with air conditioning and bathroom. the hotel is open only from November to around April.

If necessary, the police or locals will help you find alternative accommodation.

The only place to eat, other than at the Amenokal, is the small **Pirogue restaurant** which usually serves reasonably priced steak and chips. The alternative is tinned food from the stores.

EXCURSIONS BY PIROGUE

You can take interesting pirogue rides around the neighbouring **villages**; agree on the price before the trip. One worthwhile journey would be to travel by one of these canoes downstream to **Niamey** (this might only be possible when the water is high), though there is no certainty that you would find someone willing to take you.

In the 1850s Heinrich Barth, the German explorer, wrote about the area between Ayorou and Tillabery: 'The whole district is said to be greatly infested by lions and we saw the remains of four hides which a single individual of the species had torn to pieces.'

Today lions, in common with many other wild animals, no longer exist around here. However giraffes are said to roam this region and from Ayorou you can take a pirogue ride to **Hippo Pool** or the **Island of Birds**, although you cannot be sure of seeing any of the more spectacular wildlife.

ONWARD ROUTES

There is normally daily transport of some sort going to **Niamey** and **Tillabery**.

Vehicles to Mali leave several days a week, though the best time to get a lift direct to **Gao** is on Sunday after the market. The journey takes about 8 to 12 hours depending on border stops; for the most part the unsurfaced road is in poor condition.

It is 235 kms to Gao in Mali. As you go north the vegetation starts to thin out, though it still remains lush on the riverbanks. The Niger frontier post is at **Labezanga**; the rapids here hinder river transport and Barth, who passed this point in June 1853 when the water was low wrote: 'I have no doubt that this is one of the most difficult passages of the river. The name of the cape is Emnashid, "the cape of the ass" [just upstream of Labezanga] ... The most westerly branch forms a small waterfall of about 18 inches elevation, foaming along with great violence.'

There is an area of no man's land between Labezanga and the Mali customs/immigration checkpoint; from here the road continues to follow the course of the Niger and the only settlement of any reasonable size before Gao is the attractive town of **Ansongo**.

MALI

Basic Facts

Total Area: 1,240,000 sq kms.

Neighbours: Mali is a landlocked country. Algeria lies to the north, Niger and Burkina Fasso to the east, Ivory Coast and Guinea to the south and Senegal and Mauritania to the west.

Population: 6,308,320 (1976), 8,206,000 (1985 estimate) nationwide. Bamako: 404,000; Segu: 65,000; Mopti: 54,000; Sikasso: 47,000; Kayes: 45,000 (1976 figures). 20 percent of the population is urban, 10 percent is nomadic (1985).

Ethnic groups: Bambara: 1,000,000; Fulani: 450,000; Marka: 280,000; Songhai: 230,000; Malinke: 200,000; Tuareg: 240,000; Senoufo: 375,000; Dogon: 130,000 (all 1963 figures).

Capital: Bamako.

Official language: French.

Religion: Moslem: 65 percent; traditional beliefs: 30 percent; Christian 5 percent.

Independence: 1960. Formerly a French colony.

Economy: The vast majority of the country's workforce is involved in agriculture, usually at subsistence level. Only about 20 percent of the land is cultivable and the chief crops are cotton (which accounts for 40–50 percent of export revenue), rice, millet and groundnuts. Economic growth has been severely affected by droughts (the 1983–85 drought caused the death of 40–80 percent of the livestock) and this has been one reason for the human migration from the country to the towns. Mali has some mineral resources, including phosphates, uranium, gold, bauxite and manganese; however they are not yet a significant source of revenue.

Per capita GNP: US $140 (1983–85).

President: General Moussa Traore. He came to power through a coup d'etat in 1968, though he was elected president in 1979 and re-elected in 1985. The Union Democratique du Peuple Malien (UDPM) is the country's only party.

Electricity: 110/220v.

Time: GMT.

Currency: The Malian franc (FM) was abolished in 1984 and Mali's currency is now the Communaute Financiere Africaine (CFA). See Niger *Basic Facts*.

In Mali changing money is a lengthy procedure and it is advisable to get to the bank at the start of business as they are only open for a few hours a day.

Visas: Required for entry into Mali and issued one or two days after application. Mali has no representative in Britain but does have embassies in Paris and Brussels (see below). If you are following the route outlined in this book then you will find a Malian visa official in Niamey (one existed at the time of writing) and — if you are arriving from the west — a consulate in Banjul.

Visas are issued on the spot to foreigners entering Bamako by plane. According to a senior Tourist Office official, overland visitors who arrive at the Mali border without a visa are allowed into the country and asked to get the necessary entry requirements at the first main town, for example Gao, Timbuktu, Mopti, Bamako, Kayes. There is no reason to believe this is untrue, however it is still advisable to get your papers in order before reaching the border, because a frontier policeman may have his own interpretation of the formalities.

Visas are normally valid for only seven days. Extensions are easily obtainable at the main towns; they last up to two months.

Malian Embassies in France and Belgium: 89 Rue du Cherche-Midi, Paris 6. Tel: 548 5843. Rue Camille Lemmonier 112B, 1060 Brussels. Tel: 345-74-32.

Accommodation: The government campements are scattered around the country. They are usually quite basic — though adequate for travellers. For a double rates range from under $10 to around $25 depending on the standard of the place and whether one opts for a shared room, a private bathroom, air conditioning, half/full board, etc. Some towns have small, basic private 'pensions' where a bed can be found for a few dollars. The few smart provincial hotels (the Sofitel hotels in Mopti and Timbuktu) charge around $40 for a double. In Bamako there are only a limited number of places to stay for under $10 a night. The mid-range hotels in the capital are around $25 for a double with bath. Expect to pay twice that in a top hotel.

Transport: The approximate rates for the River Niger steamer:

From Gao to:

	1st Class	2nd Class	3rd Class	4th Class
Kabara (Timbuktu)	$ 60	$ 40	$25	$10
Mopti	$120	$ 80	$50	$20
Koulikoro	$160	$110	$85	$35

Much of the road transport in Mali is seasonal: Mali has 18,000 kms of classified roads and tracks, of which 7500 kms are passable at all seasons and 2000 kms are tarmac (1981). The 600-km road between Mopti (Sevare) and Gao, officially opened in 1986, is part of the Trans Saharan Highway linking Algeria to Nigeria. The government is keen to improve the Bamako-Abidjan road as this is an important link to the coast and carries 58 percent of imports and 65 percent of exports; remaining imports/exports travel on the Bamako-Dakar railway.

As a rough indication of the prices a journey from Mopti to Bamako in a 504 will cost $12. The train from Bamako to Dakar is $65 wagon-lit, $50 first class, $33 second class.

Tourist office: Societe Malienne d'Exploitation des Ressources Touristiques (SMERT), BP 222, Bamako. Tel: 22 59 42; telex: 316.

Embassies: USA, BP 34, Ave. Mohammed V, Bamako. There is no British embassy in Mali.

GAO

'As soon as I had made out that Gogo [Gao] was the place which for several centuries had been the capital of a strong and mighty empire in this region, I felt a more ardent desire to visit it than I had to reach Timbuktu. The latter no doubt, had become celebrated throughout the whole of Europe on account of the commerce which centred in it; nevertheless, I was fully aware that Timbuktu had never been more than a provincial town, although it exercised considerable influence upon the neighbouring regions from its being the seat of Mohammedan learning. But Gawo, or Gogo, had been the centre of a great national movement, from whence powerful and successful princes, such as the great Mohammed el Haj Askia, spread their conquests from Kebbi, or rather Hausa, in the east, as far as Futa in the west, and from Tawat in the north, as far as Wangara and Mosi toward the south.'

— Heinrich Barth, 1854

Songhai capital

Gao, originally called Kawkaw, was founded in the 7th C AD and by the 9th C it had become the centre of a prosperous kingdom like that of Ghana which lay further to the west. Al-Yaquibi wrote the following about Gao in AD 872.

'Then there is the kingdom of Kawkaw, which is the greatest of the realms of Sudan, the most important and powerful. All other kingdoms obey its king ... Under it there are a number of kingdoms, the rulers of which pay allegiance to the king of Kawkaw, and acknowledge his sovereignty, although they are kings themselves in their own lands.'

In the 14th C Ibn Battuta said Gao was one of the greatest centres in Sudan and nearly 200 years later Leo Africanus enthusiastically described the city's market: 'Here are exceedingly rich merchants ... It is a wonder to see what plenty of merchandise is daily brought hither, and how costly and sumptuous all things be. Horses bought in Europe for ten ducats, are sold again for forty and sometimes for fifty ducats apiece ... and a young slave of fifteen years age is sold for six ducats, and so are children sold also.'

But at the end of the 16th C the Songhai kingdom

A young girl of Gao

(see following chapter) fell to the Moroccans, and Gao, the capital, rapidly declined into what Barth described as a 'desolate abode of a small and miserable population'.

Today Gao, which was rebuilt early this century, is the downstream terminus for the River Niger steamboat (from Koulikoro and Mopti) and also the first main stop in Mali for trans-Saharan travellers coming south from Algeria (Reggane-Tessalit route).

It is a small, busy, bustling river port. The streets, set out in a grid pattern, are quite wide, but mostly unpaved, dusty and crowded; the buildings are ramshackle and of little architectural interest (this is also true of the main mosque which was originally built by Mansa Musa in the 14th C). However, Gao's charm, as with so many Sahelian towns, is the atmosphere generated by everyday life.

Not surprisingly Gao is an important market town. The Grand Marche opposite the Atlantide Hotel sells vegetables, fruits and meat, and has a section devoted to artisans and souvenir sellers. When the boat arrives the bustle of the market overflows onto the quayside, with women and children — baskets delicately balanced on their heads — selling fruits and snacks. The Petit Marche beyond the police station sells cloth, traditional crafts and a variety of domestic goods.

Points of Interest in and Around Gao

The **tomb of Askia** is about a 15-minute walk upstream from the town centre. The Askias were a dynasty of Songhai kings who had their capital in Gao and ruled from 1493 to 1591. The rather curious tomb is mud brick in the vague shape of a pyramid, with the characteristic crossbeams of Sahelian architecture sticking out at right angles. There are crude steps which half spiral to the top, from where you have quite a good view over Gao. The tomb is in a courtyard surrounded by simple attractive cloisters. You may have to ask around to find somebody to let you in.

The very small Gao **museum**, about five minutes' walk inland from the Grand Marche, mainly covers the archaeology and the present situation of the people in the region north of Gao. Exhibits include a Tuareg tent and various traditional artefacts.

Before the Sahara Lying to the northeast of Gao on the way to Kidal and Tessalit is the **Valley of Tilemsi** where there are neolithic sites dating from 1500 BC; this region used to be well-populated before it was overtaken by the Sahara desert. The Valley of Tilemsi and the neighbouring **Adrar des Iforas** region are main subjects of the Gao museum.

A short car ride northeast of Gao, on a dried up tributary of the Niger, is the **Necropole de Sane**. There is evidence of a large old tomb here, and stelae dating from the 12th C and later have also been found. The marble of one of the stelae is believed to have come from Spain.

It is possible to take **pirogue rides** on the river — just ask at the quayside. A popular excursion is to the **Dunes Rosé** (red sand dunes) 5 kms distant and on the opposite bank. There are also islands and pleasant spots on the banks in the vicinity of Gao.

PRACTICAL INFORMATION

ACCOMMODATION
The rambling colonial-style **Atlantide** is the only hotel in Gao. The building, a dusty ochre colour, has a large courtyard; the bar and dining room are solemn and dimly lit, and the bedrooms are dingy; whatever elegance it may have had is no longer there. But it has an interesting appeal, so you give it the benefit of the doubt and assume that it once had a certain style. With an element of tolerance and a romantic imagination — both so important when travelling — the conditions are quite acceptable. And the prices are inexpensive to moderate.

Behind the Atlantide there is **Paillotte camping** (small huts), and you can use the hotel's facilities. They charge about one-third the price of the Atlantide.

There is a **campsite** at the ferry point to the south of Gao.

FOOD AND ENTERTAINMENT
Typically there are several cheap eating places in town, such as the **Blackpool tea stall** — a name probably given by an English visitor, though it is difficult to think of any similarity between Gao and the northern England resort. The **Senegalese 'kitchens'** are, like elsewhere in Mali and Niger, good value.

The **bars**, eg Twist, Oasis, Desert and Escale, are sociable places to pass the evening.

OFFICIALDOM
As the capital of eastern Mali and the first significant town upstream from the Niger border, Gao is an important administrative centre.

You must **register with the police** giving details of arrival and departure. Obtain a **visa extension** if necessary (visas are usually valid for one week only; there is a fee for the extension stamp which lasts for the requested period, up to one month). **Photography permits** are available at the police station (camera details and a passport photo of yourself are required); a fee is payable. Make sure the photo permit is valid for all of Mali, not just

for the Gao district. The local treasury issues the stamps.

ONWARD ROUTES
Air services are operated by Air Mali from Gao airport, 7 kms from town, to Bamako, Goundam, Mopti and Timbuktu — one or two flights a week to each destination.

Riverboats sail from Gao to Kabara (for Timbuktu), Mopti and Koulikoro (near Bamako): see the later chapter **The River Niger Steamers**.

Gao to Timbuktu by Road
By road to Timbuktu the distance is 424 kms. There is no public road transport between Gao and Timbuktu; however private vehicles do cover this route, which runs along the eastern and northern bank of the river. The road is unsurfaced and there are sections which would probably be suited only to 4-wheel drive vehicles. During the high water season stretches of the road are impassable. At Rharous (277 kms) on the south bank there is a ferry which shuttles vehicles over to the north bank. From Rharous there is a track southwest to Mopti and another one southeast to near Gossi. Bourem (95 kms) and Bamba (232 kms) are the two main towns between Gao and Timbuktu.

Gao to Mopti by Road
Timbuktu, offers a journey of 600 kms. To the south of Gao is the ferry, capable of taking cars, which crosses the Niger. The road to Mopti (Sevare) is now surfaced.

Doro	90 kms
Gossi	162 kms
Hombori	250 kms
Douentza	398 kms
Bore	458 kms
Kona	514 kms
	(junction with road
	from Timbuktu)
Mopti	600 kms

Some form of transport leaves Gao for Mopti on most days, though with less frequency during the rainy season. The journey takes about a day. Around

Hombori are the dramatic Hombori mountains. These are outcrops of rock with many vertical faces. At the village of Hombori there is Mt Hombori Tondo, 1155 metres high. About 10 kms from Hombori is the Hand of Fatma where the needle-like rocks look like fingers.

On the way from Hombori to Douentza is the **Gandamia Escarpment**. The village of **Douentza** lies between the spectacular Gandamia and Bandiagara escarpments. From Douentza you can follow the **Bandiagara Escarpment** south. But it is over 100 kms (varies a lot depending on your route) to Sanga. You will have to find out from locals about the availability of transport and how much, if any, of the journey you would have to walk.

THE SONGHAI EMPIRE

The heartland of the Songhai empire lay along the River Niger between Kawkaw (Gao) and the Dendi region, roughly in the area of the present-day Nigeria-Niger-Benin border.

The Sorke, the community of fishermen, were originally dominant among the Songhai. Mythology represented this power as a large river beast with a golden nose ring. From time to time the beast would impose its will on the other Songhai, most of whom were farmers, and would extort tithes from them. In AD 690 a visiting foreigner was so outraged by this injustice that he killed the beast with a harpoon. He was at once elected king, and he, Za Alieman, became the founder of the Za dynasty.

The Za Dynasty

This was the first of three dynasties to rule the Songhai and it derived its name from the popular belief that 'Za min al Jemen', meaning 'He comes from Yemen'. More likely, Za Alieman was a Lamtuna Berber, or a Soninke from Ghana, or a Zaghawa nomad from the Lake Chad region. In any case the Sorke, rather than be subjected to alien rule, moved 100 kms upstream and founded Gao — but in the 9th C they were overcome by the increasingly powerful Za dynasty.

Founding of Gao

Gao rapidly rose in importance and as it was a meeting point for caravans to North Africa via Tadmekka, and Egypt via Takedda and Agadez, by the middle of the 11th C it was second in prosperity only to the state of Ghana. At this time too, influenced by traders from the north, the Za dynasty adopted Islam, though the mass of the Songhai retained their traditional beliefs.

Despite their wealth, however, the Songhai had no great military force. To their west the great state of Mali was founded by Sundiata in 1230 and by 1250 northern Songhai was under Malian hegemony. The power of Mali reached its peak during the reign of Mansa Musa, who on his return from his pilgrimage to Mecca in 1325 built a great mosque in Gao.

The Sunni Dynasty

Within a decade however the Mali garrison was driven out of Gao and the Za dynasty was overthrown by Ali Kolon who was proclaimed 'Sunni' or Liberator. The Sunni dynasty ruled for 150 years and under Sunni Ali Ber who came to the throne in 1464 Songhai became the most powerful state in West Africa.

Sunni Ali Ber, or Ali the Great, was a ruthless and brilliant soldier who, it was said, never lost a battle. In 1468 he made a brutal attack on Timbuktu, rid it of Tuareg rule, and then massacred the ulama (Moslem teachers) who he believed had been collaborating with the Tuaregs. Sunni Ali was only nominally a Moslem and despised the Moslem priests; his reputation for evil may have been exaggerated by Arab historians for this reason.

Djenne fell to Ali in 1473. This victory was the more difficult as the town is surrounded for much of the year by water and legend has it that he besieged Djenne for seven years, seven months and seven days before its inhabitants let him enter. When he did, he showed no cruelty, rather he married the mother of Djenne's former ruler.

One of Ali's most troublesome opponents were the Mossi of Yatenga, against whom he was always skirmishing. Although he never destroyed them he kept them at bay and controlled most of the Yatenga, Hombori and Bandiagara regions. He also won continual victories against his arch-enemies the Fulani of Macina who lived on the banks of the Niger between Timbuktu and Djenne.

Ali the Great's
control of the
river

The purpose of most of Sunni Ali's campaigns was to secure power along the Niger and with Gao, Timbuktu and Djenne in his hands he controlled the trading centres which fed the caravan routes in North Africa. He did not really need to go much further west and attack the heart of the crumbling state of Mali. Maybe he saw little need or maybe it was because his military strength lay in his fleet and he was therefore restricted to the river. He depended greatly on his boats — which were crewed, incidentally, by Sorke fishermen — and he even started building a canal in 1480 from Ras al-Ma on the Niger to Walata, the declining trading centre, with the intention of attacking it from the water. The passage was never cleared.

The Askia Dynasty

Ironically, Ali drowned. He was succeeded in 1493 by his son Abu Da'o who shared his father's contempt for the Moslem scholars but none of his military genius. Within months he was overthrown and killed by Mohammed Ture, known as Askia, the Usurper.

The Askias were the final Songhai dynasty and lasted almost 100 years. Askia Mohammed was a devout Moslem, a shrewd statesman and a brilliant administrator, as well as being a successful soldier. As he had no right to the throne he made a point of courting favour with the ulama. A contemporary chronicler wrote: 'Although one of the most intelligent of men he showed humility before the ulama, offering them slaves and wealth in order to assure their interests in the welfare of the Moslems as well as assist them in their submission to God and for the practice of the cult'.

But Islam was still restricted to a minority, and to ensure his acceptance by the masses, Askia Mohammed did not discourage the traditional religions.

The tomb of Askia outside Gao

Mohammed must have consolidated his position quickly because in 1497 he went on a pilgrimage to Mecca and did not return until the following year. On his journey he showed off no less wealth than had Mansa Musa, the Mali king, 175 years earlier. In Mecca he gave 100,000 dinars-worth of gold to a hostel for Sudanese pilgrims, and made such an impression that he succeeded in getting the Sherif of Mecca to appoint him Caliph of West Africa.

For the next hundred years the Songhai retained their strength in the western Sudan. Though they lacked rich resources, they gained their wealth from the trade which passed through their lands. Caravans carrying cloth, beads and most importantly salt (collected at the Taghaza salt mines) would cross the desert from North Africa to Timbuktu. There or at Djenne — the greatest of all the commercial centres – merchants would exchange their goods for gold. Gold and to a lesser extent slaves were highly prized, but the merchants never had direct contact with the sources. Local traders would barter for gold at the Akan and Benduku gold fields and then return to the market towns to exchange with the North African merchants. So the Songhai kingdom acted as a buffer between the Arab merchants and the gold fields, and the kings achieved their prosperity through levying taxes on the passing trade.

Tragedy for the Western Sudan

But in 1591 the Songhai kingdom collapsed. Sultan Mulay Ahmed el Mansur of Morocco wanted direct access to the gold mines so he sent a 4000-man army south across the desert. El-Sadi, an Arab chronicler,

commented: 'The expeditionary force found the Sudan one of God's most favoured countries in prosperity, comfort, security and vitality.' The Songhai were destroyed at the battle of Tondibi, and El-Sadi, referring to the situation after the invasion, continued: 'Security gave place to danger, prosperity made way for misery and calamity, whilst affliction and distress succeeded well being'.

The Moroccans went on to occupy Gao, Djenne and Timbuktu and they created a vice-royalty with its capital at Timbuktu. But they never developed a state power like Ghana, Mali or Songhai. They stole from the wealthy Moslems, exiled the prominent ulama, destroyed places of learning and virtually razed Gao. Also, according to El-Sadi, 'Over the length and breadth of the land people began to devour one another, raids and wars spared neither life nor wealth'.

At their height the Songhai controlled Agadez and their empire stretched from Hausaland in the east to Senegal in the west, and from just above Mossi territory in the south to the Taghaza salt mines in the desert to the north. Control of the River Niger from the Bussa rapids to the rapids of Sotuba between Bamako and Koulikoro was vital for their domination of the region. Having this stretch of river in their power the Songhai maintained authority in Gao, Timbuktu and Djenne, and trade flourished in these towns. The downfall of Songhai was tragic in its consequences for the subsequent development of the western Sudan.

THE NIGER RIVER JOURNEY

The following is a summary of the river journey from Gao to Koulikoro which is the port of Bamako, a voyage of 1308 kms. The scenery, the towns and other places of interest are mentioned in passing. But for a full description of Timbuktu, Mopti, Djenne, Dogon country, Segu and Bamako, see the later chapters devoted to these. After Bamako the route is overland to Banjul, the capital of Gambia, on the Atlantic, and a description of a journey up the Gambia River from Banjul is described.

It is of course possible to travel overland between Gao and Bamako, and this will be necessary in any case during those months when the waters of the Niger are not high. For further details see the *Practical Information* sections at the end of this and subsequent chapters.

Along the Majestic Niger

North of Gao you start to enter the desert. The land on either side of the River Niger is flat for as far as the eye can see. Generally the landscape is arid savannah or desert; very often the sand creeps right down to the water's edge, but sometimes the banks are thick with trees; irrigation schemes have developed large areas of the flood plain for rice cultivation.

High water along the Niger

I travelled by steamer from Gao to Timbuktu and on to Mopti in November. The Niger was high and the effects of the flooding were obvious. There were sections of the river that had become vast sheets of water and at times it was difficult or impossible to determine the river's edge: in the distance a patch of solid land may give the impression of being the bank, but when you look carefully you realise that beyond it there is another channel or expanse of water. So much of the land through which the River Niger flows, particularly from the Kabara region to well south of Mopti — an area which is known as the Inland Delta — is a lattice of interlacing channels and extensive marshland.

This inundation leaves small islands, quite a few supporting homesteads, though these will often be deserted until the level of water drops; horses and cattle have to wade out to their pastures and farmers

Casting a net into the Niger

paddle in their canoes to their paddy fields.

Attractive villages and homesteads are dotted along the banks of the Niger, though they are not as big or as numerous as you would expect on a river of this size and historical importance. This is partly due to the poor and seasonal roads. The buildings are made from mud brick and typically it is the unusual architecture of the mosque which catches the eye. Electricity and mains water is only in the bigger towns.

The very restful river journey is punctuated by the ports of call. A small crowd clusters around the quay-side when the boat arrives. Many have something to sell: mats, hats, fruits, nuts, brochettes, grilled fish, bread, tea, coffee. Friends and families are reunited. From the top deck of the steamer you have a detached bird's eye view of the colourful scene and gentle hub-bub below. It is unwise to walk too far from the boat as it may suddenly depart without much advance warning.

There is surprisingly little traffic on the river: the occasional pinasse or pirogue, usually travelling between neighbouring villages, or a barge, but not much else.

The Niger has majesty and the inhabitants along its banks — almost unnoticed — quietly get on with their lives. The overall atmosphere is one of calm serene strength.

Sailing to Timbuktu

Between Gao and Bourem, on the east bank, is the site of the **battle of Tondibi**. In 1591 a Moroccan army, some of the soldiers reputedly European sailors who had been captured by the Sultan of Morocco, wearily marched across the Sahara. This was a great feat in itself, though many men must have died of thirst or sheer exhaustion along the way. At Tondibi the 4000 Moroccan troops under Judah, their eunuch general, routed a Songhai force of 18,000 cavalry and 9000 infantry (some sources say the Songhai had as many as 40,000 men). The Moroccans owed their victory to their muskets, which even the huge numbers of courageous Sudanese could not match. This battle marked the downfall of the Songhai empire and led to anarchy in West Sudan.

On 4 January 1922 the Citroën Expedition, led by M Citroën himself, reached **Bourem**. These were the

Songhai Waterloo

first cars to cross the Sahara.

The narrowest part of the Niger in the Sahel region is at the **Tosaye Gorge**, just upstream of Bourem. Heinrich Barth, the explorer, was very impressed by this spot and in June (the low water season) 1853 he described it as 'that remarkable place called Tosaye where the noble Niger is compressed between steep banks to a breadth of perhaps not more than 150 yards'. He was told that the river was so deep at this point 'that a line made from the narrow strips of a whole bullock's skin was not sufficient to reach the bottom'. Just upstream of the Tosaye Gorge are **Baror and Shabor**, two great rocks in the river between which there is a narrow passage.

Legends of Egypt

This area, where the Niger suddenly changes from its easterly direction to a southeasterly course, is where the Arabs are said to have first settled on the river. It is the point of the Niger closest to Egypt and legend has it that an ancient Egyptian pharaoh once came here.

About 2500 years ago Herodotus, the Greek historian, probably not realising that the Niger turned in a

A Niger river steamer

southeasterly direction, assumed that this magnificent river that he had heard about continued east and was in fact the Upper Nile. Many eminent 19th C geographers maintained the same hypothesis right up until the mouth of the Niger was discovered (near what is today Port Harcourt, Nigeria) in 1830 by Richard and John Lander.

Bamba is probably the most historic town between Gao and Timbuktu. It has grown since Barth's day, but it has not been able to regain the importance it enjoyed during the Songhai period. 'The village at present consists of about 200 huts, built of matting and oval shaped; for, besides a small mosque there are only two or three clay buildings.' Barth continued: 'Such is the condition of this place at present, but there cannot be any doubt that it was of much more importance three centuries ago, as it is repeatedly mentioned in the history of the Songhai. At a point where the river, from having been spread, at least during the great part of the year, over a surface of several miles, is shut in by steep banks, and compressed at the narrowest point to from 600 to 700 yards, Bamba must have been of the highest importance at a time when the whole of the region along this large navigable river was comprised under the rule of a mighty kingdom of great extent'.

Arrival at Kabara

Kabara, the port for Timbuktu, is connected to the main stream of the Niger by a 3-km channel which was originally cut by Sunni Ali, the Songhai king, in the 15th C. Our steamer, the *General A Soumare*, attempted to reach Kabara by way of this canal. A flotilla of pirogues marked time, eagerly waiting and hoping that we would not make it. Although it was November the water was too low to take a vessel of this size, and as it came to a grinding halt the piroguemen immediately swarmed the *Soumare* with their small craft. Passengers lowered their baggage, goats, babies and finally themselves into the small boats. These traditional canoes then provided a shuttle sevice to Kabara.

Kabara has a small wharf and a row of bungalows. There are taxis here to take you the last 9 kms to **Timbuktu**.

Up until earlier this century unprotected travellers

The centuries-old means of transport

on the Kabara to Timbuktu road were easy targets for Tuareg villains. Felix Dubois, who passed along this route at the end of the last century, commented that 'the road half way between Kabara and Timbuktu bears a sinister reputation. The natives have given it the tragic name Our Oumaira (They hear not), meaning that neither at Timbuktu nor Kabara can the cries of the victims be heard'.

The sinister
road to
Timbuktu

If you want to visit Timbuktu then get off at Kabara and catch a later steamer. There is very little point in making a dashed visit to the town while your boat is loading and unloading — though this is how quite a few Westerners get to see the legendary city.

Before breaking your journey anywhere along the route check with Mali Navigation the timetable of the next boats.

On to Mopti and Bamako

Upstream from Kabara is the heart of the lacustrine region of the **Inland Delta**. Here there is a great network of small streams, and large, shallow seasonal lakes form on the wide, flat flood plain.

The river
divides

At **Dire**, which is the port for the important town of **Goundam**, the Niger divides into two main channels: Issa Ber (west) and Issa Barra (east); the steamer takes the western stream and stops at **Niafounke**. The two courses meet again at Lake Debo; the land between them is known as Gimbala and is renowned for the wool blankets made by its Fulani inhabitants.

Lake Debo, the Dark Lake, is the largest in the lacustrine region during the rainy season, where canoes crossing the waters from east to west lose sight of land for a whole day. The first port of call after Lake Debo is **Mopti**, the capital of the Inland Delta region. Many travellers disembark at this bustling market town: in addition to being an ideal base for trips to **Bandiagara** and **Djenne**, Mopti is linked by road to Bamako, Burkina Fasso and a host of other important destinations.

This whole area around Mopti, including Djenne, and upstream to Bamako, has featured strongly in the country's history, especially under the Kingdom of Mali and then later, from the 17th C, under the Macina and Segou kingdoms of the Fulani and the Bambarra.

Mungo Park, who was in this region in July 1796,

was moved enough by one particular spot near Sansanding to write: 'At sunset we arrived at Modiboo, a delightful village on the banks of the Niger, commanding a view of the river for many miles ... The small green islands ... and majestic breadth of the river ... render the situation one of the most enchanting in the world'. The Scotsman also thought the countryside between Segu and Sansanding bore 'a greater resemblance to the centre of England than to the middle of Africa'.

In one of the villages he visited around here Park donated a Chinese vase to the inhabitants. It was proudly put on top of the mosque's minaret and there it stayed for 100 years until the French took it away as a souvenir.

Just upstream of Sansanding is the **Markala dam** which was completed in 1947 and raised the level of the river by an average of 4 metres. River vessels pass through the 7-km canal which runs parallel to the river. The area to the north of here along the Canal du Sahel (west of the Inland Delta) is the heart of an important agro-industrial project which has its centre at Nioni. L'Office du Niger, the organisation in charge of these schemes, was established in 1932. In its first 50 years it had hoped to irrigate a million hectares, primarily for cotton and rice growing. Today less than 45,000 hectares are under cultivation.

Segu is the most important town after Mopti until you reach **Bamako** where you land at its port **Koulikoro**.

PRACTICAL INFORMATION

THE STEAMERS
During the season there are usually 3 paqueboats (steamers), each with about 100 beds, operating between Gao and Koulikoro, 57 kms north of Bamako. They are the *General A Soumare*, inaugurated in 1965; the *Tombouctou*, 1979; and the new *Kankou Moussa* (Mansa Musa), 1982.

The boats have much the same design: 3 decks, the upper 2 for cabins, bar and restaurant, and the lower one for deck passengers and cargo. The recently commissioned Kankou Moussa was built by Krupps of Germany; it has the basic facilities of any large modern river steamer — including video shows. Its main advantage over the other boats is that it is newer and cleaner.

TRAVELLING SEASON
The steamers are not in service all the year round, and if you intend to travel by boat you should be aware of the high and low water seasons of the River Niger.

From July/August to the end of November the boats operate between Gao and Koulikoro. In December and January however they operate only between Gao and Mopti. But this is only a rough guide; the water level depends on the rainfall, so in case of poor rains be on the safe side and avoid the beginning and the end of the season.

TIMETABLE
The distances are from Gao. For approximate prices see the *Mali* introductory section. It would be wise to double check these and the timetable on the spot. There are 2 services a week. Gao (departs Monday, 8pm; departs Wednesday, 8pm)

Bourem	95 kms
Bamba	206 kms
Rharous	264 kms
Kabara	408 kms departs Wednesday afternoon; departs Friday afternoon.
Dire	493 kms
Tonka	540 kms
Niafunke	579 kms
Aka	678 kms
Mopti	804 kms departs Friday morning; departs Sunday morning)
Diafarabe	926 kms
Macina	974 kms
Dioro	1038 kms
Markala	1078 kms
Segu	1128 kms
Niamina	1218 kms
Koulikoro	1308 kms (arrives Sunday morning; arrives Tuesday morning)

Though Mali Navigation tries to keep to the above schedule, delays due to breakdowns and low water can mean erratic sailings. The timetable between Gao and Mopti is liable to change during the months when the boats travel only between these two towns.

ON BOARD
Tickets and Reservations
These can be taken care of at the Mali Navigation office which is on the same street as the Atlantide Hotel by the quayside in Gao.

Classes
First Class A: double cabin, 2 beds and a wash basin.
First Class B: double cabin, bunk beds and a wash basin. Prices are slightly lower than First Class A.
Second Class: 4 people per cabin; 2 sets of bunks and a washbasin.
Third Class: 12 people in a cabin; 4 sets of triple bunks. It is a bit cramped but on the new *Kankou Moussa* conditions are not bad. On the *General A Soumare* the cabins are on the lower deck and are rather dingy. It may be preferable to sleep in the open on the upper deck, but this is likely to be an unofficial arrangement and you should not count on it.
Fourth Class: Deck space on the lower deck. Conditions are crowded and rather squalid. The lower deck also becomes a thoroughfare when the boat stops at towns along the way.

Food and Facilities
In First, Second and Third Class 3 meals a day are included in the price of the ticket. The meals are quite basic, particularly in Third Class, so it is advisable to bring along some provisions. Fourth Class passengers should provide their own food, preferably from Gao as supplies along the way can be unpredictable. There is a bar which serves beer and soft drinks; the water is filtered, but if in doubt use purifying tablets. Each class has its own communal toilet and washing and shower facilities.

BARGES AND PINASSES
Occasionally Westerners with their own car or motorbike arrange to travel on a grain **barge**. Whether you find such a vessel to suit your timetable is anyone's guess. They operate roughly during the same seasons as the steamers.

The **pinasse**, a large motorised pirogue which on average holds 30 to 50 people, takes between 7 to 10 days from Gao to Mopti. The fare is negotiable but will probably fall between that of third and fourth Class on the steamer. There is no proper sleeping accommodation on a pinasse.

TIMBUKTU

'The camels transfer their burdens to the canoes, and the vessels confide their cargoes to the camels, Timbuctoo being the place of trans-shipment. The city is merely a temporary depot, situated between the borders of the desert and the copiously watered valleys of the south, and is so completely a town of warehouses and docks that none of its merchants possesses either camel or boat. What part then do its people play if they are neither exporters or importers? They are brokers, contractors and landlords.'
— Felix Dobois, 1896

Navel on the Niger

Around AD 1100 a tribe of Tuaregs known as the Maghsharen started to graze their herds during the dry season on the banks of the Niger near a village called Hamtagal (just southwest of present-day Timbuktu). One year they discovered an oasis a short distance away from the river and so ideal was this spot that they decided to establish a permanent camp there. This small settlement was put in the charge of an old woman while the nomads were away tending their animals. The woman's name was Tomboutou, which means 'The mother with a large navel' (she may have had an umbilical hernia, a physical disorder still common in this part of the world). Some say that she was called Boutou and that Tom means 'belonging to'. Either way Timbuktu owes its name to this woman.

How Timbuktu got its name

El Sadi described the settlement's early stages of growth: 'Travellers paused there. The population increased by the power and will of God, and the people began to build themselves fixed dwellings. Caravans coming from the north and east on their way to the Mali kingdom delayed at the camp to renew their stores. A market soon formed; a high enclosure of matting was substituted for the barrier of dead thorns, and it became a meeting place for people travelling by canoe or camel'.

Although it was the Tuaregs who founded Timbuktu it was the merchants of Djenne who came here, set up shop and, with their own workmen, established the solid foundations of the historic city.

Timbuktu grew in importance and gradually the

people of Walata (the main southern Saharan caravan terminal lying to the east) started to migrate here. By the middle of the 14th C Walata was falling into ruins and, at its expense, Timbuktu started to flourish.

The Tuaregs still claimed rights to Timbuktu, but like true nomads they did not want to settle in the town; instead they left it in the charge of a subordinate governor and continued to roam the deserts, returning whenever they wanted tribute from the inhabitants.

In 1330 the people asked Mansa Musa, the King of Mali, if he would rule the town and thus put an end to the Tuareg's extortions. The great king, who had recently returned from his grand pilgrimage to Mecca, obliged, and to honour the occasion he built a palace and the Dyingereyber mosque.

The golden city

Along the route to and from Mecca Mansa Musa's wealth had impressed everybody. His abundant gold gave Mali international fame and Timbuktu became known as the pulse of his magnificent kingdom. It was after his pilgrimage that Timbuktu first gained its reputation abroad as the golden city of the interior.

The kingdom of Mali began to decline and in the first half of the 15th C Timbuktu fell back into the hands of the Tuaregs. Once again the inhabitants were bullied into paying exorbitant taxes. Oumer, the governor, sympathised with the people's pleas for justice and, besides, he had his own bone to pick with his nomad masters. He secretly invited Sunni Ali, the powerful Songhai king, to come and take control of the city. This remarkable ruler, eager to extend his domains, responded to the calls for help and in 1468 he marched to Hamtagal where he came face to face with Akil, the Tuareg chief, and his army. The nomads, realising they were no match against the Songhai force, bolted before battle ensued. They fled to Walata and with them went many of the important merchants — who at the last minute, it seems, believed their lot under the Tuaregs was better than it would be under the Songhai king.

Ali, a man notorious for his indifference towards Islam, entered Timbuktu and ruthlessly persecuted the remainder of the Moslem dignitaries because he assumed they had been in league with Akil.

After the fall of Mali and the instability of the following years, West Sudan entered upon a glorious

A caravanserai at Timbuktu

period of prosperity and security under the Songhai. It was Sunni Ali, a brilliant soldier, who laid the foundations of the great kingdom and Askia Mohammed, a shrewd and noble statesman, who extended its power over far off lands. As Sudan thrived so did Timbuktu. It was under the Askia dynasty that the city reached its zenith.

It was at this time, in the 16th C, that Leo Africanus passed through Timbuktu. He wrote: 'The rich king of Timbuktu has many plates and sceptres of gold, some whereof weigh 1300 pounds and he keeps a magnificent and well furnished court … He hath always 3000 horsemen, and a great number of footmen that shoot poisoned arrows, attending him. Here are great stores of doctors, judges, priests and other learned men, that are beautifully maintained at the king's cost and charges. And hither are brought divers manuscripts or written books out of Barbary, which are sold for more money than any merchandise.'

Later in the 16th C a European merchant in Morocco witnessed the arrival of a desert caravan, almost certainly from Timbuktu, and mentioned that it had 'such infinite treasure as I never heard of. It appears that they have more gold than any other part of the world besides'.

Troubled Centuries

But in the 17th C, after the Moroccan invasion of 1591, West Sudan plunged into disorder and Timbuktu suffered terribly. Also at one stage the area was hit by famine which reduced the inhabitants to eating the corpses of dead animals. The people were savagely oppressed and many of the ulama were put in chains and sent across the desert to Marrakesh.

The Moroccans made Timbuktu a provincial capital and used their men to govern the city. Many of these were from the army that had defeated the Songhai and some may have been Europeans drafted into the Moroccan force. Many of the soldiers intermarried with the locals and their descendants became known as the Arma. Today there are about 15,000 Arma, nearly all Moslem, living in the Timbuktu region.

The Moroccans had neither any real desire nor the strength to control Sudan and soon they lost their grip on Timbuktu. The city, exposed and difficult to defend, had nearly always been ruled from outside

A young Tuareg woman of Timbuktu

and once again it was fought over by several different tribes during the centuries following the invasion. Most prominent among these were the Mossi, the Fulani, the Toucoleur — and, of course, the Tuaregs, who hovered round the outskirts of the city causing havoc to the inhabitants and anyone who might threaten their authority.

A general mood of fear and repression hung over Timbuktu. Naturally the economy floundered; trade and the trans-Saharan caravans were never on the scale as they were during the Songhai period, and the majority of the inhabitants were forced to a low standard of living.

This was more or less the situation right up until the French occupation in 1893. From accounts given to him by locals, Felix Dubois, who visited Timbuktu in 1896, described the atmosphere of the place during the period of the Tuareg menace:

'The poorest and wealthiest alone remained faithful to the city. The first, living in straw huts, possessed nothing, and consequently had nothing to lose. The second, the opulent merchants, could, owing to their great fortunes, manage to endure these annoyances, and the emigration of the smaller traders, moreover, permitted them to augment their business, and therefore their profits.

Timbuktu the mysterious

'No one ever gets accustomed to pillage and ill-treatment however, whatever the compensations may be; and to avoid being robbed in the open street, and seeing their houses turned upside down, the inhabitants adopted a new manner of living. They transformed their garments and dwellings, and ceasing to be Timbuctoo the Great, they became Timbuctoo the Mysterious.

'Instead of the imposing white turbans of the natives and the beautiful dark ones (made of shining tissues) of the Moors, the people cover their heads with unappetising rags, or cheap caps.

'The houses are disguised like their owners, and, to escape the visits of the veiled men, all appearance of wealth and prosperity is avoided. I will not assert that they are voluntarily defaced, but time and weather are allowed to work their way upon them unhindered.'

And the appearance in Dubois' time, as related below, is much the same as today.

'By these means the town very soon acquired a tumbled down and battered appearance. Everything seems to be falling into the streets, except the doors — those obstinately closed doors that had so astonished me on my arrival. They are the objects of the most studied care, and are set up regardless of cost. Heavy planks of a very hard wood are brought from a distance for this purpose, and are adorned with armour like any gentleman of Agincourt. Thus barricaded, the inhabitants, under the cover of simulated misery, live the silent life of the cloisters.'

European Adventurers

This is probably what Timbuktu was like when the first explorers arrived here in the early and middle part of the last century. They were naturally disappointed. It was popularly believed in Europe that Timbuktu the Mysterious was still Timbuktu the Great. It must have been sickening for the truly intrepid adventurers — Laing, Caillie, Barth — to wearily trudge thousands of kilometres through appalling conditions surrounded by fierce hostility, only to find that their magnificent goal had in fact a 'tumbled down and battered appearance'.

Lifting the veil
It seems that Alfred Tennyson had been correct when he made a dig at those who supported the fashionable idea that Timbuktu was an Eldorado. The following is a passage from his poem 'Timbuctoo', published before any explorers had publicly revealed their first-hand accounts of the city.

Wide Afric, doth thy sun
Lighten, thy hills unfold a city as fair
As those which starred the night o' the elder world?
Or is the rumour of thy Timbuctoo
A dream as frail as those of ancient time?
... the time is well-nigh come
When I must render up this glorious home
To keen Discovery: soon your brilliant towers
Shall darken with the waving of her wand;
Darken, and shrink and shiver into huts,
Black specks amid a waste of dreary sand,
Low-built, mud-wall'd, barbarian settlements.

Nearly 50 Europeans attempted to reach Timbuktu between the late 16th C and the 1870s. Only three of them — Gordon Laing, Rene Caillie and Heinrich Barth — are known for certain to have succeeded. Their stories are told in the appendix at the end of this book.

Timbuktu Today: Points of Interest

Timbuktu excelled as a centre of commerce, religion and scholarship. Architecture and the arts were never its strong point and it is unlikely that the city ever boasted any truly grand buildings.

Wandering the sandy streets

Today Timbuktu is in much the same state as it was when Laing, Caillie, Barth and Dubois visited it in the 19th C. The present population is estimated at around 20,000, which is larger than in Barth's day, but smaller than it was at its peak. Generally this grey mud brick town is in a poor state of repair, sad, drab, dusty, devoid of trees and not particularly impressive; a once proud, prosperous, legendary city is now neglected because nobody seems to care. However, Timbuktu is not unpleasant and it is a joy to wander the sandy streets of such a historic place, especially with the knowledge that it has changed little in the last hundred, maybe several hundred, years. The **houses of Gordon Laing, Rene Caillie** (both on the same street) **and Heinrich Barth** still stand and are commemorated by plaques.

Mosques

The three main mosques are Timbuktu's greatest heritage. An old Sudanese proverb says: 'Salt comes from the north, gold from the south, and silver from the country of the white man, but the word of God and the treasures of wisdom are only to be found in Timbuktu'. The *Tarikh es Sudan*, an important 17th C historical work by El Sadi, a scholar in Timbuktu and Djenne, claims: 'Never has Timbuktu been sullied by worship of idols nor by rendering homage to any other deity than the merciful God. It is the dwelling place of wise men, the servants of the Most High, and the perpetual habitation of saints and ascetics'.

From Timbuktu Islam radiated to the rest of Sudan. Highly respected, pious and erudite marabouts, some of whom were said to perform miracles, taught here. One of the greatest was Sidi Yehia (1373–1462), who is buried under the recently restored mosque in the centre of town bearing his name. Near the **Sidi Yehia Mosque** is a courtyard known as Tomboutou Koi Batouma; it was here, supposedly, that the old woman

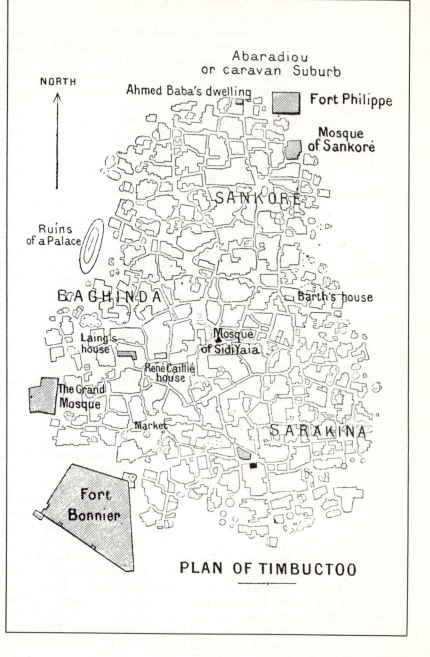

Abaradiou
or caravan Suburb

NORTH

Ahmed Baba's dwelling   Fort Philippe

Mosque
of Sankoré

SANKORÉ

Ruins
of a Palace

BAGHINDA   Barth's house

Laing's
house   Mosque
                     of Sidi Yaia

        René Caillié
        house

The Grand
Mosque

        Market   SARAKINA

Fort
Bonnier

PLAN OF TIMBUCTOO

Dubois' map of Timbuktu

101

after whom Timbuktu is named handed out water to weary travellers.

The **Sankore Mosque**, built by a wealthy woman, was also a university. It attracted students, *talibas*, from all over this part of the Moslem world. Today the sight of boys sitting with their blackboards reciting passages of the Koran is particularly common in Timbuktu and Djenne. The most religious families lived in the quarter around the Sankore Mosque. The Grand Mosque, the **Dyingereyber**, was originally built in 1336 by El Saheli, an Andalusian architect who returned with Mansa Musa from Cairo. It is believed that he introduced mud bricks into West Sudan. He also built a mosque in Gao. The Dyingereyber fell into ruins and was reconstructed at a later date. It is worth climbing its 15-metre minaret for a panoramic view over the town.

These mosques are not very large, nor architecturally impressive or in good repair. But they are Timbuktu's grandest and most historic (pre-19th C) buildings. In no way do they compare with the mosques at Djenne or Mopti, but these two towns are fortunate in having resources of clay while the surrounds of Timbuktu are devoid of such construction materials.

The **grand market** is by Timbuktu's busy central square. It is underneath a large blue hangar, both incongruous and an eyesore. The market mainly sells fruits and vegetables. Most of Timbuktu's shops, Air Mali's office and the taxi stop are in the neighbouring square. The **small market** is a short distance to the west; there is a section here where the artisans work and sell their handicrafts. Timbuktu is particularly well known for its Tuareg leather work and also embroidered galabiyyas. A supermarket, again completely out of place, is just to the south of the small market. In the 1850s Barth recorded: 'All the calico which I saw bore the name of one and the same Manchester firm printed upon it in Arabic letters ... All cutlery in Timbuktu is of English workmanship'.

The **gardens** or terraces of Timbuktu, a lush area of greenery, are in the west of the town. In the north is the **Abaradio quarter** where the caravans used to stop. Even as recently as the late 19th C 50,000 to 60,000 camels would arrive here each year. Today you may see a few small caravans still travelling to or from the salt mines at Taudeni.

Laing's house at Timbuktu

Tuaregs have small camps in the environs of Timbuktu. The women and children come into town and will offer you handicrafts. There are usually a couple of men hanging around the Campement who will take you on their camels to their camps in the desert — you can even spend some days out there with them. The Tuareg, especially around Timbuktu, are hard bargainers, so the price you pay for their wares will be the measure of your firmness and skill.

PRACTICAL INFORMATION

ACCOMMODATION AND FOOD

Timbuktu has 2 **hotels**. There is the inexpensive, tourist class **Le Campement**, PO Box 49; Tel: 7. This is a typical government-owned hotel, rather sombre, colonial in style and falling into disrepair. But it is not unpleasant and is well situated on the edge of town with the desert as its back garden. The attractive annex block, with the rooms surrounding a courtyard, is neglected and in need of restoration. Rooms are cheaper here.

The other is the more expensive first class **Azali**, PO Box 64. It is part of the French Sofitel group through whom (and also Novotel) bookings may be made. New, small, tastefully decorated, it caters for tourists who come on short excursions from Bamako, and Western aid workers. The Azali is a bit out of town in the desert, about a 5-minute walk from the Campement. It has the advantage of air conditioning.

Locals may well put you up in their **houses** at a cheaper rate.

Both hotels have **restaurants**. In town most places close early, so finding food in the evening can be difficult. Also try the market, shops and supermarket. Behind the post office, near the Place Independence, is the **Kaleme Bar**, possibly the only bar in town (besides the hotels) to serve alcohol.

Because of Timbuktu's inaccessibility, shortage of agricultural land and few natural resources, prices here are generally higher than elsewhere.

SERVICES

Timbuktu has a **post office**, a newly-opened **bank** (both near the Place Independence), and a small **SMERT** (tourist) office near the Campement.

GETTING ABOUT TOWN

Everything in Timbuktu is within walking distance. **Taxis** to Kabara and elsewhere can be picked up in the square near the grand market.

In recent years SMERT has been trying to attract tourists to Timbuktu. But only 2 or 3 of the half dozen to dozen Westerners on the river steamer will actually disembark at Kabara. Sometimes a small excursion arrives by plane from Bamako, but most tourists make the cursory visit only to say 'I have been to Timbuktu'.

Timbuktu is one of the poorest towns in Mali, and tourists are regarded, particularly by children, as an extra source of income. Here, as at a growing number of places along the route, the children will pester you, the *Nasara* (Christian) for 'un cadeau', 'un Bic', 'un bonbon' or money. In return, some of them will offer their services as a guide, which is a good (though possibly illegal) way of seeing the town.

TRAVEL OUT OF TIMBUKTU

Road transport available to the public is not that regular from Timbuktu, especially in the high water season. None of the roads from the town (except to Kabara) are surfaced and some of them are impassable during the wet time of year. One such route is to Mopti via Sarafere.

Parts of the route further west via Nampala to Segu are also impassable during the high water season. Trucks occasionally travel to the salt mines of Taudeni, 700 kms to the north; permission from the police is necessary before going there.

The **steamer** arrives and leaves from Kabara, or from the canal which links the port to the Niger. If you are in Timbuktu it can be difficult to find out exactly when it leaves.

Timbuktu has a domestic airport with 1 or 2 Air Mali **flights** a week to Bamako, Gao, Goundam and Mopti.

EXCURSIONS

Pirogues can be hired from Kabara for **trips on the River Niger**.

100 kms west of Timbuktu is **Lake Faguibine**. Its true blue waters, surrounded by white sand, measure 120 kms by 25 kms, making it one of the biggest lakes in West Africa. Lake Faguibine is a delightfully serene and quiet place to spend a few days. SMERT can arrange transport, via Goundam, to the lake, but there is no recognised accommodation in the area. The main villages on the southern shore from east to west are Bintagougon, Mbouma, Goumsao and, on the western tip when the water is high, Ras el Ma, the place which Sunni Ali planned to connect by canal to the Niger.

Dire has a solar power station which helps facilitate irrigation and provide electricity for the locals. Dire is also the port for Goundam which lies a few kilometres to its northwest.

Goundam is an important administrative centre for the surrounding farming area.

ONWARD ROUTES

The road from Timbuktu to Mopti is usually impassable for more months of the year than the Timbuktu to Segu route via Lere. Thus during the high water season it may be necessary for those with motor vehicles to take the western Lere-Nioni-Sansanding-Segu route and then double back to Mopti via San along the all-weather surfaced road.

Also there is certainly a chance that *all* roads between Timbuktu and Mopti or Segu will be impassable between July and November and certain sections may be closed right up until February depending on the extent of the rains.

Timbuktu to Mopti by Road
The overall distance is 434 kms.

Goundam	97 kms
Tonka	136 kms
Niafounke	184 kms

Niafounke is on the west bank of the Issa Ber channel of the River Niger; on the east bank of the Issa Barra channel there is the village of Sarafere. During the low water season there is a track from Niafounke to Sarafere, and then south to Korientze, a total just short of 100 kms. It is 150 kms from Korientze to Mopti; the road improves and from the village of Kona (about halfway) it is surfaced.

Timbuktu to Segu by Road
This route via Lere and Nampala covers 717 kms.

Goundam	97 kms
Tonka	136 kms
Niafounke	184 kms
Lere	320 kms
Junction of road south to Diora	388 kms
Nampala	412 kms
	(just south of the Mauritian border)
Junction of road going west	555 kms
	(just south of Kogoni)
Nioni	610 kms
Sansanding	679 kms
Segu	717 kms

MOPTI

There seems to be a tremendous temptation for tourism promoters throughout the world to compare any canal- or water-dominated town with Venice. Thus we have 'Leningrad, the Venice of the USSR', 'Stockholm, the Venice of Sweden', 'Amsterdam, the Venice of Holland', and so on. With less justification, Mopti, which is situated on three small islands at the confluence of the rivers Niger and Bani, has been dubbed 'the Venice of Mali and West Africa'.

Mopti was only a small fishing village when it was conquered by the French in 1893. By 1905 a colonial administrator had arrived and a few years later the trading companies set up shop. Today Mopti vies with Segu to be Mali's second town after Bamako; it has the highest population density in the country and is also the commercial capital of central and eastern Mali.

With these statistics you might imagine Mopti to be unpleasantly congested and full of factories and office blocks. In fact places like that do not exist in Mali. Mopti is a delightful, busy market town with a population of 54,000. It is an artisan's centre and an ideal base for trips to Djenne and Bandiagara. The town of Sevare, 12 kms to the east, is sometimes regarded as part of Mopti; it is of little interest to the traveller.

Points of Interest in and around Mopti
Children, besides wanting to introduce you to their 'uncle' or 'brother' who sells 'antiques', may well offer to show you around the **neighbouring villages**. The trip means hiring a pirogue with the young boy and his 'brother', the boatman. Punting along the River Bani, stopping off at traditional Fulani and Bozo fishing villages, is a pleasant and interesting way to spend half or a full day. Small clusters of **Tuareg tents** also dot the banks; these nomad families have moved here because of the increasing hardships in the desert. The price of such a trip, which is negotiable, is inexpensive.

The spectacular mud-built **mosque** in the old part of Mopti on the other side of the causeway has a similar design to the one in Djenne but is on a smaller scale. Non-Moslems may not enter.

On Thursdays Mopti becomes one big **market**.

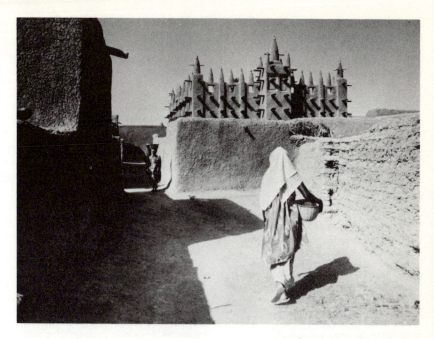

A small mosque in a village near Mopti

When the river is high pirogues and pinasses skirt the three-sided harbour. The quay, sloping from the road to the water's edge, is a blaze of colour and bustle; a wide variety of things, in particular spices, vegetables, fruit and reed work, is sold here. On the far side and beyond the Bozo restaurant, women from the local villages sell their smoked fish to the merchants. The small market, where local cloth, blankets, crafts and traditional objets d'art are sold, is in and around a courtyard in what is known as the 'commercial centre' (the area behind the bank). Tailors here will make you clothes to order. For the rest of the week Mopti's markets still function, but at a more subdued level. Mopti is one of the best places in Mali to buy handicrafts and cloth.

PRACTICAL INFORMATION

ACCOMMODATION
Mopti's top hotel, the smart **Kanaga** (PO Box 224), is on the corniche about ½ km from the town centre. Like the Azali in Timbuktu, it is run by Sofitel through whom reservations can be made; the

standard, style and price range are similar, ie prices are moderate. All rooms are air conditioned, with shower.

The government-run **Campement** is well patronised as it is neither too expensive nor too basic. There are the usual Campement features: gloomy, austere dining/bar area, large contained courtyard, modest rooms, pleasant atmosphere and friendly staff. Prices vary depending on air conditioning and shower/bath facilities, but are about a third less than the Kanaga, and include breakfast and lunch or dinner too (you may be able to negotiate a lower price by not taking the 'obligatory' meal). The Campement is next to the police station.

The **Oriental**, a small local rest house with half a dozen rooms provides very basic accommodation very cheaply. It is across the causeway in the old town and is popular with travellers. Also in the old town is the **Bar Mali Hotel**; the building is interesting but squalid and not recommended for accommodation.

The **Motel de Sevare** is 12 kms east of town, near the airport. Rooms have fan, shower and WC, and cost about the same as at the Campement.

Children, if they see you with your bags, will come up and offer you **lodging**, occasionally on a boat which can be cheaper and more interesting than staying at a hotel.

FOOD
Besides those at the hotels, there are 2 popular restaurants in Mopti. On a little promontory at the harbour entrance is the **Bozo**. Its situation is attractive: slightly raised, water on 3 sides, overlooking the harbour and the busy market; it is outdoors, casual, unpretentious and good value for money. The food, usually rice and fish, is good and cheap. It is also a haunt for souvenir sellers.

The other restaurant is the **Nuits de Chine** near the BP station on the corner of the harbour. The name, decor and boss are Chinese, but the food most definitely is not. Steak and chicken with chips and delicious Dogon onions are the specialty. The room is dim and the atmosphere mildly decadent. Like the Bozo the food is good

value. Both restaurants serve cold beers and soft drinks.

A variety of foods can be bought from **roadside vendors** throughout Mopti. Tea stalls are open till quite late.

TRAVEL OUT OF MOPTI
Mopti is an important port of call for the **steamer**. It is also possible to take a **pinasse** from here to Gao.

The airport is at Sevare, about 12 kms east of town. There are **flights** once or twice a week to Bamako, Gao, Goundam and Timbuktu.

If travelling by **road**, go to the main taxi park just to the south of the harbour. There is a regular flow of traffic to destinations throughout Mali and also to neighbouring countries. Some public transport services originate and terminate at Sevare.

EXCURSIONS
SMERT organises excursions to the **Bandiagara Escarpment** (Songo, Sanga, Bandiagara) and to **Djenne**, but they are expensive. Taxis leave frequently for Bandiagara from the main taxi park, so you can organise the trip yourself. It takes 1½ hours to cover the 75 kms, though more quickly if the road has now been surfaced.

ONWARD ROUTES
Mopti to Djenne by Road
Taxis leave from opposite the Campement on Monday mornings (Monday is market day in Djenne) and take about 2 hours to cover the 132 kms. There is no guarantee of finding transport any other day of the week. During the rainy season you may not be able to reach Djenne by road.

Mopti to Djenne by River
An enjoyable alternative is to take the pinasse which leaves for Djenne from the harbour early on Friday morning. The journey takes the best part of a day.

Mopti to Gao via Hombori
Usually there are trucks or Land Rovers leaving most days from the Texaco garage near the Mali Navigation office. The distance is 600 kms, the road is now surfaced and the journey can be accomplished in a day or so.

DJENNE

'They turned ... silently pointing to some object that was invisible to me; then with voices barely audible from emotion, they murmered, "Jenne!" ... Here was something that I had never seen before, either, and shall never see again, namely, a negro surprised and affected, not by some European invention, but by a spectacle of his own country. I hastened forward, and stood astonished in my turn; for the first time in these regions I was astounded by the work of man ... Jenne is the jewel of the valley of the Niger.'

— Felix Dubois, 1896

Djenne was founded halfway through the 13th C by the Soninke and soon after, when King Kunburu converted to Islam, it became an important place for Koranic scholarship. The king asked the ulama to pray that the city would prosper as a thriving, cosmopolitan commercial centre. His wish was granted:

The Grand Mosque at Djenne

Djenne established significant trade links along the River Niger with Timbuktu and developed as an important market. El Sadi in the *Tarikh* went so far as to say: 'Jenne is one of the greatest Moslem markets, where traders carrying salt from the mines of Tagheza meet traders with gold of Bitu [Akan forests] ... It is because of this blessed town [Djenne] that caravans came to Timbuktu from all points of the horizon.'

Europeans trading on the West African shores must have heard about Djenne's fabulous gold market from black merchants. For this reason they named the Guinea coast — where they were involved in bartering for gold — and subsequently the English 'Guinea' coin, after this city. All the same, rumours of Timbuktu's magnificence eclipsed those of Djenne's.

In the 17th C Djenne's golden era began to wane; though it continued to be an important centre, particularly for Islamic studies.

Situated on the River Bani, Djenne is virtually an island for most of the year. Formerly this was to the city's advantage as it provided a water route to Timbuktu as well as a natural defence. But the trends of trade have changed and today Djenne stands isolated. Not linked to the outside world by proper roads it has missed the opportunity to develop. Untarnished by modernisation, Djenne is one of the most fascinating places to visit in West Africa.

Unchanged and fascinating

In 1828 Rene Caillie became the first European to enter Djenne and his description of its market, the city, the houses and general character shows that it has changed remarkably little in the last 150 years.

Rene Caillie in Djenne

Extracts from Caillie's 19th C book *Travels through Central Africa to Timbuktu* give today's visitor a reasonable picture of present-day Djenne.

'The town of Jenne is full of bustle and animation; every day numerous caravans of merchants are arriving and departing with all kinds of useful productions.

Bustle and animation

'I paid a visit to the market; I was surprised at the number of the people I saw there. It is well supplied with all the necessaries of life, and is constantly crowded by a multitude of strangers and the inhabitants of the neighbouring villages, who attend it to sell their produce, and to purchase salt and other commodities.

'There are several rows of dealers both male and female. Some erect little palisades of straw, to protect themselves from the excessive heat of the sun; over these they throw a pagne [a length of cloth] and thus form a small hut. Their goods are laid out in little baskets, placed on large round panniers.

'In going round the market I observed some shops pretty well stocked with European commodities, which sell at a very high price ...

'There are also butchers in the market, who lay out their meat in much the same way as their brethren in Europe. They also thrust skewers through little pieces of meat, which they smoke-dry and sell retail. Great quantities of fish, fresh as well as dried, are brought to this market, in which are also to be had earthern pots, calabashes, mats and salt ...

'There are a great number of hawkers in the streets ... They sell stuffs made in the country, cured provisions, colat [kola] nuts, honey, vegetable and animal butter, milk and firewood.'

Large daily markets are now something of the past. However Caillie's description could well apply to the present weekly market which is held every Monday in front of the mosque. It is certainly worth coinciding your visit to Djenne with this lively and colourful event.

Merchants and houses

'The Moorish merchants resident in Jenne ... occupy the best houses, which have besides the advantage of being situated near the market. The principal trade of the place is in their hands.

'The houses are built of bricks dried in the sun. The sand of the isle of Jenne is mixed with a little clay, and it is employed to make bricks of a round form which are sufficiently solid. The houses are as large as those of European villages. The greater part have only one story. ... They are all terraced, have no windows externally, and the apartments receive no air except from an inner court ...

'In Jenne there is a mosque built of earth, surmounted by two massive but not high towers; it is rudely constructed, though very large. It is abandoned to thousands of swallows, which build their nests in it. This occasions a very disagreeable smell, to avoid which, the custom of saying prayers in a small outer court has become common. In the environs of the mosque ... I always observed a number of beggars,

111

reduced to mendicity by old age, blindness or other infirmities.'

The Great Mosque

In 1830, soon after Caillie's visit, Cheikou Amadou, the Fulani ruler of Djenne, destroyed this 11th C mosque. Some say that this fanatical Moslem chief razed the holy place because, as a young Koranic student, he had been shocked that trade had distracted so many of Djenne's people from their religious duties. He vowed that one day when he became king he would teach the inhabitants of the city a lesson. He kept his promise by pulling down the Grand Mosque and building a new capital — which he called Hamdallai ('Praise be to Allah') — on the other side of the River Bani.

The present Grand Mosque was built in 1905 in much the same style as the old place of worship described by Caillie. Every few years it is rendered by children. This magnificant, huge mosque is famous throughout the world for its crude, bizarre but extremely elegant architecture.

To gain entry into the mosque you may have to find a local boy to act as your guide. The imam may ask you to contribute something to the coffers.

Caillie also talked about the advanced state of Djenne. Everyone was employed in a useful trade; most of the inhabitants could read, no one went barefoot — not even the children of the slaves; people lived very well: they ate rice boiled with fresh meat. The streets, though unpaved, were swept daily. Caillie

Blowing one's nose in safety and style

wrote with relief: 'I was pleased to find at Jenne that one might use a pocket handkerchief without being ridiculed; for the inhabitants themselves use it, whereas, in the countries through which I had previously passed, it would have been dangerous to suffer such a thing to be seen'.

Today Djenne's street life may seem no different from that of any other Malian provincial town. However there is a distinguished aura about the place because of its unique situation and fine unspoilt traditional architecture. Djenne is of more interest to the tourist than other historical towns like Gao and Timbuktu.

Points of Interest in and around Djenne

Besides seeing the **Grand Mosque** and **market**, it is worth strolling around the **backstreets**. Artisans skil-

Entrance to the Grand Mosque

113

fully ply their crafts: wood, gold and silver objets d'art, old and new, can be bought; but the prices in Djenne may well be inflated compared to elsewhere in the country, so be prepared to bargain. The **Marabout's House** (the oldest building in Djenne) and the young students reciting passages from the Koran are reminders that Djenne is an important seat of Islamic learning. There is also the place, though it is nothing spectacular, where many years ago a beautiful young virgin was sacrificed so as to save Djenne from a horrific catastrophe.

If you do not want a guide just walk about town and ask locals to point out the various places.

The fertile area around Djenne supports many delightful fishing and farming **villages**. You can get to some of them on foot or by mobilette (which you can hire in Djenne), or, depending on the season, by pirogue.

Excavating the ancient city

Over the last few years excavations have been in progress at the site of the ancient city of **Jeno**, which lies about 3 kms from Djenne. Further research has to be made before the archaeologists can be unequivocal in their theories; however it is believed that Jeno was founded around the 3rd C BC, reached its most prosperous period between AD 700 and 1000, and was eventually abandoned around 1400.

It is possible that when Islam was introduced to this area the Moslem converts wanted to separate themselves from the pagans. They therefore established a new city, Djenne, and gradually Jeno was depopulated and fell to ruin.

You have to get permission from the commissioner of police in Djenne to visit Jeno.

PRACTICAL INFORMATION

ACCOMMODATION AND FOOD

The accommodation in Djenne is a SMERT-run **hotel** and the rather basic government **Campement**, with a restaurant, which is opposite the President's residence.

There are 1 or 2 small cafés which serve rice, fish and meat dishes and many street stalls selling a variety of food in much the same way as Rene Caillie described.

TRAVEL

For getting to Djenne, see Mopti. After Djenne's Monday market you can catch a **taxi** back to Mopti, or early on Tuesday morning you can take the **pinasse**: this takes the better part of the day, stopping at many villages along the way, before reaching Mopti. There is no other guaranteed transport. There may be transport going south to Segu.

THE DOGON

Dogon Country

The Dogon are principally cultivators who live in an area covering 50,000 sq kms in southwest Mali. To a Westerner they are probably the most interesting of Mali's ethnic groups. Part of their lands is the Bandiagara Escarpment, 75 kms east of Mopti, which is about 200 kms long and runs roughly parallel to the River Niger.

Cliffside villages

Many villages cling dramatically and picturesquely to the side of the almost sheer 500- to 600-metre high cliffs. The original reason for living here was as protection against hostile tribes, but after the French colonised the region earlier this century, the villagers spilled down onto the flat sandy savannah plains known as the Seno.

In the 1970s Dutch archaeologists discovered evidence of ancient granaries near the village of Sanga. They estimated by carbon 14 dating that the area was inhabited around the 3rd C BC; they named their findings the Toloy Culture. There seems to have been a gap between this era and the arrival of the Tellem people in the 11th C AD.

The Tellem were small — sometimes referred to as the 'little red people' — but the popular belief that they were pygmies has not been satisfactorily substantiated. Also the Dogon notion that these people lived high up above the villages in small, barely accessible caves chiselled out of the cliffs is more than likely inaccurate. Archaeologists think the Tellem used the caves as granaries, for refuge when under severe attack and for burial ceremonies (as still practiced by the Dogon).

In the 15th C the Dogon migrated — probably to escape the threat of Islam — from Mande country in the west to the Bandiagara Escarpment. Most experts believe the Dogon lived alongside the Tellem until they drove them out in the 17th C. The Tellem fled to northern Burkina Fasso where their descendants are the Kurumba people.

Although the Dogon suffered against the superior French forces at the end of the last century, it was not until the battle of Tabi in 1920 that they were put under the yoke of colonialism.

Dogon Art and the Myth of Creation

The unique Dogon art is sought after by visitors to
Mali as well as by galleries throughout the world.
Symbolism is an intrinsic part of their art and architecture and to understand it a knowledge of their
religion and cosmology is necessary.

Dogon believe that Amma was the supreme crea-
tor. He created the earth and then had intercourse
with her. This resulted in a fox, Dyougou Serou; but
after a second attempt, twins, a boy and a girl were
born and taken up to heaven — they were known as
Nommos.

The power of speech lay in the skirt of the earth.
Dyougou Serou, wanting the ability to talk, had intercourse with her (Dyougou, ashamed of this act, is
often shown covering his eyes with his hands). The
earth's purity was lost through this incestuous act, so
Amma decided to create a man and woman by himself. The couple had children and grandchildren, eight
in all, who are the original Dogon ancestors. They
became Nommos and went to heaven.

Amma sacrificed one of the Nommos to cleanse the
earth. His body was scattered on the ground, thus
making it fertile. He was then resurrected and along
with the other Nommos, animals, plants and miner-
als, he was put in a granary and sent down to earth on
a rainbow.

When they arrived another Nommo was sacrificed
and turned into the serpent Lebe, who symbolises
earth. It was Lebe who led the Dogon from Mande
country to the Bandiagara Escarpment. The Lebe cult,
like most cults, is supervised by Hogons who are
important old men in the community.

One day Lebe came across some youths who were
wrongly dressed. He reprimanded them — but in the
Dogon tongue, not in the language of the spirits. He
died at once, thus introducing death which until then
was unknown to the Dogon.

The art and rituals of the Dogons have a strong
association with death and spirits.

Masked Dances

Houses, statues, stools, locks and most other artefacts
carry symbolic meaning in their designs. Even the
traditional layout of the village is anthropomorphic —
in the shape of a man.

A Dogon granary

Death and dancing

But the Dogon are most famous for their masks. With the arrival of death — as related in the myth above — the Dogon established masked dance rituals to take care of the spirits. The idea was that the spirits, in limbo after death, could attach themselves to something tangible before being put to rest with the other ancestors.

The Awa mask society, formed of men in the village, is in charge of the masked dances. The most important ceremony is the Sigui, which is held every 60 years (the last was held in the late 1960s) to commemorate the passing of a generation. A Great Mask, Imanana, is carved in the shape of a postrate serpent with a rectangular head. This can be up to 12 metres in length and is only used at Siguis or funerals. During the Sigui the story of the creation and how death was introduced is related; there is also a plea to Lebe for forgiveness because of the way death came to earth.

Every few years there is an anniversary, known as Dama, for those who have died since the last Dama. On these occasions important masked dances are performed to convey the spirits of the dead to the world of the ancestors.

There are also personal funerals: the Great Mask is brought down from the caves and taken to the house of the dead person. A chicken is attached to the mask, thus providing food for Lebe. In this ritual the mask acknowledges the deceased and he, through his family, in turn pays his respects. A couple of days later a masked dance is performed. Usually there are five dancers; four wear bede (young woman) masks and the fifth a sirige (multi-storied house) mask, which can be up to 7 metres in height. The dance, which like all dances follows a particular choreography, finishes with the sirige dancer nodding his head and touching either side of the deceased's funeral blanket with the top of his mask. The idea is to ask the pardon of the dead person, because it was man who caused death to be introduced into the world.

Types of mask

There are about 80 masks in all and these are divided into six categories: Dogon people, non-Dogon people, birds, mammals, reptiles and objects. Some of the most common masks are the Karanga (bird), the satimbe (woman), pulloyana (Peul, ie Fulani, woman), dyomma (rabbit), no (bull), tene tana (stilt walker), sirige (house), wallu (antelope) and bede (young woman).

Nowadays dances are often put on at places like Sanga for the growing number of tourists. Though these are based on traditional dances, it is more than likely that they are adapted to give greater floor time to elaborate masks and dramatic choreography. An exciting dance, authentic or not, is what the visitor pays to see and consequently the true meaning of the tradition becomes blurred in the mind of young Dogon dancers.

The Gona dance is popular: dancers wearing the karanga mask jump high in the air and touch the ground with the top of their mask. Another favourite is when sirige masked dancers perform to the Bimmili Galu beat. Here the man tilts his head so that his tall mask is parallel to the ground and then spins around on the spot very quickly. Particular beats accompany the different masks.

Nowadays only a small percentage of Dogon, usually the Hogons, have an accurate and deep knowledge of the meaning of their art and rituals.

Buying Dogon Art

There is a tremendous demand from collectors and tourists for Dogon works of art. Consequently many of the finer pieces have been taken from the villages and now craftsmen are churning out masks, statues and other objets d'art simply to satisfy the market. Dealers may try to convince you that these reproductions are old and valuable artefacts and thus ask for a higher price. All the same, just because a piece is new, though possibly conditioned to look of an earlier period, does not mean that it lacks beauty and craftsmanship.

Tellem figures The wooden Tellem statues, usually with arms raised above the head (symbolising a Nommo asking for rain and thus forgiveness) are popular souvenirs.

Art from the Bandiagara Escarpment can be divided into Tellem Proper (11th to 15th C) Tellem-Dogon Transitional (15th to 17th C) and Dogon (18th C onwards). It is nearly impossible to find statues from the first two periods. Usually dealers will admit that their Tellem figures are modern, but styled in the traditional Tellem fashion; be sceptical of those who claim their crafts really come from the early eras.

119

Dogon Markets

Markets tend to get going around midday and throughout the morning men with laden donkeys and crocodile-files of women with baskets stacked high on their heads trickle into the market area and take their positions. The market attracts people from many kilometres around: it is not opulent nor is there an abundance of goods, but transactions take place and the scene is animated, happy and colourful.

Typically the market is made up of rows of squat wooden-framed, millet stalk-covered shelters. Men and women sit under these covers with their merchandise: the delicious small Dogon onions, peanuts, millet, chilis, rice, fruits, spices, dried fish are all neatly displayed in small piles. The itinerant salesman who moves from one market to the next has a stall with plastic trinkets, torches, batteries, rubber shoes and the ubiquitous 'Kung Fu' or 'Bob Marley Lives' T-shirts.

Bob Marley T-shirts

In the morning a cow and sheep are slaughtered and throughout the day grilled meat is available to order. The atmosphere is festive (which is quite unusual for the Sahel) — maybe this is because of kojo (or chakalow). The Dogon — who have a strong non-Islamic heritage — brew a potent millet beer called kojo (known by various names and made elsewhere in West Africa). The beer seems an important part of the market; brewed by women, it is put, still fizzy and fermenting, into large earthenware pots. The designated drinking area is usually the shade of a large baobab or mango tree, around which men will cluster and joke and catch up on the week's news over a few calabashes of thirst-quenching kojo.

Millet beer

With a few exceptions markets are not held on set days of the week, but every five days. It can be difficult to find out the right day when you are not in the village itself; this is one of the reasons why it is useful to have a guide when travelling in Dogon country.

A slaughtered cow at Douru market

FROM MOPTI TO BANDIAGARA

Dogon daytrip

About three-quarters of the way from Mopti to Bandiagara the village of **Songo** — the first of the Dogon settlements — is signposted as 4 kms to the left. It is quite typical of the Dogon villages: the unique mud and stone architecture, narrow lanes, the toguna (the meeting place for elders), the weavers, a small mosque, and then above is the falaise (cliff), which has some of the best examples of rock paintings in the Dogon country. Visitors to Mopti who have not the time to go to the Bandiagara cliffs proper — the heart of Dogon country — often come here for half a day to get an idea of this unique culture.

On the main road once again there is a track off to the right (before you reach Bandiagara) leading to **Deguembere**. This is where the legendary El Hadj Omer, founder of the 19th C Toucoleur empire, was supposedly killed by fire in a cave in 1864.

Bandiagara, the main town in Dogon country, is an administrative centre with a police headquarters, school, hospital and Christian mission. The majority of the population are Dogon, but there are also a substantial number of Fulani inhabitants.

Your base for explorations

For the visitor Bandiagara's main function is as a base and starting point for trips around Dogon country; it is also worth coinciding your stay with the lively market which is held every Friday and Monday. Shops sell basic provisions which may be useful for the trip. Before setting off it is worth buying a small supply of non-perishable food, some kind of water flask, and sweets and kola nuts for presents.

The police — their headquarters is near the Campement — like visitors to register with them before travelling around this region.

PRACTICAL INFORMATION

ACCOMMODATION AND FOOD

Across the river there is a very basic government **Campement** with 5 rooms, a bar and a restaurant. Toilet and washing facilities are communal. Rooms are inexpensive.

By the river is the **Kansaye Hotel** run by an *ancien combattant* named Kansaye. In this part of the world anciens combattant (war veterans) are Malians and other West Africans who fought for France during the First and Second World Wars in

Europe, North Africa, or wherever else they were needed. After being demobbed many returned with a small war pension to their home villages where they now command tremendous local respect.

The hotel is basic and the rooms have yet to be finished, but the atmosphere is friendly and Mr Kansaye is knowledgable about the Dogon country. Excess baggage can be left here if you are going to trek around the cliffs.

There are several small local **restaurants**, **bakeries** and **food stalls** in the town.

GUIDES

Young boys, usually in their early teens, come up to you as soon as you arrive in Bandiagara and offer their services as guides to the Dogon country.

Before selecting your guide ascertain whether he knows the route along the escarpment, on what days the markets are held and whether he has friends and relations in the villages.

The guide's greatest value, however, is as an interpreter: French into the local language. In their eagerness to be employed the boys may exaggerate their abilities, so use discretion in your choice. Rates of payment, which are low, are negotiable and in addition be prepared to pay the lad's expenses — which would amount to the nominal price of a couple of meals a day.

It is possible to make the trip without a guide, but travelling is much easier, and more interesting, if you have one.

EXPLORING THE BANDIAGARA ESCARPMENT

The best way to see the Bandiagara Escarpment is on foot. The walk is long but not that demanding if you are reasonably fit; track shoes or even a good pair of sandals are adequate footwear.

Although Dogon country attracts tourism the only Western influence in the villages seems to be the occasional transistor radio, wristwatch and sunglasses. There is no mains water or electricity and donkeys are the means of transport along the foot of the escarpment. Do not expect to find any medical assistance here.

Drinking water is drawn from deep wells at the villages and is generally clean; if you have doubts then add purifying tablets. It is worth carrying a water flask.

Taking up residence in a Dogon village

When you arrive in a village you should be introduced to the headman, who will find you a hut to sleep in and somebody to prepare your meals. Expect to pay for this: it may not be regarded as payment, rather as an exchange of tokens between host and guest. Your guide can advise you on the price. Millet is the most common food, but there is also rice and a limited variety of vegetables; meat is understandably more expensive and the chicken or goat will be brought for your approval before being slaughtered and cooked. Kojo (or chakalow), a local millet beer, is fairly potent, thirst-quenching and certainly worth trying.

The Dogon are hospitable: the older generations quietly and politely accept visitors, though deep down they may resent tourism and the lure of the cities which seems to be attracting their young men and thus destroying the traditional way of life.

Villages are divided into *quartiers*, each with its own toguna (meeting place for the elders) and collection of stone-walled compounds. Along the escarpment it is apparently the animists — often reluctant to allow outsiders to wander around their dwellings — who live on the cliff face. Above them are the old Tellem caves. The settlements on the plain tend to be predominantly Moslem; most villages have a small mosque, though the faith may be no more than nominal.

Cliff dwellings at Teli along the Bandiagara Escarpment

The architecture is traditional and has strong associations with Dogon mythology. The houses are basic and made of mud brick — as are the unique tall thin granaries with their millet stalk thatch. The family house, ginna, is where offerings to the ancestors are left in niches which have been cut into the walls. The ginna of the hogon, a village elder and elected priest, is particularly special. Very important is the toguna, the meeting place for the village elders. Traditionally this low structure is supported by eight carved wooden pillars, representing the eight original ancestors, which gradually spiral, thus symbolising the mythical serpent Lebe. The villages are laid out anthropomorphically, ie in the shape of a man, and the toguna represents the head.

Visiting a Showcase Village

Mali's National Tourist Office, SMERT, organises tours to the Bandiagara Escarpment from Mopti. These are either day excursions to Bandiagara and Songo or slightly longer trips to Bandiagara and Sanga. In the case of the latter expedition you travel by Land Rover with an official driver/guide and stay at the government campement. Although this is a quick and easy way of seeing Dogon country it has the disadvantage of being expensive and also it allows only a rushed glimpse at (particularly in the case of Sanga) a traditional village which has in any case been exposed to tourism. In addition there are the shortcomings of travelling in a group.

Travelling with a group

Sanga is a showpiece Dogon village for tourists. I have never been there, but apparently it is attractive and still retains its traditional architecture and way of life, despite close contact with Westerners. In 1930 an American, Reverend Francis McKinney, established a Christian mission in Sanga; it was also here that the French ethnographer Marcel Giraule based himself from the 1930s until his death in 1956. His studies announced the Dogon, until then a little known group of people, to the rest of the world and intrigued anthropoligists and Africa enthusiasts.

If you want to visit Sanga without SMERT then it is best to take the truck which leaves Bandiagara the day before or the same day as Sanga's market day (you should be able to find out the market day from locals in Bandiagara). The road is poor and the distance is

A man of Ende village

around 45 kms. On arrival at Sanga you may have to pay a small 'tourist tax' to a government representative.

Sanga is on the plateau, a short distance from the cliff which along this stretch of the escarpment is about 500 metres high. There are several recognised **scenic routes** from Sanga to neighbouring villages: Le Petit Tour: Sanga to Gogoli (on the edge of the plateau), 7 kms; Le Moyen Tour: Sanga to Gogoli and Banani (on the face of the cliff and on the plain), 10 kms; and Le Grand Tour: Gogoli, Banani and Ireli (on the face of the cliff and on the plain), 15 kms. The distances refer to the round trip from Sanga. The natural tunnel at **Bongo** should be included on these trips. It is probably wise to go with a local; in fact it may be obligatory to have an official guide to whom a set fee will have to be paid. The aforementioned villages are typically Dogon and they should be on your itinerary if you visit Sanga. Incidentally, Banani is the village depicted on the 1000 FM note.

A Trek Through the Heart of Dogon Country

Setting off on your own

An alternative — or in addition to the Sanga trip — is to go from Bandiagara to the cliff face at Kani Kombole and follow the escarpment northeast. It is about 25 kms from Bandiagara to Djuigibombo and then another 25 kms via Kani Komboli along the foot of the cliffs to Douru. Allow at least three to four days for the journey — anything less would be too rushed. If you want to continue from Douru to Sanga allow another three to four days for the 30-odd kms.

The well-defined dirt road runs along the top of the plateau from Bandigara southeast to Djuigibombo and if walked at a brisk pace the distance should be covered in a morning. The terrain is flat and the vegetation is bush savannah with baobabs, kieta and kapok trees. You pass by a couple of villages; in the distance beyond Tegourou there is a heavily wooded area marking the site of a small European-built dam. Irrigation, either as a result of damming or from streams and wells, is important on the plateau.

Djuigibombo, on a slight hill, is built on rock; high stone walls surround the compounds; the buildings (which include a small church, with about half a dozen mud pews and an altar) are made out of mud and stone; there are a couple of spikey baobabs and maybe a few other trees. The overall effect is stark and grey.

The villagers, their clothes devoid of finery and with their traditional deep blue cloth pagnes providing the only hint of colour, blend into the habitat. This is not a reflection of dullness, if anything it emphasises the difficult environment in which the Dogon live. However below Djuigibombo, clustered along the banks of the narrow stream, are lush irrigated fields which during the season are rich with fruits and vegetables: mangoes, guavas, chilis, tomatoes and most importantly the Dogon onions.

View from the top of the cliff

It is about 5 kms from Djuigibombo until you suddenly reach the edge of the cliff; from here there is a marvellous view across the flat sandy seno (plain). The cliff is almost sheer, but with a little care the descent can be walked without much trouble.

Kani Kombole is quite typical: the village is divided into several quarters on the plain — each one separated by a few hundred metres — and then other quarters extending up the cliff face. Above them are the old Tellem caves. Apparently there is an old man born about 1846 (!) living in one of the cliff face settlements.

Following along the foot of the escarpment in a

northeast direction it is about 4 kms to **Teli**, the next village. Though the ground is sandy it is firm enough not to cause any real difficulty in walking. The cliff dwellings at Teli are some of the most interesting along the Kani Kombole to Douru stretch.

Walia, the next village, is not far and then a few kilometres on there is **Ende**; it is possible to ascend the cliff from here to **Soningue**. Along the plain you pass the dramatically-profiled headland and then a string of villages: **Bagoulou, Yabatalou, Doundouru** (also noted for its picturesque cliff dwellings), **Konsagou** and then **Gimini** from where it is a scenic 5 km-walk up the cliff and along the plateau to Douru.

Douru, an important market town, is on the edge of the plateau and has the significant advantage of having a road, albeit very poor, to Bandiagara. It is certainly worth coinciding your visit with the market day; besides this being a lively and a social occasion, it is also the only day you can depend on getting transport — on the onion truck — back to Bandiagara, 25 kms to the west.

In a separate quarter away from the main village is a cluster of shabby breeze block bungalows — a school, a dispensary, the police headquarters; these are the only Western-style buildings along the route since Bandiagara. Next to them is the onion market. Throughout the morning on market day there is practically a continuous line of women arriving here from the onion fields which are next to the resevoir 1½ kms away. The women, clad in their characteristic deep Dogon blue pagne, have an elegant deportment as they balance several heavy baskets of onions on their heads. Merchants buy from the women, then pile the onions in large mounds ready to be sacked, weighed and put on the onion truck to Bandiagara that evening. These delicious onions, a little bigger than a grape, are an important cash crop for the Dogon.

Onions and more onions

The main market is very active and typically Dogon; for the cliff dwellers it is the chance to have contact with people and goods from Bandiagara and Mopti.

If you intend to continue your journey along the foot of the cliffs then descend to **Nombori**. I never covered this section of the escarpment, but I am told that the settlements are very striking; the route passes villages like **Tereli, Yaye, Ireli, Pegue** and **Banani** and

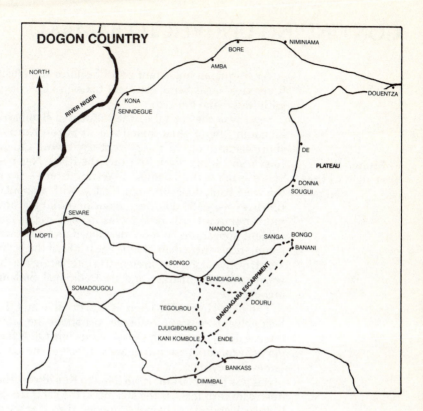

then up to **Sanga**. You can mount the cliffs at either
Ireli or Banani.

CONTINUING UPRIVER TO BAMAKO

After Mopti, an important port of call for the Niger River steamer is **Segu**. Frequent taxis also link Segu with Mopti and Bamako.

Segu was the capital of the influential Bambarra kingdom (the original capital was at Segou Koro, a short distance out of the present-day town). On 20

Mungo Park's first sight of the Niger

July 1796 Mungo Park first saw the River Niger — 'twice as big as the Thames at Westminister' — from the west bank opposite Segu. Today, with a population in excess of 50,000, Segu is one of the largest and most important provincial towns in Mali and at face value it appears to be more developed and a greater commercial centre than Mopti. The banks of the Niger are attractive along this stretch; also interesting are the town's Monday market and its traditional Sudanic architecture.

The new Hotel GTM here is inexpensive and the best value; rooms at L'Auberge cost about the same but are dingy, though the garden is delightful. A few very cheap, very basic rooms are available at the Chez James Bassey Bar.

It is less than 200 kms from Segu to **Koulikoro**, the upstream terminal for the steamers; the cataracts at Sotuba, just north of Bamako, prevent river transport continuing further (though there are boats from Bamako to Guinea). From Koulikoro frequent taxis and a daily train cover the final 57 kms to the capital.

Crocodile river

In local language Bama means crocodile and Ko means river. **Bamako** has long been an important trading post. In 1806 when Mungo Park passed through here it was a fishing and market village with a population of 6000. By the end of the century the French had colonised the town. In 1904 they linked Bamako to Kayes by rail and four years later the capital of Haut Senegal-Niger was moved from Kayes to Bamako. More recently the capital has grown at a fast rate: in 1960 the estimated population was 120,000; today it has easily tripled, perhaps even quadrupled.

Rapid urban growth is common in Africa and other Third World countries. Untypically Bamako does not appear to have an exploding construction programme, usually evident by sprouting skyscrapers at

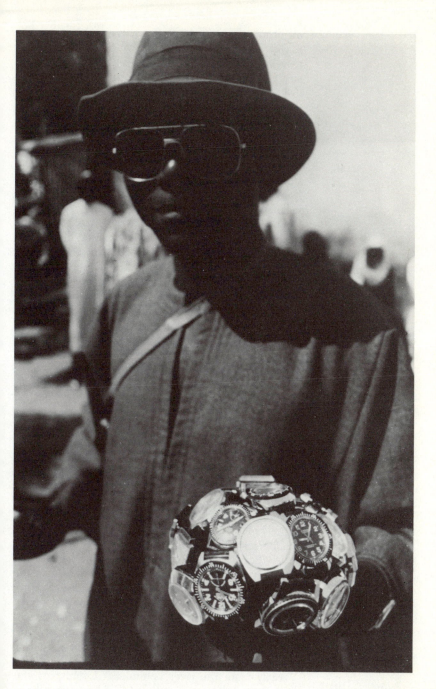

A street vendor at Segu

different stages of completion silhouetted against the skyline. Bamako is a small, busy city with crowded tree-lined avenues and a fairly high population density. Congestion is becoming a concern, though happily it is nowhere near as bad as in Lagos. At present the top two hotels, several commercial buildings and banks and the elegant new mosque are the only modern buildings amongst the streets of mud brick dwellings.

Points of Interest in Bamako

Bamako does not have very much to offer the traveller in the way of sights or things to do.

The triangular **Central Market**, with its pink traditional-style gateways, is interesting. This comparatively small area is crowded with stalls selling spices, handicrafts, souvenirs and domestic goods. Nearby, under the hangar, is the main fruit, vegetable and meat market. Market activities and atmosphere spill out a further 100 to 200 metres around the Central Market. The area to the north, west and south is the commercial centre, full of small shops, stalls, hawkers, souvenir sellers. To the east is the very busy Boulevard de Peuple with its electrical repair stands, bicycle and scooter shops, clothes stalls and taxis.

Going up the street in front of the mosque is the **Artisans' Market**. Here craftsmen work in wood (including ebony), silver, leather, bone and other materials, producing a wide range of ornaments and handicrafts which can be bought on the spot at the small kiosks — which also sell work imported from elsewhere in Mali, including masks from the Dogon region. The market has a director of arts who will happily give you guidance on any purchases.

Kibera Village near L'Amitie Hotel is where craft apprentices weave, sculpt, make shoes, bags and jewellery (to order if required). At **Darsalam**, near the railway line, and also next to the Omnisport stadium, tisserands (weavers) work on their traditional looms. The market at **Medina Coura**, by the Omnisport stadium too, specialises in baskets, pots and leatherwork. Next to the Artisans' Market is the **Musée et Maison de l'Artisan** which holds art exhibitions.

Away from the river behind the Omnisport stadium is the hill known as **Point G**. The seven hills of

The bridge at Bamako: a rare span across the Niger

Seven hills Bamako were named in colonial times after the first seven letters of the alphabet. The first six seem to have faded into obscurity, but the seventh is still known as Point G. This wooded hill and the area around it enjoys scenic walks and a panoramic view over Bamako and the River Niger. From here you also appreciate that Bamako is undeveloped compared to most African capitals. Point G is a 10- to 15-minute taxi ride from the centre of town.

In the same direction along the pleasant wide tree-lined Avenue de la Liberté are the **Zoo** and **Botanical Gardens**, about half an hour's walk from town. Both display a minimal amount of species, but there are plans for development. The main attractions at the zoo are the lion and eagle.

The **National Museum** is an attractively designed building on the Avenue de la Libertié where artefacts from around Mali are exhibited.

ACCOMMODATION

There are 2 high-standard hotels in Bamako: **Hotel l'Amitie**, PO Box 1720; Tel: (223) 224321; telex: 433 AMIHOTEL. And **Hotel le Grand**, Avenue Van Vollenhoven, PO Box 104; Tel: 222481; telex: NO483.

Overlooking the river Niger, **l'Amitie** is Bamako's — probably the country's — only skyscraper and certainly the capital's smartest hotel. It has a swimming pool, tennis court, nightclub and other facilities you would expect to find in a top hotel. **The Grand**, near the railway station, has a good reputation and is popular with visiting businessmen. It provides the same facilities as l'Amitie, but on a smaller, more modest scale. Less expensive, than l'Amitie.

Bamako has a handful of moderately-priced hotels, their rooms with air conditioning and baths: **Les Hirondelles**, on the Koulikoro Road, not central; **Le Terminus**, by the old aerodrome, again not central; **Le Lido**, popular because of its pleasant setting and swimming pool, but about 5 kms west out of town along Kasse Keita Avenue; **Le Dakan**, fairly central in the Niarela district of town; **Le Motel**, about 4 kms from the centre, PO Box 911; Tel: 93622/24.

There are a couple of less expensive central hotels: **Le Majestic**, Avenue du Fleuve; **Hotel de la Gare**, at the railway station.

The two 'cheap' central hotels, **Pension-net Djoliba** near the American Embassy, and **Bar Mali**, Avenue Mamadou Konate, are expensive for the standard they provide.

Realising the lack of cheap, reliable accommodation in Bamako, 2 non-profit making institutions have opened their doors to low budget visitors. The **Maison des Jeunes**, by the river near the bridge, has dormitories with beds. However vacancies are only available when visiting delegations or youth groups are not using the building. **The Foyer d'Accueil** (sometimes known as the Catholic Mission Hostel), Rue El Hadj Ousmane Bagayoke near the Bar Mali Hotel, is run by Catholic nuns and also provides dormitory facilities.

As yet there is no official **campsite**; ask SMERT for up-to-date details.

FOOD

The top hotels have the best and most expensive restaurants; however eat-as-much-as-you-like breakfast buffets at places like the Grand Hotel can be good value. As for the cheaper hotels, the restaurants at the Majestic (La Sangha) and the Hotel de la Gare are not bad value.

The following restaurants are reasonably priced, popular, central and recommended. Compared to the Niamey garden restaurants they are smarter — though not necessarily better — and cater for a predominently Westernised clientele. Many resemble French cafés and dishes tend to be European. Most of them serve alcohol: **Le Chantilly**, Avenue du Fleuve; the **Bar Berry** and the **Central near Place des Souvenirs**; **Black and White**, behind Populaire Pharmacie de Mali on the Avenue du Fleuve; **Savane Royal** by Vox cinema; the **Mediterranée** near the Central restaurant; **Le Bol de Jade** (Chinese and Vietnamese cuisine) Rue BDM — road of the BDM bank; the more expensive **La Gondole** on Avenue de la Nation, and **La Phoenicia** (patisseries, teas, ice cream) up

LEGEND

1	Hotel l'Amitie	10	Railway Station	20	Surete
2	Hotel le Grand	11	Banque BMCD	21	Point G
3	Hotel Majestic	12	American Embassy	22	Zoo
4	Bar Mali	13	French Embassy	23	Botanical Gardens
5	Foyer d'Accueil (Catholic Mission)	14	Central Market	24	Post Office
6	Maison des Jeunes	15	Mosque	25	Post Office
7	Banque BDM	16	Artisans' Market	26	Banque BIAO
8	Banque du Mali	17	Darsalam	27	Cathedral
9	3 Caimans	18	Omnisport Stadium		
		19	SMERT		

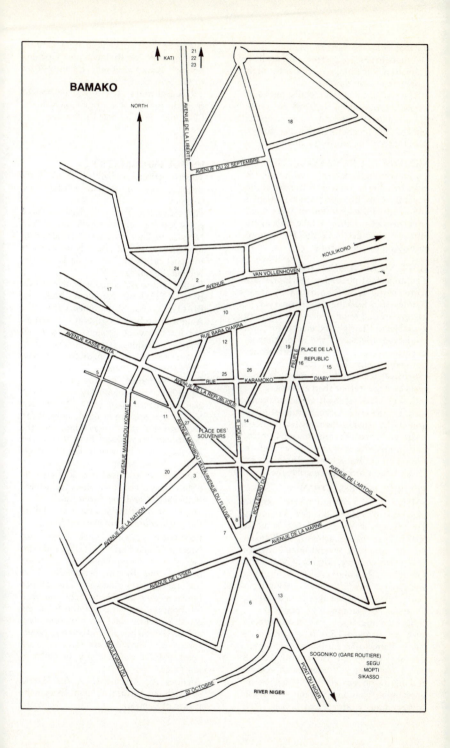

BAMAKO

the road from the Bank du Mali.

A more expensive restaurant is at the **3 Caimans** nightclub (open October through June) by the Pont du Niger.

The typical small **cafés, stalls**, men and women on the side of the road, etc, serve the usual variety of local foods: beignets, smoked fish, brochettes, stew, rice dishes. Also there are of course the **markets**.

ARRIVING AT BAMAKO
If you arrive in Bamako by taxi brousse it is more than likely you will be dropped at the Sogoniko Gare Routiere, which is about 8 kms south of the town centre. Here there are many taxis waiting to take passengers into the city. Establish the fare before embarking on the journey.

GETTING AROUND TOWN
The important places for the tourist are more central in Bamako than they are in Niamey, thus **walking** is the easiest way of getting around town. Collective **taxis** are available and fairly inexpensive: just hail them from the side of the road. Alternatively there are private taxis in the Place des Souvenirs, but they tend to be quite expensive. Cabbies know most destinations by name rather than address.

Collective taxis going to set destinations, such as Sogoniko Gare Routiere, leave from the Dabanani (crossroads) on the Boulevard du Peuple near the Artisan Centre. Confirm the prices with the driver before embarking on the journey. Ask locals or SMERT for a rough price guideline.

TOURIST INFORMATION
SMERT is the acronym for Societe Malienne d'Exploitation des Resources Touristiques, in other words Mali's tourist board. Their headquarters is in Bamako but they also have several small branches around the country, notably at Mopti and Timbuktu. Their staff are very helpful and will assist in any difficulties ranging from visa formalities to hiring a vehicle, taking excursions or planning an expedition.

SMERT organises several **excursions** such as Bamako-Timbuktu-Bamako (3 days); Bamako-Mopti-Bamako (5 days); Bamako-Timbuktu-Mopti-Bamako (8 days). These tend to be quite expensive, and there is no reason why if you have the time and inclination you cannot do these trips, and many others, by yourself.

The SMERT office is in Boulevard du Peuple, opposite the mosque. Opening hours: 7.30am to 2.30pm; Fridays, 7.30am to 12.30pm; closed Sundays.

Detailed **maps** of Mali can be bought from the Institute Geographique National (IGN) near the Gondole Restaurant.

USEFUL INFORMATION
Tourist office: See SMERT, above. Both they and the Surete issue photography permits.

Post office: Rue Karamoko Diaby. It has a poste restante service. Open 8am to 2pm Monday to Thursday, also Saturday; 8am to noon Friday. The philately bureau is at the post office in Avenue de la Liberte, beyond the railway line.

Banks: There are 4 main banks: BIAO, BMCD, BDM and Banque du Mali. The BIAO in Avenue Mohammed V (near the American Embassy) is the most convenient for changing foreign currency and travellers cheques. Bank hours are from 7.30am to 2.30pm Monday to Thursday, also Saturday; 7.30am to 12.30pm Friday.

Surete Nationale, Avenue de la Nation. Open 8am to 2pm Monday to Thursday, also Saturday; 7.30am to 12.30pm Friday. Visa extensions are available here: it can take several days, depending on the department's workload. Even if your visa is valid it may be wise to get the Surete in Bamako to stamp your passport. You should get an exit visa before leaving Mali. SMERT may assist you in these formalities. Both SMERT and the Surete issue photography permits; make sure it is valid for the whole country, not just one area.

Embassies: Algeria, Guinea, Mauritania, Nigeria, Ghana, France, the USA and West Germany have embassies in Bamako. Senegal and Britain periodically have honorary representatives. The French Embassy may be able to help you with information and visas for the following countries which have no representatives in Mali (but do not depend on this): Benin, Togo, Niger, Burkina Fasso and the Ivory Coast. SMERT will give you the embassy addresses.

Airlines: Air Afrique, UTA, Air Algerie, Air Mali and Aeroflot all have offices in the centre of Bamako.

TRAVEL OUT OF BAMAKO

Roads link Bamako to Guinea, the Ivory Coast, Burkina Fasso and Mauritania (find out about the conditions of the road from Nioro du Sahel to Mauritania before attempting this route), as well as to places all around Mali.

Public vehicles operate to Nioro du Sahel, Timbuktu, Mopti and Sikasso. Check with SMERT about road conditions to Nioro du Sahel and Timbuktu, and where to find transport to these destinations. Most public transport leaves from the Sogoniko Gare Routiere, which is about 8 kms out of Bamako on the south bank of the River Niger.

Collective taxis for Sogoniko leave from the Dabanani (crossroads) on the Boulevard du Peuple, near the Artisans' Centre. There are also **private taxis** which can be hired from Place des Souvenirs. The latter are far more expensive.

Bamako's **airport** is 15 kms southeast of the city at Senou. Check the taxi tariff and airport tax before setting out. Air Mali has at least one flight a week from Bamako to these **domestic destinations**: Kayes, Nioro du Sahel, Mopti, Goundam, Timbuktu and Gao. These services can be heavily booked, so reserve well in advance if possible. There are also **tourist excursion flights** to such places as Timbuktu; see SMERT for details. Without too much inconvenience it is possible to reach any **international destination** from Bamako, Paris being the principal European destination via which transfers can be made.

There are also **boats** to Kankan in Guinea, and **trains** to Dakar in Senegal (see Onward Routes below). For the route to Kayes in western Mali and on into Gambia, see the following chapter.

ONWARD ROUTES

By Boat up the River Niger into Guinea

The boat, a 20-metre steel barge, leaves Bamako roughly every fortnight during the high water season (August to December approximately) for Kankan in Guinea. The journey takes about 5 days and covers 385 kms.

The ports of call with their distances from Bamako:

Kourouba	90 kms
Kangara	102 kms
Banankoro	143 kms
Balandougou	159 kms (Guinea frontier)
Dialakoro	181 kms
Siguiri	211 kms
Bate Niafadji	329 kms
Kankan	385 kms

There is one class, fares are low and conditions on the barge are very basic: you sleep on mats, there are crude toilet facilities and though food is served you should bring some of your own provisions.

The **Mali Navigation** office is on the riverbank a short walk beyond the 3 Caimans nightclub. The company's hours of business are 7.30am to 2.30pm Monday to Thursday, also Saturday; 7.30am to 12.30pm Friday; closed Sunday.

Check at the Guinea Embassy about visa formalities.

Bamako to Dakar by Train

In 1904 the French constructed a railway line which linked Dakar on the Atlantic with Bamako deep in the interior of their West African colonies. The line is as important now for freight and passenger movements as it was then, especially as there is no proper road along the full length of this route. The journey is scheduled to take 27½ hours. The ordinary service leaves Bamako daily except Wednesday and Saturday when an express service operates. Often additional trains operate from Bamako to Kayes, Kayes to Tambacounda, and Tambacounda to Dakar.

The trains are pulled by diesel engines. The express is fairly new and comfortable, while the older ordinary service is rather shabby but certainly bearable for the day's journey to Kayes. Both have 1st and 2nd class, also sleepers which are of a reasonably high standard.

Bookings, which include seat reservations for the wagons-lits (sleepers) and 1st class, should be made as early in advance as possible. Seats in 2nd class cannot be reserved, so arrive early if you want to secure a seat. A fare reduction is possible if you can prove you are a student.

From Bamako to Koulikoro

There is also a daily **train** service from Bamako to Koulikoro, the upstream terminus for river traffic to Gao. It departs at 6.30pm and arrives at 8pm.

BAMAKO TO KAYES

For the most part the route passes through hilly terrain thick with luxuriant vegetation. The only direct transport covering the 500-odd kms between Bamako and Kayes is the train. Road vehicles have to go via Nioro du Sahel; many of the tracks are impassable during the rains. If you intend to travel around this area it is worth seeing SMERT for further information on the national parks, campement and hotel facilities, the condition of the roads and the availability of public transport.

Between Bamako and Kayes there is a series of rapids and waterfalls (distances are from Bamako): at 270 kms are the Billy falls; 358 kms the rapids at Kale; at 380 kms is the village of **Bafoulabe** which is a base, with campement, for travels around this scenic region.

Source of the Niger

There is a road from Bafoulabe to the Fouta Djalon highland region of Guinea, where the River Niger has its source. The Gouina falls (430 kms) are on the River Senegal, as are the Felou rapids (495 kms) which have lost some of their beauty since the construction of a hydro-electricity station. 15 kms south of Kayes is the Paparah waterfall.

Vicinity of Bamako

There are several places in the vicinity of Bamako, such as the valley of Oyako and the Sotuba causeway, which are of touristic interest but are best visited during the dry weather. SMERT will give you the information about these and other local scenic sights and the best times of the year to see them.

The scenic Manding Plateau is to the southwest of Bamako.

Vicinity of Kayes

The former gold producing area of Bambuk lies west and south of Kayes between the Faleme and Bafing rivers. It was from here that the Sudanese merchants, particularly during the era of the Kingdom of Ghana, gathered gold and traded it with the trans-Saharan merchants. Thanks to gold bearing places like this the Sudanese kingdom prospered and the prolific trade across the desert flourished.

Young women of western Mali

The whole area south of the railway line is attractive and rugged. There is a rough road which runs south of Kayes parallel to the Senegal border and then into Guinea at the Fouta Djalon highlands. 15 kms along this road is the Paparah waterfall. At the village of Dialafara there are rock drawings. Further on at Yatera there is a junction and a road north to Bafoulabe; some 50 kms south of Yatera, after the village of Nerena, is Kenieba where there is a small campement.

Arrival at Kayes

Kayes was the former administrative capital and terminus for traffic on the River Senegal; however since the Dakar-Bamako railway line was extended to Bamako its importance has declined. It is one of the hottest towns in Mali and well known for its diverse population. A short distance from Kayes is Medine where the French built a fort in 1855 and were held under siege by El Hadj Omer.

PRACTICAL INFORMATION

ACCOMMODATION AND FOOD
The **Hotel de Rail**, opposite the station, is large, pleasant and moderately-priced. Cheaper and basic accommodation is found at the **Hotel de la Pharmacie**, **Hotel Amical** and **Hotel L'Amitie**.

Small **cafés** can be found in town.

OTHER THINGS
Try to **change any surplus Malian francs** here or at Kidira rather than in Senegal where people are not very interested in Malian currency.

If you have not already had an **exit permit** stamped in your passport at Bamako, have it done here.

ONWARD ROUTES
The train crosses the border into Senegal at Kidira, west of Kayes. From there a road follows the River Senegal to **St Louis** on the Atlantic while another runs alongside the railway line to **Tambacounda**. It is this route you should be following if you are heading for **Dakar** or **Banjul**.

By **rail** the distance from Kayes to Tambacounda is 285 kms, with principal stops at Kidira (105 kms) and Goudiry (172 kms).

WESTERN MALI

Northwest of Bamako, about a third of the way to the Mauritanian border, are several parks and game reservations: the Fina, Badinko and Kongassambougou reservations and the Boucle du Baoule National Park. In total they spread over 771,000 hectares. Nearly half of this area is covered by the **Boucle du Baoule National Park**, where there are traditional villages farming millet, cotton and groundnuts and wildlife which includes elephant, giraffe, buffalo and lion.

Campements can be found at Missira, Madina and Baoule.

Enchanting prospect

This is the wooded savannah region of Kaarta, through which Mungo Park travelled in January 1796 on his way to the River Niger. On one occasion the Scot's explorer climbed to the top of the hills and described the panoramic view: 'I had a most enchanting prospect of the country. The number of towns and villages, and the extensive cultivation around them, surpassed everything I had yet seen in Africa.'

Sections of the Bamako-Nioro du Sahel-Kayes roads are impassable during the rains.

100 kms north of Bamako along this road is Tioribougou; 15 kms southwest of here are **Lakes Ouenga and Kolani** which are known for their traditional fishing (particularly active in April). Turn left at Kolokani, 124 kms from Bamako, for the Missira campement. **Kolokani** is an administrative centre with a campement and a colourful market.

A little over 200 kms on from Kolokani, at the village of Diema, there is a track to the west which avoids Nioro du Sahel and joins up with the Kayes road; this shortcut saves 75 kms.

Just short of the Mauritanian border — a total of 432 kms from Bamako — is Nioro du Sahel. Northeast of here was Diara, an important trading town of the former Kingdom of Ghana. The site of the ancient capital of Koumbe Saleh is much further to the east — north of the Malian-Mauritanian border town of Nara.

Nioro du Sahel, founded towards the end of the 17th C, was an important administrative centre but declined when the French established their head-quarters at Kayes at the end of the last century. It is a pleasant town with a colourful mixture of ethnic groups. There is a campement and an airport for internal flights. Along with Kayes, it is the hottest town in Mali. Of particular interest here is the old Mosque.

Into Mauritania

The tracks leading into Mauritania are poor and extra care should be taken, particularly between July and October (it may be wise to avoid travelling during this period). 230 kms north of Nioro is the desert oasis of **Aioun el Atrouss**.

I am uncertain of the frequency of vehicles travelling here or anywhere else in Mauritania, but it seems that once you have your visa (this you should be able to get in Bamako — or Banjul or Dakar if you are coming from the other direction) your best bet is just to get up to Nioro and hope that there is reliable transport going in your direction.

At the time of writing visas were being issued at Mauritanian embassies and the border was open. It should be realised that this could change without much notice, so try to get up-to-date information wherever possible.

PRACTICAL INFORMATION

ONWARD ROUTES
Two routes run southwest from Nioro du Sahel to Kayes; this, the southern one, is shorter and in better condition:

Birou	41kms
Sandere	107kms (Junction of road east to Diema)
Dialaka	168 kms
Kayes	251 kms

SENEGAL

Basic Facts

Total Area: 196,000 sq kms.

Neighbours: Mauritania to the north, Mali to the east, Guinea and Guinea Bissau to the south and the Atlantic Ocean to the west. Gambia sticks into the side of Senegal like a finger.

Population: 6.4 million nationwide (1984 estimate). Dakar: 800,000; Theis: 120,000; Koalack: 100,000; St Louis: 90,000; Ziguinchor: 60,000 (all figures are for 1978 and are estimates). 35 percent of the population is urban.

Ethnic groups: Wolof: 709,000; Fulani: 324,000; Serer: 306,000; Toucouleur: 248,000; Diola: 115,000 (1960 figures).

Capital: Dakar.

Official language: French.

Religion: 90 percent Moslem, the remainder Christians, with some animists in the south.

Independence: 1960. Formerly a French colony.

Economy: The Senegalese economy is essentially agricultural with groundnuts (Senegal is one of the world's leading producers of groundnuts) accounting for a high percentage of exports. In recent years the increased cultivation of cotton, rice and sugar has helped diversify the country's agriculture. The cattle population has been reduced by successive droughts. The fishing industry has grown significantly and tuna, sardine and shellfish are exported. Phosphates, the country's main mineral resource, is an important export commodity. Senegal has yet to tap its iron ore deposits. In recent years tourism has grown rapidly and it is now a valuable source of income.

Per capita GNP: US $370 per annum (1983–85).

President: Abou Diouf has been leader of Senegal since 1980. Parti Socialiste Senegalais (PS) is the ruling party.

Electricity: 220v.

Time: GMT.

Currency: The unit of currency is the franc CFA (see Niger).

Visas: Required for entry into Senegal and issued one to two days after application. They should be obtainable in neighbouring West African countries as well as in London (see below). The visa is normally valid for one month and extensions are easily available in Senegal.

Senegalese Embassy in London: 11 Phillimore Gardens, London W8. Tel: 01-937 0925/6.

Accommodation: Good budget accommodation is difficult to find. In Dakar a room in a reasonable pension will cost $15 to $20. Mid-range hotels will charge $20 to $40 a night. At the top end of the market Senegal has some very good hotels (business and tourist hotels in Dakar and along the coast, eg Club Mediterranée), but be prepared to pay $50 to $100 for a double.

Transport: Senegal has 14,000 kms of road (1982), of which 25 percent is tarmacked. 504s operate from Tambacounda to Dakar ($12) and Banjul via Koalack ($12). There is rail transport between Dakar and Bamako (see Mali *Basic Facts*). The river Senegal is navigable between St Louis and Kayes (Mali) between August and December; there will be improvements in navigability once the Manatali Dam has been completed. The Senegal is navigable up to Kaedi for six months of the year and up to Rosso and Podor throughout the year. Sections of the rivers Saloun and Casamance are also navigable.

Tourist office: Secretariat d'Etat au Tourisme, Rond Point de Madeleine, BP 4049, Dakar. Tel: 22 22 26.

Embassies: British, 20 Rue du Dr Guillet, BP 6025, Dakar. Tel: 21 73 92; telex: 548. USA, Ave. Jean XXIII, BP 49, Dakar. Tel: 21 42 95; telex: 517.

PASSING THROUGH SENEGAL

East Senegal is flat savannah, quite rich in vegetation and with many baobab trees. **Tambacounda** (often abbreviated to Tamba) is the capital of this region and a good place to get off the train if you do not want to go direct to Dakar. It is an important crossroads for travellers. Apart from the Bamako-Dakar train stopping here, there is also a surfaced road linking Tamba to the coast. And you can head south to **Niokolo-Kobo National Park**.

The park, 144 kms southeast of Tambacounda, covers 800,000 hectares. Three rivers, including the Gambia, flow through it giving rise to lush, varied vegetation throughout the year. Elephant, lion, panther, buffalo, hippo and crocodile inhabit the park, it is claimed; at any rate their presence is not obvious and more usually wildlife enthusiasts will have to be satisfied looking at monkeys, wild pig, gazelle and antelope. Numerous species of colourful and beautiful birds also make their homes here.

One of the best parks along the route

Along with Parc du W (see Niger), Niokolo-Koba is the best nature reserve along the route followed in this book.

PRACTICAL INFORMATION

GENERAL
After Mali you are suddenly hit by the comparatively high level of development and prosperity of Senegal. Expect costs to be a bit higher too.

TAMBACOUNDA
The only **hotel** is the moderate Asta Kebe, 2 kms out of town. The police, who are very helpful, may assist you in finding other accommodation.

There is a **bank** here.

NIOKOLO-KOBA NATIONAL PARK
The park is expensive to stay in. Typically, the French have built stylish **camps** to cater for their tourists. If you have your own equipment you can make your own camp, though get the permission of a park ranger first. There is a park admission fee. The best way of getting around the park is by **car**, but they are expensive to hire.

There are **hotels** at Badi, the village of Niokolo Koba, and at Simenti where there is a **landing strip**.

Information is available at the tourist office in Dakar or at the Hotel Asta Kebe in Tambacounda.

ONWARD ROUTES
There are frequent taxis brousse from Tambacounda to **Dakar** (about 5 hours) and **Kaolack** (about 3 hours), both in Senegal. From either place it is easy to get transport to **Banjul**, the capital of Gambia. Obviously Gambia is more quickly reached from Kaolack from where it takes another 2 to 3 hours to Banjul via the Barra ferry.

Senegal borders Gambia to both north and south, and an alternative route from Tambacounda is to go by road to Velingara from where you can hop over to Basse-Sante-Su, an important upriver town in Gambia, or continue to Kolda and on to Ziguinchor, capital of Senegal's beautiful **Casamance region**.

Casamance, which covers the western part of south Senegal, is very popular with French tourists, most of whom drive here from Dakar via Banjul, Farafenni or Tambacounda. The most popular places are **Ziguinchor** on the River Casamance, and the area from here up to and including **Cap Skerring**.

GAMBIA

Basic Facts

Total Area: 11,295 sq kms.

Neighbours: Gambia is bordered to the north, east and south by Senegal and to the west by the Atlantic Ocean.

Population: 695,886 nationwide (1985 estimate). Banjul: 39,500; Serrekunda/Bakau: 34,382; Gunjur: 4677; Sukuta: 3844; Farafenni: 3778 (1973).

Ethnic groups: Mandinka 40 percent; Fula 13 percent; Wolof 13 percent; Jola 7 percent; Serahuli 7 percent.

Capital: Banjul.

Official language: English.

Religion: Moslem: 90 percent; the remainder of the population is almost all Christian, though there are some animists, especially from the Jola tribe.

Independence: 1965. Commonwealth member.

Economy: 80 percent of the workforce is involved in agriculture. Groundnuts are the chief crop and account for 90 percent of exports. Tourism is an expanding industry and accounts for 7 percent of the GDP.

Per capita GNP: US $230 (1983–85).

President: Sir Dawda Jawara has been president since independence. His party is the People's Progressive Party.

Electricity: 220v.

Time: GMT.

Currency: The unit of currency is the Dalasi (D). 100 bututs = 1 Dalasi. Coins: 1, 5, 10, 25, 50 butut and 1 Dalasi. Notes: 1, 5, 10 and 25 Dalasi.
£1 = 11D; US $1 = 7D. Approximate 1988 rates.

Visas: British citizens do not need visas to enter Gambia. You are allowed an initial three or four week period of stay; the Ministry of the Interior (on the corner of Anglesea Street and Dobson Street) will grant you an extension for a small charge.

Gambian High Commission in Britain: 57 Kensington Court, London W8. Tel: 01-937 6316.

Accommodation: Hotels — catering almost exclusively for the package tourist — are along the coast. Rates range from $35 to $75 a double — this may include meals. In Banjul there are a few mid-range hotels ($25 double) and a couple of basic lodges (around $10 a night). Inland only a very few hotels can be found; they tend to be basic ($10 to $20 a room) and cater for the local business traveller. Elsewhere — as in all the remoter parts of the Sahel – you may have to rely on local hospitality.

Transport: Gambia has 2360 kms of classified roads and tracks, though some of these are seasonal and only 20 percent are tarmacked. 504s provide transport from Banjul to the eastern extremity of the country; the Banjul to Basse fare is about $10. A variety of vessels provide excursions up the River Gambia.

Tourist office: Apollo Hotel Extension, Orange Street, Banjul. Tel: 28472; telex: 2204.

Embassies and High Commissions: British, 48 Atlantic Road, POB 507, Fajara; Tel: 95133; telex: 2211. USA, Pipeline Road, Fajara-Serekunda. Tel: 92858.

Tourism in Gambia is relatively new, but in the last few years the number of visitors has rocketed. Plane-loads of package holidaymakers, mainly Scandinavian and British, land in Banjul eager to soak up the sun on the sand in an African setting. The vast majority come during the high season which is between October and April.

Kenya is the other black African country to which Britons go in search of beach resorts and it also has the advantage of spectacular scenery and game reserves. Gambia's wildlife is mainly the smaller animals, though ornithologists will not be disappointed as the banks of the River Gambia are known throughout the world for their abundance of birds — over 400 species.

Small is beautiful

Gambia has a 'small is beautiful' charm. It is one of the smallest countries in Africa (11,295 square kms), and with an average breadth of 35 kms and length of 300 kms it is like a long finger poking into the side of Senegal. Gambia has 50 kms of Atlantic coastline, most of it palm-fringed beach and hardly built on; otherwise Gambia is its river, and a boat trip into the interior is, along with its beaches, Gambia's greatest attraction. But the people too need to be mentioned: their warmth and hospitality put a smile to the sunshine and create an almost calypso atmosphere normally associated with a Caribbean island.

The warm smile of a Gambian woman

BANJUL

Suppressing the slave trade

In 1807 the British abolished slavery. Even so this did not wholly prevent merchants trying to ship their human cargo across the Atlantic. Initially Colonel Charles MacCarthy, Governor-in-Chief of West African territories, wanted to occupy James Island and monitor the trade along the River Gambia from there. Captain Alexander Grant was sent with some African Corps soldiers to establish the base; however, he rejected the island as too small and too far from the mouth of the river. Instead he chose Banjul Island which is at the point where the Gambia flows into the Atlantic. He leased the island from the King of Kombo and on 23 April 1816 it was renamed St Mary.

The site was little more than sand and mangrove and general conditions were unhealthy; building material had to be brought downstream from Dog Island. Though the island was probably intended only as a temporary military station, a town was quickly built and named Bathurst after the Colonial Secretary of that time. Two main streets, Wellington and Buckle (the latter named after the Colonial Engineer who planned the town) ran parallel to the river. They were joined by six smaller streets — Blucher, Picton, Anglesley, Hill, Orange and Cotton (named after Wellington's aides and, in the case of Blucher, the man who saved his bacon at Waterloo). At the western end of town a square was laid out and named after Governor MacCarthy; beyond this area was Government House.

Bathurst became a trading centre for upriver merchants and also a port of call for ships travelling along the West African coast. But profits from Gambia were fairly low — at least until groundnut exports got underway — and that, coupled with the many deaths and cases of illness among the colonials, forced the British to question the value of their presence in the country. As an economy measure they on more than one occasion put Gambia under the control of the governor of Sierra Leone, another British colony further south along the coast.

Nevertheless Britain hung onto its small colony and during the Second World War Bathurst was used by the Royal Navy and the RAF as a stopping point

The Albert Market in Banjul

enroute to the East.

In 1973, three years after Independence, Bathurst was renamed Banjul. Today Banjul is remarkably undeveloped for a capital city, though admittedly a lot of business now takes place in the satallite town of **Small-scale** Serekunda — and anyway Gambia is a small country. **capital** Unlike fast-growing Niamey, Bamako and Dakar, there are few signs of large sums of money being allocated for modern construction programmes. From the Barra ferry, Banjul, partly obscured by the thick vegetation along the shore, looks little more than a backwater trading town; like everything else about Gambia it is pleasantly small in scale.

Especially after visiting Niger, Mali and Senegal the British influence in Gambia is very striking and for many visitors this familiarity reinforces the capital's cosy charm. This ranges from expressions such, as 'Dash me a dollar' (give me a delasi) or 'Let's go chop chop' (let's go and eat) — common idioms in former British West African colonies — to Banjul's street names, its fish and chip restaurant and its cricket pitch in MacCarthy Square.

Few tourists actually stay in Banjul (except at the Atlantic Hotel), but though it has few sights it is quite an interesting place to visit.

PRACTICAL INFORMATION

ACCOMMODATION

The **top hotels** on the Kombo St Mary Peninsula depend on the European package tourist for their business.

From Banjul going west to Bakau and then from Bakau to Fajara and on to Kotu, Bijilo and many miles beyond is more or less unbroken, unspoilt beach. There are about 10 hotels along the 17 kms of coast between Banjul and the new Senegambia Hotel. All of these are on the beach, most have swimming pools, bedrooms are air-conditioned and have their own bathrooms, and there is some kind of evening entertainment. Standards and prices vary to an extent, but as they are monitored by tour operators they do not drop below a certain level. These travel companies are mainly British, Scandinavian and German and each one tends to use particular hotels. Consequently the hotels have different European national atmospheres.

Atlantic Hotel, PO Box 296, Marina Drive, Banjul. Tel: 8601; telex: GV 2250. Pool, disco, tennis, air-conditioned rooms with bath — and many other facilities. The Atlantic is probably the best hotel in Gambia. The centre of town — either past the President's Palace or via the fish-market — is only a short stroll along the beach. It has a predominantly British clientele.

Along the coast towards Denton Bridge you come to the **Wadner Beach Hotel**, PO Box 377, Cape Road. Tel: 8239; telex: 2219 GV. Right on the beach, this is a very pleasant, moderately-priced place. The rooms (some air-conditioned, all with bath or shower) are in thatched buildings set in tropical gardens. There is a pool, tennis court and nightclub too.

Around Bakau there are the **Sunwing** at Cape Point, the **African Village** and the **Tropic Gardens** hotels. Further down the beach, just beyond the American ambassador's residence in the Fajara area, are the **Fajara, Bungalow Beach, Bakotu** and several other hotels as yet unopened. A few kilometres or so on from Fajara is one of Gambia's newest and largest hotels, the **Senegambia**; it is a smart, modern rather attractive hotel complex and most of the clientele are Scandinavian.

If you intend to spend some time at one of these hotels it is worth finding out about all-inclusive package tours from your travel agent. This is obvious if you want a two- or three-week holiday solely in Gambia. However it is also worth bearing in mind that some people arrive on a tour and after their holiday forefeit the return flight and continue their travels within Africa (or the other way round). This can work out cheaper than paying for the hotel on a day to day basis.

Many of the hotels drop their prices during the low season (between May and October).

Cheaper hotels, all in Banjul, include the **Carlton** (PO Box 639, Independence Drive. Tel: 258), the **Adonis** (PO Box 377, 23 Wellington Street. Tel: 262) and the **Apollo** (PO Box 419, 33 Buckle Street. Tel: 8184). These are primarily for the individual visitor and businessman of Banjul. Rooms are usually air-conditioned with bath.

There is a dearth of good **low-budget**

LEGEND

1	Adonis Hotel	6	Albert Market	13	Ministry of the Interior
2	Atlantic Hotel	7	Post Office	14	Tourist Office
3	Apollo Hotel	8	Standard Bank		
4	State House	9	Barra Ferry Terminal		
	(President's Palace)	10	Gambia Ports Authority		
5	Quadrangle	11	Football Stadium		
		12	Central Bank		

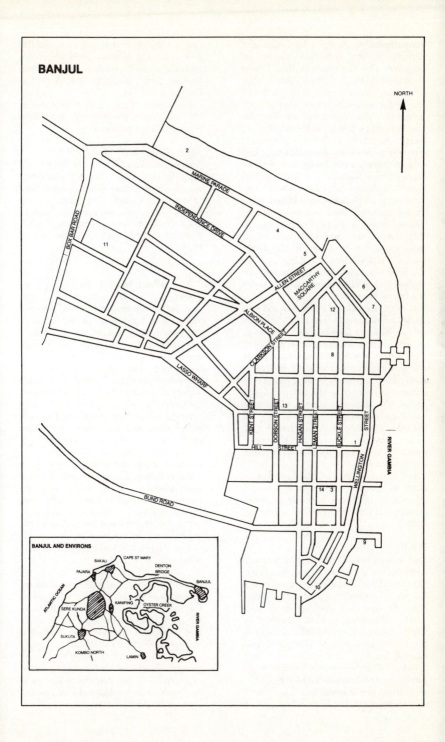

BANJUL

NORTH

BOX BAR ROAD

MARINE PARADE

INDEPENDENCE DRIVE

2

11

4

5

ALLEN STREET

MACCARTHY SQUARE

6

ALBION PLACE

12

7

CLARKSON STREET

8

LASSO WHARF

KENT STREET

DOBSON STREET

13

HAGAN STREET

LEMAN STREET

BUCKLE STREET

STREET

HILL STREET

1

WELLINGTON

RIVER GAMBIA

14 3

9

BUND ROAD

10

BANJUL AND ENVIRONS

CAPE ST MARY

BAKAU

DENTON BRIDGE

FAJARA

BANJUL

ATLANTIC OCEAN

KANIFING

OYSTER CREEK

SERE KUNDA

RIVER GAMBIA

SUKUTA

KOMBO NORTH

LAMIN

accommodation, probably because of the scarcity of the individual low-budget traveller. The **Government Rest House** behind the Catholic Cathedral has, for the time being, been converted into a hostel for the Senegalese police and therefore no longer provides accommodation. There is the **Traveller's Lodge** in Dobson Street, but it is rather drab with hardboard partitions dividing the cubicles (the owners have a new, better and cheaper lodge in Sere Kunda). The **Taranga**, Hill Street, is shabby but clean. Also in this category is **Uncle Joe's Guest House**; it is a pleasantly 'well lived in' small private house, owned by the portly Uncle Joe, an informative and hospitable gentleman who spent several years in the 1950s studying and working in England.

These places will lack private bath or shower and air conditioning; usually there is a fan on the ceiling.

If these are still too expensive and you do not mind being in Barra, on the north side of the River Gambia, then there is an old **government lodge** next to Fort Bullen. This small, wooden colonial-style guest house situated at the mouth of the river is rarely used, seemingly because few people know about the place. Maybe it is thought unsuitable accommodation, as running water and electricity are now defunct. All the same it is quiet and clean, though a bit musty, and its ridiculously low price indicates that it is a leftover from a bygone era.

Bakau, where many expatriates live, is close to the most popular beaches. I imagine it will not be long before cheap accommodation will open here for the traveller.

FOOD
Each season heralds new restaurants and nightclubs in the Bakau-Fajara area. They, like the cuisines in the hotels, cater for the European demand; the food is predominately Western as is the pop music, and what confirms that you are holidaying in Africa rather than the Mediterranean is the Gambian staff and the token traditional decor.

In Banjul the restaurants with European menus are the **Tropical Nightclub**, Clarkson Street; the **Braustable**, Leman Street — package tourists are usually taken to

one of these after their city tour; and the **Fish and Chip Express**, good fish, chips and salad at a reasonable price, which is in Leman Street opposite the American Peace Corps Centre.

Local foods, snacks and fruits are sold on the side of the street or in cheap cafés throughout the peninsula.

ACTIVITIES AND EXCURSIONS
Tourist markets, known as bengdulala (singular bengdula) — which in Mandingo means 'meeting place' — sell a large variety of souvenirs; Gambia is particularly noted for its batiks and wood carvings. Most of the large hotels have a bengdula. There is also one on the beach beyond the Atlantic Hotel.

The **Albert Market**, built in Russell Street by the British, consists of narrow, dark paths with rows of crowded cramped stalls. The building does not cover a particularly large area and now the market has spilt onto the road behind and borders the beach area where the fishermen keep their boats. The Albert is very much a domestic market for Gambians. A whole variety of goods are sold: pots, pans, shoes, cloth, fruits, etc. Also, and this is now typical in urban African markets, there are men selling digital watches, transistors calculators and other electrical gadgets.

The Albert Market has many small cafés and these are probably the cheapest places to eat in Banjul. The most common dish is stewed lamb and 'French' bread and in the mornings many office workers stop here to have breakfast on their way to work.

The Market was damaged by fire in 1986 and has since undergone a facelift.

The Albert Market closes in the mid afternoon.

The clean, sandy, sun-soaked **beaches** are the main attraction for most visitors to Gambia. The best one is near Bijilo — which is almost deserted, though fairly inaccessible. Or, if you want to be close to the hotels, then try the stretch at Fajara.

At dawn a handful of Gambians jog along the beach outside the Atlantic Hotel near Banjul; in the evening children and local teams play football and hold training sessions on the firm sand.

Despite the increased number of tourists the beaches of the Kombo-St Mary Peninsula are by no means overcrowded. And if you go a little further down the coast there is kilometre after kilometre of palm fringed beaches almost untrodden from one day to the next.

However, a couple of points of warning: the currents in the Atlantic can get quite strong; and second, there have been a few isolated cases of theft on the beach and consequently guards are posted near the hotels during the day. It is advisable not to walk along the beach after dark.

Oyster Creek is the mangrove swamp area to the west of Banjul. Private yachts and fishermen moored near Denton Bridge, or at Old Jeshwang, often take visitors along the network of channels which cut through the thick mangrove vegetation of Oyster Creek. A keen bird watching friend said this excursion is a must for ornithologists who do not have the chance to travel up the River Gambia. Organised trips are laid on by the tour operators; alternatively go there yourself (take the Bakau or Sere Kunda bus/taxi and ask to be dropped off at Denton Bridge). The yacht owners charge a lot; the price of hiring a fisherman and his canoe is negotiable.

Other excursions and shows offered by the tour companies include visits to traditional local **villages**. The constant flow of foreigners has somewhat tarnished the pristineness of these places and turned them into showpieces.

Also there are **ethnic dances** at the hotels — these are colourful, gay and popular; excursions by truck into the **bush**; and a variety of beach/sea activities like **windsurfing** and **sea fishing**.

Further afield there is a day-trip (during the tourist season) by yacht to **Fort James Island** and **Albreda** (near **Juffure**).

Abuko Nature Reserve is 24 kms southwest of Banjul. The wildlife at this small reserve is limited to hippos, baboons, chimps and smaller animals; however there is a wide variety of flora and birds.

Organised excursions to the park leave from the main hotels. Consult the tourist office for further information if you want

to go independently. Cars are left outside the gates and tours are conducted on foot. There is an entrance fee.

GETTING AROUND THE BANJUL AREA

Banjul itself is so small that **walking** will get you anywhere easily.

Taxis and minibuses operate throughout the day between Banjul, Bakau, Sere Kunda and Brikama. For **minibuses** to **Bakau**, go to Independence Avenue opposite the Anglican cathedral; for **Sere Kunda**, catch one on Grant Street opposite MacCarthy Square; for **Brikama**, minibuses leave from the junction of Albion Place and Grant Street.

Taxis can be hailed along any street. Taxis with a 'Tourist Taxi' card in their window have a set tariff between places. All the same, confirm the fare before setting off.

USEFUL INFORMATION

The **tourist office** is next to the Apollo Hotel on Orange Street: 8am to 2.45pm, Monday to Thursday; 8am to 12.45pm, Friday and Saturday. **Photography permits** are not at this moment necessary, though check with the tourist office for up-to-date information.

The **post office** is on Russell Street next to the Albert Market: 8am to 2.45pm, Monday to Thursday; 8am to 12.45pm, Friday and Saturday.

There are 3 commercial **banks** in Banjul: the Standard Bank, the International Bank for Industry and Commerce, and the Commerce and Development Bank. The **Standard Bank** in Buckle Street is where most visitors change their money; the bank has a branch in Basse. Street dealers at the ferry dock offer better rates than the banks for hard currency cash, though this is illegal. Change sufficient money before embarking on a journey inland as apart from the bank at Basse you will have to rely on finding some enterprising merchant. Bank hours are from 8am to 1pm, Monday to Thursday; 8 to 11am, Friday and Saturday.

The **Ministry of the Interior** is on the corner of Anglesea and Dobson Streets. Commonwealth citizens do not need a visa to enter Gambia. You are allowed a period of stay, usually 3 weeks or a month, after which the Ministry will grant you an extension. Hours are from 8am to 2.45pm, Monday to Thursday; 8am to 12.45pm, Friday and Saturday.

Visas for the following West African countries are available from their embassies or national representatives in Banjul: Guinea, Hagan Street; Guinea Bisseau, Hill Street; Mali, corner of Grant Street and Lasso Wharf; Mauritania, Clarkson Street; Nigeria, Buckle Street (but note that you might have difficulty getting a Nigerian visa from here); Senegal, corner of Buckle and Cameroon Streets; and Sierra Leone, Hagan Street.

The **American Embassy** is in Pipeline Road, Fajara-Serekunda. Tel: 92858. The **British High Commission** is at 48 Atlantic Road, Fajara (PO Box 507). Phone 95133.

ONWARD ROUTES WITHIN GAMBIA
The following chapter describes a journey up the Gambia River and provides some practical information.

ONWARD ROUTES TO SENEGAL AND MALI
It is first helpful to know that the **ferry** across the mouth of the Gambia River from Banjul to Barra leaves every 2 hours between dawn and dusk from the ferry terminal off Wellington Street. The trip takes about 20 minutes and is very cheap. Cars are carried.

To Senegal
Collective taxis leave to the Casamance region in **south Senegal** from next to the Box Bar stadium or from the taxi station at Brikama.

For **Dakar**, Peugeot 504s depart from the taxi park at Barra. They start setting off when the first ferry arrives from Banjul and continue regularly until the early to middle afternoon. The journey, on a good surfaced road via Kaolack, takes around 5 hours. You pass through customs and immigration posts on entering Senegal.

There are regular **flights** from Banjul to Dakar.

To Mali
There are several **overland** options. Take a taxi to Dakar and from there a train leaving at noon on Tuesday and Friday to Bamako. Or, if you want to avoid Dakar, go by taxi from Barra to Tambacounda (change at Kaolack) — a total of around 6 hours — and then catch the train to Kayes and Bamako. A third option is to go from Basse (in upriver Gambia) to Velingara which is just inside the south Senegal border. From there you can take a taxi to Tambacounda and then the train on to Mali. There is very little road transport between Kayes and Bamako.

There are no **flights** from Banjul to Mali. You would have to go, say, to Dakar first from where you could fly to Bamako.

JOURNEY UP THE GAMBIA RIVER

Mangroves along the Gambia River

If you are going upriver and then returning to Banjul I suggest you travel one way by boat and the other way by land.

The River Gambia is several kilometres wide at its mouth and as you penetrate deeper into the heart of darkness the banks, rich in mangrove trees and tropical vegetation, gradually close in on your boat. At Basse, the furthest passenger steamers will travel, the river is only 100 metres wide. This, and the dense vegetation on the banks, give it a more intimate atmosphere than the River Niger.

Compared to the River Niger everything about the River Gambia — its size, the steamer, the bustle of activities at its ports — is on a small scale.

By road or river? The boat trip up the Gambia may well be romantic and exciting; the scenery from the river is interesting and the journey relaxing. But you are detached. If you travel by road, not only is it easier to visit the places of interest, but also you can stay in the villages and wander the countryside where few foreigners bother to venture.

The north bank, particularly east of Georgetown, remains little affected by Westerners. The south bank, with its surfaced road linked to Banjul, is more developed.

The Lower Reaches of the Gambia River

In 1827 Commodore Bullen, who had fought at the battle of Trafalgar, supervised the building of a British fort at **Barra**. The construction met with local opposition which culminated in the Barra War, and it was not until the French sent a warship to help their fellow Europeans that the British managed to complete the fort in 1831. The cannons positioned here, in addition to those in Banjul (outside the President's Palace), helped protect the entrance to the River Gambia and prevent illegal slave ships reaching the ocean. The interior of the rather unspectacular Fort Bullen can only be visited with special permission (see the tourist office).

About 10 kms east of Barra is **Berending** where crocodiles bask in a sacred pool.

Before the British built fortifications at the mouth of the river the strategic point from which traffic along the Gambia was controlled was **Fort James Island**, 24 kms upstream from Banjul. Portuguese sailors had landed here in 1456 and it soon became a trading post. A Baltic noble, James Duke of Courland, built the first fort in 1651, but ten years later the British captured the island and named it for the heir to the throne, the future King James II.

Outposts of global conflict

In 1681 the French established a trading station at **Albreda**, opposite Fort James Island, and for the next 100 years there was continuous rivalry between the French and British along the Gambia River. It was in 1779, while the French and British were engaged in their broad struggle which, among other things, saw the independence of the thirteen British colonies in North America, that the French managed to destroy the British fort on the island. Nevertheless, at the Treaty of Versailles in 1783 the British were given control of the Gambia River. But Fort James Island was left in ruins and today, with its abandoned

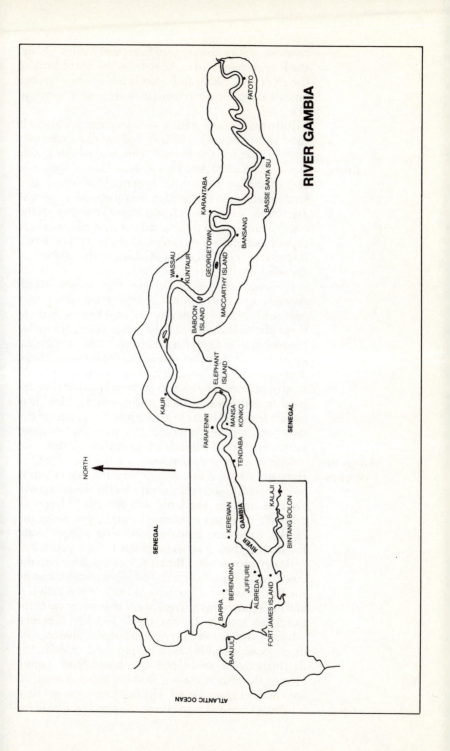

RIVER GAMBIA

cannons, it is a gravestone of European rivalry. Oddly, the French remained in Albreda on the north bank of the river until 1857, and what is left of their trading houses along the waterfront makes for an interesting visit.

Roots

Juffure is a five-minute walk inland from Albreda. It used to be known as Jillifrey and was an important trading post for the British. This was where Kunte Kinte, ancestor of Alex Haley, the author of *Roots*, was carried off as a slave to America 200 years ago. Understandably the village has become a tourist attraction. You can visit Kunte Kinte's compound, the nearby ruins of the trading station where he was kept captive and other places linked to the story. Locals will introduce you to relations of Haley's who still live in the village.

It would be sensible to see Fort James Island, Albreda and Juffure all in one trip; some tour operators offer a half-day excursion which visits these three places. If you want to be independent, then a far cheaper way is to take a taxi from Barra to Albreda; Juffure is just the other side of the road from Albreda. You can see Fort James Island from the river bank; local fishermen take visitors to the island, but they are used to tourists and their prices may be high. It is unsafe for small boats to go out into the middle of the river when the water is choppy. The steamer normally stops at Albreda on its upriver voyage.

Mangrove swamps

Mangrove is at its densest from the mouth of the river to around Kaur. Above here the vegetation is more mixed. If you really want a feel of the mangrove swamps and see the birds and possibly a hippo or crocodile, then get a boatman to take you along the creeks. Kerewan, Tendaba, Kaur and villages along the Bintang Bolon are good places to base yourself.

Bolon means creek: **Bintang**, a village 8 kms up the creek, was originally established as a trading station by the British Guinea Company in 1652. In the 18th C it and other posts on the creek were important bases for European traders. Up the creek you find **Gereeja**, which was a former Portuguese outpost; **Bwiam**, site of a locally significant iron pot; and **Kalaji**, the destination for small pleasure boats from Banjul (during the tourist season). Bintang Bolon is about 50 kms upriver from Banjul. The easiest way to get here is to take a taxi and turn off the main road and head for

An old trading house at Albreda

a village on the creek. The alternative is to go on a river excursion.

Just west of **Kerewan** you have to take a ferry across the creek. There are interesting pirogue rides through the mangrove swamps around Kerewan.

Quite a few tourists get off the steamer at **Tendaba Camp** and then rejoin it on its return journey. The camp — about all there is here — is run by a Swede and can accommodate 100 people in mock traditional huts. The conditions are adequate, though nothing fancy. There is a restaurant, a well stocked bar and a swimming pool. Land Rover trips to the nearby villages and priogue rides up the creeks are the main attractions for guests. Tendaba Camp can be reached by road or river: see the tourist office in Banjul about reservations. At **Batelling**, about 8 kms southwest of Tendaba by road, there are abandoned cannons, which formerly helped defend the trading posts.

The busy Trans-Gambian Highway — passing through **Farafenni** and **Mansa Konko** — links north Senegal with its southern region of Casamance. Ferries still operate between the river banks; the

Gambian government is reluctant to build a bridge as this would hinder navigation and reduce the toll levy. Farafenni has a couple of small hotels. Soma, about 2 kms south of Mansa Konko, is a main pick up point for transport to Banjul or places to the east.

The waters of the Gambia River are affected by salinity as far upstream as **Elephant Island**, which is about 150 kms from the ocean.

Groundnuts (peanuts) are Gambia's main cash crop and export. The nut was brought over from Brazil to Europe in the 16th C and then introduced to Gambia by the Portuguese. It did not become a trade item until the 19th C; today over 90 million kilos (with shells) are cultivated annually.

Groundnuts: the happy season

Planting is in April and May — the fields are usually inland from the river — and harvesting in October. At this time of the year extra labourers, known as 'strange farmers', drift in from the neighbouring countries to help with the gathering. In November and December the groundnuts are taken to the market and winnowed, weighed and stacked to dry. This is sometimes referred to as the 'happy season' because the months of hard work have come to an end and the farmers now have some money in their pockets.

For the tourist it is an interesting and colourful time to visit inland Gambia; also the weather is at its best.

December heralds the trade season. Ocean-going ships of 3000 tons can come upstream as far as **Kaur** to collect their cargo. On the water's edge at Kaur there is a decorticating (husking) plant, but the main part of this small, rural town is a couple of kilometres inland. Many of the shops belonging to the old trading companies are now deserted; this reminder of the former European merchants is very typical of villages all along the River Gambia.

Kaur is a pleasant place to spend a day or two: a couple of rows of whitewashed shops, an active market, an open-air cinema and a couple of bars are the notable features of the town; there is no hotel, but the bars usually have spare rooms. It is worth taking a ride in a dug-out which ferries locals up the mangrove creeks to the neighbouring villages and paddy fields.

The Upper Reaches of the River

European ships used to come up as far as **Kuntaur** to

Groundnut packing at Kaur

collect groundnuts. But since 1970 the river has become too silted to accommodate such vessels, and today Kaur is the furtherest inland they can venture. **Baboon Island**, just up from Kuntaur, is a fairly new national park: see the tourist office in Banjul for further information.

Ancient megalithic circles

The megaliths found in Senegal and Gambia are unique in Africa. In Gambia the stone circles have a diameter of between 3 and 6 metres and are mostly found on the north bank of the river. They are formed of 10 to 20 laterite stones which were cut from neighbouring hills and weigh up to 9000 kilos; they stand between one half and 2.5 metres high and have diameters of just over a metre.

Wassau, a couple of kilometers north of Kuntaur, is one of the more accessible and interesting sites. The 11 circles here are known to date from AD 750, possibly earlier; their purpose is uncertain, but the finding of skeletons underground within the circle suggests they were burial places.

Gambians, proud of their ancestral roots, may try and encourage you to visit the circles. Certainly they do not compare to anything like Stonehenge and to the layman they may be of little interest.

In 1823 Captain Grant leased Lemain Island from the local chief and renamed it MacCarthy Island. A garrison of troops was despatched here to protect the upstream traders and their interests. **Georgetown** — the only town — is on the north side of the island. It has always been a significant administrative centre, though it lost much of its importance when proper roads were established along the banks of the river. MacCarthy Island and Georgetown are quiet and delightfully laid back. Much of the 10-km long island grows rice and groundnuts; there is a prison, ruins of a slave compound, trading stores, a famous boys' school, a rest house, a new guest house called the Baobolong at the east end of Georgetown and a row of shops and bars. Ferries connect the north and south sides of the 2.5-km wide island with the mainland.

Bansang is a south bank taxi stop and ferry crossing; it has a bustling shanty-town atmosphere and, except for by the river, it is not particularly attractive. The main feature here is the hospital.

Karantaba is on the site of what was formerly the village of Pisinia, where Mungo Park based himself in

One of the ancient stone circles at Wassau

167

1795 before travelling east in search of the River Niger and again in 1805 when he attempted to make further discoveries. Pisinia must have been quite a typical upriver trading factory. Park describes the set-up: 'Pisania is a small village in the king of Yany's dominions, established by British subjects as a factory for trade, and inhabited solely by them and their black servants. It is situated on the banks of the Gambia, sixteen miles above Jonkakonda. The white residents, at the time of my arrival there, consisted only of Dr Laidley, and two gentlemen who were brothers, of the name of Ainslie, but their domestics were numerous. They enjoyed perfect security under the king's protection; and being highly esteemed and respected by the natives at large, wanted no accommodation or comfort which the country could supply; and the greatest part of the trade in slaves, ivory, and gold, was in their hands'.

Mungo Park's base camp

The English were the dominant European traders — the French, Danes and Americans also had interests — along the River Gambia. However, business seems to have diminished by the time Park arrived; only two to three ships would arrive from England each year with exports of under £20,000.

While staying at Dr Laidley's, Park wrote about the local system of trading and it is worth taking the opportunity here to quote him, as he gives us an idea as to how and what kind of transactions took place: 'The commodities exported to the Gambia from Europe consist chiefly of fire-arms and ammunition, ironware, spirituous liqours, tobacco, cotton caps, a small quantity of broad cloth, and a few articles of the manufacture of Manchester; a small assortment of India goods, with some glass beads, amber, and other trifles, for which are taken in exchange, slaves, gold dust, ivory, bees-wax, and hides. Slaves are the chief article, but the whole number which at this time are annually exported from the Gambia by all nations, is supposed to be under one thousand.

Slaves: the chief article of trade

'Most of these unfortunate victims are brought to the coast in periodical caravans, many of them from very remote inland countries, for the language which they speak is not understood by the inhabitants of the maritime districts . . . On their arrival at the coast, if no immediate opportunity offers of selling them to advantage, they are distributed among the neighbouring villages until a slave ship arrives, or until they can be sold to black traders, who sometimes purchase on speculation. In the meanwhile, the poor wretches are kept constantly fettered, two and two of them being chained together, and employed in the labours of the field; and I am sorry to add, are very scantily fed, as well as harshly treated. The price of a slave varies according to the number of purchasers from Europe and the arrival of caravans from the interior; but in general I reckon that a young and healthy male, from sixteen to twenty-five years of age, may be estimated on the spot from £18 to £20 sterling'.

Today Karantaba, divided into different quarters, is a typical middle-sized Gambian village; Karantaba Wharftown has a small shop, run by the headman, and a basic dispensary — making this a place of some importance. But there is no electricity or running water and the former trading shops above the wharf (post Mungo Park) stand deserted.

Karantaba is on a quiet bend of the river and is surrounded by woods (incidentaly there are very pleasant walks in the wooded regions on the north bank of upriver Gambia). There is little reason why the average Westerner should want to stop in Karantaba; however a few make an effort to visit the small obelisk which was erected in Mungo Park's honour. This tatty memorial is in a cleared patch a short walk out of the village; it can also be seen from the river if you do not want to get off the boat.

Basse Santa Su (Basse for short) is the main upriver town. It is very much an active commerical centre: there is a bank, many shops, a cinema, bars, a crowded market, two hotels (the Apollo is the least expensive), a ferry which carries cars and a fast-flowing taxi service. But once again the main charm of the town is its waterfront along which there are old attractive trading shops.

Fatoto is the most eastern administrative town in Gambia. The vegetation on the banks of the river here is dense, lush and very attractive.

PRACTICAL INFORMATION

TRAVELLING UPRIVER BY ROAD
Service Taxis
Taxis depart from Thomas Street, next to the Box Bar Stadium off Independence Drive (or from the big car park in Sere Kunda) to **south bank destinations** such as Soma, MacCarthy Island (Georgetown), Bansang and Basse; most taxis leave early in the morning as the journey to, for example, Basse takes the best part of a day. To go on to Fatoto you would probably have to change at Basse.

Taxis leave from Barra to **north bank destinations** such as Juffure, Kerewan, Kaur, Kuntaur and MacCarthy Island (Georgetown). Beyond here you would probably have to change transport.

Cross-river Ferries
There are many ferry points along the River Gambia; the following are the principle ones which take **passengers and cars**: Banjul to Barra; Farafenni to Soma (this is the main Trans-Gambian route linking north and south Senegal); Georgetown (ferries link MacCarthy Island to both banks of the river); and Basse, which is the furthest upstream that vehicles can cross the River Gambia.

In villages along the river ferrymen, often with no more than a manually-operated small tub barge or a canoe, carry **passengers only** from one bank to the other.

The Road along the Southern Bank
The excellent surfaced road which runs along the south side of the river from Banjul to Basse is the main route of communication into the interior. A perfectly good road, unsurfaced at present, continues from Basse to Fatoto. In addition to the usual pick-up vans there is a constant flow of Peugeot 504 taxis along this route, and a new bus service.

The Road along the Northern Bank
The road following the northern bank of the river is gravelled and waiting to be surfaced. It is therefore not as good as the southern road. After MacCarthy Island stretches of it are track (still suitable for vehicles, though travelling is sometimes difficult during the rainy season). Transport is usually pick-up vans and is slower and less frequent, particularly east of MacCarthy Island, than on the southern road. But this should not be a deterrant: you should not have to wait more than several hours for transport anywhere along the river banks.

TRAVELLING UPRIVER BY BOAT
The Steamer
The *Lady Wright*, a packet boat, used to carry passengers, mail and freight up and down the river. It became famous among philatelists because it served as a mobile post office, with its own stamp, for villages along the river. The boat now lies unused in the Banjul docks.

The *Lady Chilel*, named after the wife of President Sir Dawda Jawara, was the new steamer which came into operation in 1978. It has recently sunk, but its replacement is likely to have similar facilities: air-conditioned first class cabins with their own loo, shower and wash basin and either 2 or 4 berths; enough cabin space to accommodate 40 passengers; benches on the ground level deck — also used by deck passengers for sleeping.

Meals: Continental or English breakfast, lunch and dinner are served in the restaurant; deck passengers should bring their own provisions as these meals are quite expensive and the chances of finding food at ports of call are unpredictable.

Most cabin passengers are European holidaymakers on an excursion. Compared to the steamers on the River Niger in Mali, the River Gambia steamer is small, far less crowded and caters predominantly for the tourist; there are proportionately fewer local/deck passengers because Gambians tend to opt for more reliable and quicker road transport — a choice hardly open to Malians.

Timetable: During the season — from November to April/May — the steamer leaves Banjul every Tuesday (for the rest of the year it is once a month) at midday. It goes upstream as far as Basse and is back in

Banjul, having travelled through the nights, on Friday afternoon.

The following are the ports of call with their distances from Banjul:

Albreda	24 kms
Kerewan	59 kms
Kemoto	67 kms
Tendaba	99 kms
Yelitenda	128 kms
Bamballi	152 kms
Sambang	161 kms
Kankunda	166 kms
Kaur	182 kms
Carrol's Wharf	200 kms
Kudang	208 kms
Nianimaro	216 kms
Kuntaur	228 kms
Barajali	244 kms
Sapu	251 kms
Georgetown	265 kms
Bansang	281 kms
Karantaba	300 kms
Diabugu	332 kms
Kossemer	339 kms
Basse	361 kms

Cabin accommodation should be reserved as far in advance as possible from the Gambian Port Authorities at the southern end of Wellington Street, Banjul.

Alternative River Transport

You can charter **privately-owned yachts**, eg the *Spirit of Galicia*, to take you up the river. The beauty of this is that you are in a small group and you can go wherever you want. These excursions have become a very popular way of seeing Gambia and now tour operators are reserving the yachts a long time in advance as an extra for their clients.

Trips like this are expensive; out of season the price may drop — that is if they are in operation — and space is more likely to be available. Alternatively you could probably hop along most of the river in small **local boats**.

APPENDIX

THE AFRICAN ASSOCIATION AND ITS EARLY EXPLORERS

At the St Alban's Tavern on 7 June 1788, 12 highly distinguished gentlemen inaugurated a society which they called the Association for Promoting the Discovery of the Inland Parts of the Continent of Africa. Though their interests were primarily scientific — the president was the eminent botanist Sir Joseph Banks — they at this stage wanted to learn anything they could about the vast, uncharted interior of Africa.

John Ledyard, an American, was the first explorer the African Association (as it became known) commissioned. He had already lived with American Indians, sailed around the world with Captain Cook and walked from Hamburg to Siberia — only to be expelled by the Empress Catherine — before being asked by Banks to traverse the Sahara desert. It was suggested that he head south from Cairo and then westwards. Asked when he would be ready to leave he replied 'Tomorrow'. A little more time however was needed for preparations and on 30 June 1788 Ledyard left London. He died of an overdose of medicine in Cairo before beginning his journey of discovery.

Around the same time the African Association employed Simon Lucas, an Englishman who had once been enslaved in Morocco, to travel from Tripoli to the Fezzan and then to Gambia or the Guinea Coast via Timbuktu or Agadez. Lucas never got further than the North African coast before he returned home.

In 1790 Banks enlisted the services of Major Daniel Houghton, a 50-year-old bankrupt Irishman who, it was rumoured, was keen to travel so as to escape his creditors. Houghton struck into the interior along the River Gambia, but between the course of this river and that of the Niger he met his death at the hands of the Moors.

The next adventurer the African Association recruited was a young Scotsman named Mungo Park.

MUNGO PARK'S FIRST JOURNEY INTO THE INTERIOR OF AFRICA

Mungo Park was born at Foulshiels, Scotland, in 1771, the son of a well-to-do farmer. At 21 he graduated as a doctor from the University of Edinburgh and served for a year as assistant surgeon on a ship bound for Sumatra. On his return he offered his services to the African Association. Young, strong, healthy and without dependants, and most of all ambitious to travel and explore, his offer was readily accepted.

Arrival in Gambia

In June 1795 Park set foot on Gambian soil at Jillifree (present day Juffure).

'My instructions were very plain and concise. I was directed, on my arrival in Africa "to pass on to the river Niger, either by the way of Bambouk, or by such other route as should be found convenient. That I should ascertain the course, and, if possible, the rise and termination of that river. That I should use my utmost exertions to visit the principal towns or cities in its neighbourhood, particularly Timbuctoo and Houssa; and that I should be afterwards at liberty to return to Europe, either by the way of the Gambia, or by such other route, as, under all the then existing circumstances of my situation and prospects, should appear to me to be most advisable"'.

Into the Forest

In the company of a freed Jamaican slave called Johnson and a young black man named Demba, Park began his search for the Niger.

'I had now before me a boundless forest, and a country the inhabitants of which were strangers to civilised life, and to most of whom a white man was an object of curiosity or plunder. I reflected that I had parted from the last European I might probably behold, and perhaps quitted for ever the comforts of Christian society.'

Mumbo Jumbo

After a few days travelling Park arrived at Kolar in the kingdom of Woolli (about 25 kms west of Tambacounda) a 'considerable town' where hanging on a tree he noticed 'a sort of masquerade habit, made of the bark of trees, which I was told on inquiry belonged to Mumbo Jumbo'.

When a man found his wives squabbling amongst themselves he, or his representative, would disguise himself by donning the Mumbo Jumbo cloak. He would then call for a village assembly, his intention being to punish his troublemaking wife.

'The ceremony commences with songs and dances, which continue till midnight, about which time Mumbo Jumbo fixes on the offender. The unfortunate victim being thereupon immediately seized, stripped naked, tied to a post, and severely scourged with Mumbo's rod, amidst the shouts and derision of the whole assembly; and it is remarkable that the rest of the women are the loudest in their exclamations on this occasion against their unhappy sister. Daylight puts an end to this indecent and unmanly revel.'

A week later the small expedition entered the kingdom of Bondou. Park noted: 'I cannot, however, take leave of Woolli, without observing that I was everywhere well received by the natives; and that the fatigues of the day were generally alleviated by a hearty welcome at night'.

A wonderful machine

Park was received hospitably at Fatteconda, the capital of Bondou. Amongst other things, he presented the king — to his delight — with an umbrella which the old gentleman 'repeatedly furled and unfurled, to the great admiration of himself and his two attendants who could not for sometime comprehend the use of this wonderful machine'.

But the king seems to have had a penchant for

European goods and Park's blue coat, particularly the yellow buttons, caught his fancy. Park was conscious that the 'request of an African prince, in his own dominion, particularly when made to a stranger, was little short of a command ... As it was against my interest to offend him by a refusal, I very quietly took off my coat, the only good one in my possession and laid it at his feet'.

Invitation to a harem

Park himself was also naturally a source of curiousity; he was led to the harem where the women — alarmed by his whiteness and peculiar features — thought he must have been dipped in milk when he was young and had his nose 'pinched every day till it had acquired its present unsightly and unnatural conformation'.

The expedition did eventually face hostility. On more than one occasion Park was robbed or was forced to pay extortionate levies to pass through various territories. Even so, despite minimal funds, he stoically pushed on.

Local Shenanigans

Park rested a few days at a village called Teesee, where he noticed that the 'present inhabitants, though they possess both cattle and corn in abundance, are not over nice in articles of diet; rats, moles, squirrels, snakes, locusts, etc, are eaten without scruple by the highest and the lowest ... Another custom still more extroardinary, is that no woman is allowed to eat an egg. This prohibition, whether arising from ancient superstition or from the craftiness of some old Bushreen [village elder] who loved eggs himself, is rigidly adhered to, and nothing will more affront a woman of Teesee than to offer her an egg ... The men eat eggs without scruple in the presence of their wives'.

Here Park also witnessed what was tantamount to a court case. A young man had recently married a beautiful girl and, as he was soon to appear in battle, he asked the old village priest to give him some saphies (usually writings from the Koran which act as charms). The preist agreed, but claimed that the saphies would be more effective if the young man avoided any nuptial intercourse with his bride for the space of six weeks. The husband — without telling his spouse the reason — faithfully abided by the instructions.

Rumours began going around Teesee that the priest was more intimate with the young wife than he ought to be. The husband disregarded such talk — after all, he rationalised, the priest was an honourable man as well as his friend.

But the stories intensified until one day the young man asked his bride if there was any truth in these tales, to which she confessed that the priest had seduced her.

The old man was found guilty by the village elders and was given the choice of being sentenced to slavery or paying two slaves for his freedom. However, the young man thought the punishment too severe and demanded that his former friend should be publicly flogged instead.

Troubled Lands

Battles and skirmishes between neighbouring kingdoms were common according to Park, and during his stay in Teesee tension was building up between two neighbouring states, Kasson and Kajaaga. An envoy from Abdulkader, King of Foota Torra, a land in the west, arrived at Teesee and announced 'that unless all the peoples of Kasson would embrace the Mohemedan religion, and evince their conversion by saying eleven public prayers, he [the King of Foota Torra] could not possibly stand neuter in the present contest, but would certainly join his arms to those of Kajaaga'.

The inhabitants debated the matter amongst themselves and reluctantly 'one and all publicly offered up eleven prayers, which were considered a sufficient testimony of their having renounced paganism, and embraced the doctrines of the Prophet'.

Over the centuries thousands were bullied into accepting Islam in this manner. For many this conversion was only nominal and today whole communities claim to be Moslems, but without necessarily following the strict codes of faith.

The expedition slowly continued its journey eastwards, though it had to make detours to avoid troubled areas. Early in February it reached Kemmoo; Park was shown a hut where he could rest. 'I had scarcely seated myself in this spacious apartment, when the mob entered; it was found impossible to keep them out, and I was surrounded by as many as the hut could contain. When the first party, however, had seen me, and asked a few questions, they retired to make room for another company; and in this manner the hut was filled and emptied thirteen different times.'

A war was brewing in the area immediately to the east so, on the advice of the local chief Daisy, Park headed north into the Moorish kingdom of Ludamar. The aggressive nature of the Moors became increasingly clear to Park and at Funingkedy a small band of mounted Moors descended on the village, herded up the locals' cattle, selected 16 of the finest bullocks and then galloped back home with their spoils. The villagers, about 500 in all, cowered and put up no resistance as the five raiders behaved as they pleased. One boy, however, did throw a spear and as a result, was shot in the leg by the Moors. Amid the cries of his distraught mother, the lad was brought to Park, who recommended the amputation of the limb. The horrified congregation immediately believed him to be a cannibal for suggesting such an operation. The boy died, but not before the priest had made him repeat 'There is but one God, and Mohammed is his Prophet'. Thus the mother was assured 'that her son had given sufficient evidence of his faith, and would be happy in a future state'.

Park accused of cannibalism

Encounter with the Moors
Park tried to avoid contact with the Moors though at one village they surrounded his hut 'and treated me with the greatest insolence. They hissed, shouted, and abused me; they even spat in my face with a view to irritate me, and afford them a pretext for seizing my baggage', and eventually they 'opened my bundles, and robbed me of everything they fancied'.

A few days later Park was confronted by a band of Moors who had orders to take him and his companions to Ali, Sheikh of Ludamar. After several days of travel they arrived at Benowm which 'presented to the eye a great number of dirty-looking tents scattered without order, over a large space of ground; and among the tents appeared large herds of camels, cattle, and goats'.

Park was brought in front of Ali, who 'was sitting upon a black leather cushion, clipping a few hairs from his upper lip; a female attendant holding up a looking-glass before him. He appeared to be an old man of

Arab cast, with a long white beard; and he had a sullen and indignant aspect'. Incidentally, Park himself had an impressive beard and Felix Dubois, a Frenchman who travelled this area at the end of the 19th C, heard locals refer to Park as Bonciba-tigui, 'the man with the large beard' (literally: *batigui*, owner; *bonci*, beard; *ba*, large).

Christians and swine

Once again Park was the subject of intense curiosity, and had to unbutton his waistcoat to display his whiteness, and his toes and fingers were counted for 'they doubted whether I was in truth a human being'. That evening the Scotsman was shown to a hut where, tied to one of the uprights, was a hog. Ali had earlier tried, unsuccessfully, to bait Park with this animal because he believed there must be natural hostility between Christians and swine.

The following day, 13 March 1796, Park recorded in his diary: 'With the returning day commenced the same round of insults and irritations: the boys assembled to beat the hog, and the men and women to plague the Christian. It is impossible for me to describe the behaviour of a people who study mischief as a science, and exult in the miseries and misfortune of their fellow creatures ... I was a stranger, I was unprotected and I was a Christian; each of these circumstances is sufficient to drive every spark of humanity from the heart of a Moor ... but never did any period of my life pass away so heavily: from sunrise to sunset was I obliged to suffer, with an unruffled countenance, the insults of the rudest savages on earth'.

A council of the senior men tried to decide what to do with the Christian, whom they also suspected was a spy; some wanted to put him to death, others elected to cut off his right hand; but eventually, the unanimous verdict was to pluck out his eyes, 'which they said resembled those of a cat'.

The sentence was to be deferred, however, until Ali's wife, Fatima, who was away at the time, had satisified her curiosity and seen a white man.

Park in captivity

The days in captivity tediously bore on. Park suffered bouts of fever, continual insults and the constant fear that he may be put to death. There was one rather amusing incident Park allowed himself to treat light-heartedly: 'The curiosity of the Moorish ladies had been very troublesome to me ever since my arrival at Benowm; and on the evening of the 25th (whether from the instigation of others, or impelled by their own ungovernable curiosity, or merely out of frolic, I cannot affirm), a party of them came into my hut, and gave me plainly to understand that the object of their visit was to ascertain, by actual inspection, whether the rite of circumcision extended to the Nazarenes (Christians), as well as to the followers of Mahomet. The reader will easily judge of my surprise at this unexpected declaration; and in order to avoid the proposed scrutiny, I thought it best to treat the business jocularly. I observed to them, that it was not customary in my country to give ocular demonstration in such cases, before so many beautiful women; but that if all of them would retire, except the young lady to whom I pointed (selecting the youngest and handsomest), I would satisfy her curiosity. The ladies enjoyed the jest, and went away laughing heartily; and the young damsel herself to whom I had given the preference (though she did not avail herself of the privilege of inspection), seemed no way displeased at the compliment, for she soon afterwards sent me some meal and milk for my supper'.

Ali moved camp to Bubaker and it was here that Park was first presented to Fatima, 'a woman of Arab cast, with long black hair, and remarkably corpulent', who was quite cordial after she had overcome her initial shock of seeing a Christian.

Fat is beautiful   It is worth taking the opportunity here to mention how, according to Park, the Moors viewed their women: 'They [women] are regarded, I believe, as an inferior species of animal, and seem to be brought up for no other purpose than that of administrating to the sensual pleasures of their imperious masters. Voluptuousness is, therefore, considered their chief accomplishment, and slavish submissions as their indispensible duty ... The Moors have singular ideas of feminine perfection ... Corpulence and beauty appear to be terms nearly synonymous. A woman, of even moderate pretensions, must be one who cannot walk without a slave under each arm to support her, and a perfect beauty is a load for a camel'.

To reach this state of obesity mothers forced their young daughters to eat great quantities of kouskous and drink bowls of camel's milk. Park remembered an incident: 'I have seen a poor girl sit crying, with a bowl at her lips, more than an hour, and her mother, with a stick in her hand, watching her all the while, and using the stick without mercy, whenever she observed that her daughter was not swallowing'.

The country here was drier and more desolate than at Benowm; the desert stretched into the distance, the trees were stunted, 'hungry cattle licked up withered grass, while the camels and goats picked off the scanty foliage'. The season had reached its hottest and water was very scarce; at times Park was reduced to begging for refreshments, but usually the Moors would just abuse him. Asleep the Scotsman would joyously dream of the clear, cool gurgling streams of home, 'but alas! disappointment awakened me, and I found myself a lonely captive, perishing of thirst, amidst the wilds of Africa'.

After two months of captivity Park finally escaped while Ali was preoccupied with fighting some of his local enemies.

Escape to the Niger

Park was now alone — Demba had been taken for slavery by Ali and Johnson had gone his own way.

Travelling by night and living off whatever he could find he struggled on eastwards and only after he felt he was out of Moorish spheres of influence did he seek the company of other travellers. One evening his two Sudanese companions told him they would reach the Joliba (the local name for the Niger) the following day. Park was ready before sunrise the next morning; by 8am he saw the smoke above Segu and shortly after he fell in line with some refugees from Kaarta whom he had met previously. Suddenly one of them called out '"Geo Affili", "see the water" ... and, looking forward, I saw with infinite pleasure the great object of my mission — the long sought for majestic Niger, glittering to the morning sun, as broad as the Thames at Westminster, and flowing slowly to the eastward'.

The direction of the course had long been a mystery. Quite incredibly Leo Africanus, the 16th C traveller, had claimed the Joliba flowed west.

Having reached the Niger Park headed downstream to his next goal, Timbuktu. But, to his great disappointment, he learnt that 'Timbuctoo, the great object of my search, is altogether in possession of that savage and merciless people [Moors], who allow no

The river flows east

180

Christian to live there'. At the village of Silla he decided to turn back: '... I had a short paroxysm of fever during the night. Worn down by sickness, exhausted with hunger and fatigue, half naked, and without any article of value by which I might procure provision, clothes, or lodging, I began to reflect seriously on my situation. I was now convinced, by painful experience, that the obstacles to my further progress were insurmountable.'

The Way Back

It was now July 1796. Park's return journey was, if anything, more hazardous than his outbound trip. It was the rainy season and the bad weather made travelling more difficult and led to the prevalence of diseases. Famine had struck the Manding country and the situation was so appalling that mothers were selling their children to their chiefs in return for corn. All the same, Park, as he was out of funds, had to rely on the hospitality of locals for his survival, though on one occasion he earned his food and lodging by writing a saphie for his landlord on a blackboard. So as to get the full effect of the charm his superstitious host washed the writing with a little water, said a few prayers, then drank the concoction; to make sure he had not missed a word he licked the board dry.

At the small village of Kamalia in Manding country, Park became the guest of Karfa Taura, a merchant who was taking slaves from the interior to Gambia. Park decided to resume his journey with the slave coffle after the rains. In exchange for hospitality he offered to pay Karfa the price of one prime slave when they reached Gambia.

Travels with a slave caravan

The fever which affected many during the rains nearly killed Park, but after a slow recovery, he was eager to continue his journey. However the day of departure was constantly postponed. 'And here I may remark, that loss of time is an object of no great importance in the eyes of a Negro ... so long as he can spend the present moment with any degree of comfort, he gives himself very little concern about the future'.

Park passed his time by talking to the slaves. Most of them had been prisoners of wars — captured in Kaarta by the Bambarran army — who were taken to Segu, where some had been kept in irons for three

Does the white man eat slaves?

years, and then onto Yamina, Bamako or Kancaba where they were bartered for gold dust. They continually asked whether Christians were cannibals, believing that white men would eat them once they crossed the salt waters. Such fears may have been an inducement to attempt escape, but their shackles minimised the opportunities to run off. A pair of heavy fetters would be locked on to the left leg of one man and the right leg of another; the men could lift these irons with a length of string, thus enabling them to walk slowly. Every four slaves were fastened together by their necks with a strong rope of twisted thongs or sometimes an iron chain; at night fetters were put around their hands.

They finally got going half way through April 1797 and a little over six weeks later they arrived at Jindey on the banks of the River Gambia where Park recalled that 'eighteen months before, I had parted from my friend Dr Laidley [the British trader who had been Park's initial contact and host in Gambia], an interval during which I had not beheld the face of a Christian, nor once heard the delightful sound of my native language'.

Less than a fortnight later, on 17 July, Park boarded an American vessel bound for South Carolina which, due to damage, had to dock at Antigua. From here he caught another ship to England and on 22 December 1797 Park landed at Falmouth.

MUNGO PARK'S SECOND JOURNEY INTO THE INTERIOR OF AFRICA

On his return to England Mungo Park saw to the publication of his *Travels* and as a result he received public recognition for his heroic expedition and discovery. He married and took up the post of a country practitioner in the town of Peebles.

Restless desire to return to Africa

But Park became restless; despite his harrowing experiences, he — in common with so many of the great explorers — longed to return to the lands where he had suffered so much and had almost died.

In 1804 the opportunity arose. The British government, believing that it was in their interest to make further explorations in West Africa, asked Park to take an expedition along the River Niger. He accepted and was given the following brief: 'The great object of your journey will be to pursue the course of this river to the utmost possible distance to which it can be traced'.

In April the expedition — comprising Park, Anderson his brother-in-law and second in command, Martyn a junior officer, Scott a draughtsman, four carpenters whose job it was to build a boat when they reached the River Niger and 35 soldiers — landed in Gambia at Kaye, just downstream from Pisinia. Later that month the team, which now included black porters and guides, marched off from Pisinia eastwards bound for the River Niger.

Park wrote to a friend with great optimism and confidence: 'Everything at present looks as favourable as I could wish, and if all things go well, this day six weeks I expect to drink all your healths in the water of the Niger'.

The Expedition Beset with Misfortune

But from the start the expedition was struck by unfortunate incidents. There were two main problems. First, because of unforseeable delays, they set off into the interior in the hot season — noted for its hurricanes — and during the course of their journey they were overtaken by the heavy annual rains. On 10 June 1805 the rain fell and Park recorded in his journal: 'The rain had not commenced three minutes before many of the soldiers were affected by vomiting, others fell asleep as if half intoxicated'.

The other misfortune was the quality of the soldiers. They were unfit and indifferent to their task and there was no discipline as neither Park nor Anderson were professional soldiers or experienced leaders. Men got lost, search parties were sent to look for them **Malaria and** and this resulted in more delays. The sick, usually **dysentery** suffering from malaria or dysentery, were often left in the villages to recover or die. Park, himself racked by illness, showed obsessive determination and on 10 August his diary relates the following incident: 'Found many soldiers sitting, and Mr Anderson lying under a bush, apparently dying. Took him on my back, and carried him across the stream, which came up to my middle. Carried over the load of the ass which I drove, got over the ass, Mr Anderson's horse, etc. Found myself much fatigued, having crossed the stream sixteen times'.

On 19 August — almost four months, and not six weeks as hoped, after they had left the River Gambia — the party climbed the hills which seperate the River Niger and River Senegal. Park happily wrote that evening '. . . and coming to the brow of the hill, I once more saw the Niger rolling its immense stream along the plain!' But a great price had been paid for the achievement; Park somberly continued his journal: '. . . when I reflected that three-fourths of the soldiers had died on their march, and that in addition to our weakly state, we had no carpenters to build the boats in which we proposed to prosecute our discoveries, the prospect seemed somewhat gloomy'.

Along the Niger

They reached the Niger at Bamako and pushed on downstream to the large market town of Sansanding where, being short of cowrie shells, the local currency, Park set up shop and offered for sale a 'choice assortment of European articles'. With their earnings they bought an old pirogue and 'with eighteen days' hard labour, changed the Bambarra canoe into His Majesty's schooner *Joliba* [the local name for the River Niger]; the length forty feet, breadth six feet; being flat bottomed, draws only one foot water when loaded'.

Before departure Park reported to the Colonial

Secretary: 'We had no contest whatever with the natives, nor was any one of us killed by wild animals or any other accidents; and yet I am sorry to say that of forty-four Europeans who left Gambia in perfect health, five only at present are alive, viz. three soldiers (one deranged in mind), Lieutenant Martyn and myself. . . . My dear friend Mr Anderson and likewise Mr Scott are both dead; but though all Europeans who are with me should die, and though I were myself half dead, I would still persevere; and if I could not succeed in the object of my journey, I would at last die on the Niger'.

The same day he wrote to his wife: 'I do not intend to stop or land anywhere, till we reach the coast, which I suppose will be sometime in the end of January. We shall then embark in the first vessel to England . . . I think it not unlikely but I will be in England before you receive this'.

This was his last communication with England.

The Search for Park

Throughout 1806 vague rumours that the expedition had perished reached the British settlements on the coast. Eventually the Governor of Senegal enlisted Issaco, Park's former guide, to go into the interior and find out for certain what had happened. Issaco set off in January 1810 and did not return until September the following year. In a village near Sansanding he met Amadi Fatoumi, who had accompanied Park on his Niger voyage; it is from Fatoumi's account that we learn the fate of HM *Joliba* and its crew.

When the *Joliba* left Sansanding there were nine persons on board, which included three slaves, ample provisions for a long journey and 15 muskets with adequate supplies of ammunition. In Lake Debo they were attacked by three canoes, but they managed to fend off their assailants; again around Kabara they fought off further onslaughts. Fatoumi cited another incident: 'Passed by a village, the residence of King Gotoijege; after passing which we counted sixty canoes coming after us, which we repulsed, and killed a great number of men. Seeing so many men killed, and our superiority over them, I took hold of Martyn's hand, saying "Martyn, let us cease firing, for we have killed too many already"; on which Martyn wanted to kill me, had not Mr Park interfered'.

It would seem that the bedraggled, disease-ridden remainder of the expedition were by now half-crazed and Park, their leader, was as obsessed as ever to reach his goal. But their unwarranted hostility left the peoples of the River Niger with bitter memories of Mungo Park, as Gordon Laing, a later explorer, was to discover 25 years after.

Bitter memories

While he was in In Salah Laing wrote: 'An extremely ridiculous report has gone abroad here that I am the late Mungo Park, the Christian who made war upon the people inhabiting the banks of the Niger, who killed several, and wounded many Tuareg... I may even say, how selfish was it in Park to attempt making a discovery in this land, at the expense of the blood of its inhabitants, and to the exclusion of all after communication: how unjustified was such conduct! What answer am I to make to the question which will be often put to me? — What right had you, or if it was not you, What right had your countryman to fire upon and kill our people? I fear I will be in much trouble after leaving Timbuctoo'.

At Yaour just north of Bussa, Fatoumi left the expedition as his duties were now completed. Park had either forgotten to give presents to the local king or they had been mislaid. Either way the result was the same: the King of Yaour sent a band of soldiers to await the HM *Joliba* a short distance downstream at the Bussa rapids; on reaching this point Park negotiated the main channel, but the boat got stuck. The enemy were standing on the rocks above them and opened fire, mercilessly bombarding the crew with lances, pikes, arrows and stones.

Last moments

Fatoumi recounted the final minutes of the tragic expedition: 'Mr Park defended himself for a long time; two of his slaves at the stern of the canoe were killed; they threw everything they had in the canoe into the river, and kept firing; but being overpowered by numbers and fatigue, and unable to keep up the canoe against the current, and probability of escaping, Mr Park took hold of one of the white men, and jumped into the water; Martyn did the same, and they were drowned in the stream attempting to escape'.

GORDON LAING: THE FIRST EUROPEAN TO REACH TIMBUKTU

Gordon Laing, son of an Edinburgh schoolmaster, was born in 1794. At the age of 17 he joined the West Indies Infantry Regiment and was eventually posted with them to Sierra Leone.

Freetown, the capital, was a feverish place — a 'White Man's Grave' where between 1822 and 1830 1470 Europeans, out of a population of 2000 whites, died of disease. The fear of falling ill detered many foreigners from settling along the coast; even those who were there for a short stay were flirting with death, as a contemporary English sailors' song warned:

> Beware and take care of the Bight of Benin,
> For one that comes out there are forty goes in.

Having led survey parties on behalf of the army into Guinea Laing was given permission by Lord Bathurst, the Colonial Secretary, to take an expedition into the interior for the purpose of scientific research. Laing wanted to set off from the West African coast, but his orders were that any attempt of discovery should be made from the north coast, and so in May 1825 he arrived in Tripoli.

The Race for Timbuktu

Hugh Clapperton, the seasoned Scottish explorer, who had just returned to England from his Bornu expedition, must have been disappointed to hear that a fresh recruit was on his way out to search for Timbuktu and the mouth of the Niger. Clapperton felt that he had a right to these discoveries and consequently a deep rivalry broke out between him and his fellow townsman Laing.

Clapperton and Caillie

Around the same time a young Frenchman, Rene Caillie, unknown to any official body, was living with Moors, learning their ways and thus preparing himself for his own journey to Timbuktu.

In December 1824 an award of what amounted to 10,000 francs had been offered to the first person to reach Timbuktu and return to Europe. This prize, with all its various honours (unknown to Caillie at the

time), encouraged the race to the fabled city of the African interior.

Laing's start from North Africa

In Tripoli Laing was well received by Hanmer Warrington, the British consul, whose duty it was to host British explorers and help them with their ventures.

Eager to get going, Laing was frustrated by the Pasha who refused to let him leave Tripoli without payment. The Scotsman's initial costing for the expedition was £143, which the Colonial Office granted him. This proved to be a ridiculously low sum and eventually, unknown to the Colonial Office, it was agreed that the Pasha should receive £2500 (£500 before Laing left Tripoli, £500 on his reaching Ghadames, £500 when he got to Tuat and £1000 when he arrived at Timbuktu). Lord Bathurst was furious when he learnt about this huge expenditure. But Laing, trying to justify such a payment, wrote: 'I consider protection and safety will be as fully ensured to me as if I were merely on tour through the secure districts of my ever blessed and happy country'.

False Confidence

How wrong he was. Between him and his goal lay one of the harshest parts of the Sahara, a land though which hostile tribes who hated Christians freely roamed.

On 18 July 1825 — four days after his marriage to Warrington's daughter — Laing set off. The expedition, known as the Timbuktu Mission, consisted of Laing, Jack de Bore, his West Indian servant, Rogers and Harris, two African boat builders, an interpreter and 11 camels. Sheikh Babani, who claimed that he had frequently visited Timbuktu over the last 30 years, was given £1000 by the Pasha to take the party to the city; he said the journey would take only two and a half months.

Laing was confident and without a hint of modesty he wrote: 'I shall do more than has ever been done before, and show myself to be what I have always considered myself, a man of enterprise and genius'. His notes were eventually lost, so most of the information we have about his journey come from his letters to Warrington.

At the start of the trip Laing wore Turkish clothes for convenience, but just in case anybody thought that he was cheating by trying to disguise himself or that he was repudiating his religion for the sake of adventure, he informed Warrington: 'Lest it should be supposed that we attempt to pass ourselves for what we really are not, it is my intention to read prayers to my three attendants always on Sunday, on which day we shall appear dressed as Englishmen'.

Along the way Laing desperately missed Emma his wife; he was plagued by fever, by people demanding money, and by his obsession to beat Clapperton to Timbuktu and to the mouth of the Niger. Having arrived in Ghadames he mentioned in a letter that 'Clapperton may well have stayed at home if the termination of the Niger is his object. It is destined for me and neither a Pearce [another explorer] nor a Clapperton can interfere with me'. Around the same time Clapperton's second African mission was landing on the west coast.

At Ghadames Laing was warmly received: 'A large deputation met about three miles from the town and accompanied us with acclamations expressive of the warmest welcome, and although we are not yet two hours in quarters, my house is filled with provisions of every description'.

After about a five week stay the Timbuktu Mission eventually left Ghadames on 3 November 1825 bound for In Salah 800 kms to the southwest. The party had been joined in Ghadames by Hatita, a guide who had worked with Clapperton and whose services Warrington and Laing thought would be indispensible.

Things Fall Apart

But Laing was gradually losing control of his subordinates: Rogers and Harris were chasing the local women and were more a nuisance than they were worth; Hatita, who had been paid money up front, was reluctant to go to In Salah; and Babani, 'one of the finest fellows I ever saw', as Warrington had written to Bathurst, was in fact a rogue — as Laing informed the Consul when he wrote to Tripoli about the hardships of the journey: 'This is not exactly the way I ought to travel for the sum of $4000. I ought to have been placed beyond the reach of risk; and the sheik [Babani] might have brought us an escort of twenty men all the way for the sum of $400 instead he has with him two slaves'.

Also Laing began to realise that to the west the Pasha had no real influence beyond Ghadames. The region into which they were travelling was controlled by small bands of Tuareg nomads, who survived on the plunder and tribute of the passing caravans: 'Whatever they demand must be given them'. The Pasha had warned Laing before the journey: 'If you wish to go that road, you must open the door with a silver key'.

The Timbuktu Mission arrived at In Salah on 2 December; the local sheikh received Laing with extreme hospitality: 'I am glad you have come – here is my house for you and here is my son, who will attend you wherever you wish to go; look upon the country as your own, and do whatever you wish; there is nothing too good for you, etc, etc.' The inquisitive inhabitants, who had never seen a white man before, mobbed Laing and he had to stand on the roof of his house while everybody gazed up at him.

Desert Caravan

In Salah was an important crossroads for caravans. When Laing arrived many people were congregated here waiting to go to Timbuktu (in fact the In Salah-Timbuktu route at this stage was not used that frequently). However nobody wanted to move on for fear of being caught up in a bitter conflict which was raging between the Ahagger Tuaregs and the Ulad Delim to the south.

Some, it seemed, initially believed that the white man would escort them safely through the troubled land; but there were also those who after a while objected to the presence of a Christian in their town. One Tuareg approached Laing and claimed that he had been shot in the cheek by somebody from Mungo Park's expedition and that Laing was in fact Park himself.

The proposed caravan to Timbuktu consisted of 350 camels and 150 men, many of whom were armed. Even so the risk of losing all, including their lives, at the hands of a bunch of belligerent nomads, dissuaded them from setting foot out of In Salah.

Irritated by this attitude Laing set off alone. Embarassed by their lack of courage the caravan followed him.

Laing was homesick and lonely: 'I so much despair of hearing again from Tripoli that I no longer look back: my whole ideas, my thoughts, my prospects are "forward", for I cannot enjoy a moment of happiness till I return... In former days I used to derive the greatest of earthly enjoyment from living alone: my thoughts took the most fascinating direction ... Times are changed. I am now almost afraid to trust myself with the full swing of thought, and for the first time in my life I express a wish that I had with me a companion de voyage'.

Terrors of the Sahara

The caravan pushed south through one of the most perilous sections of the Sahara. Reports that the Ulad Delim were lying in wait terrified everybody and they would have all about-turned to In Salah if it had not been for Laing's insistence that they continue. One day a small band of Tuaregs fell in line with the caravan and indicated that they would provide protection.

They were now travelling at the fair rate of 32 kms a day 'over a desert of sand as flat as a bowling green'. Everything was going smoothly, Laing confidently wrote home: 'My prospects are bright, and expectations sanguine: I do not calculate upon the most trifling difficulty between me and my return to England'.

It was now the end of January 1826 and Clapperton was in Yorubaland. Approaching Timbuktu from different directions Clapperton and Laing were roughly equidistant from the city. But Laing's optimism was ill founded; one cannot blame the man for writing with such enthusiasm and hope when things were starting to look up. Sadly, it seems he was tempting fate.

One day Babani persuaded Laing's men to give him their guns and ammunition. The following night the Tuareg escort surrounded Laing's tents and butchered the inhabitants. Several were killed and only the Scotsman's West African servant escaped unhurt. Babani, who must have been in cahoots with these Tuaregs, was not touched; similarly the rest of the caravan were left alone.

It was a miracle that Laing survived. With little opportunity to treat his wounds he struggled to keep up with the caravan. Slumped on his camel he plodded 650 kms southeast to the oasis of Sidi el Muktar. Here he was able to recuperate, but it was not until the beginning of May 1826 that he was well enough to write to Warrington (it took over two years for this letter, written in an almost illegible scrawl, to reach Tripoli). The letter included a horrifying list of the explorer's wounds.

'I shall acquaint you with the number and nature of my wounds, in all amounting to twenty-four, eighteen of which are exceedingly severe — To begin from the top, I have five sabre cuts on the crown of the head and three on the left temple, all fractures from which much bone has come away, one on my left cheek which fractured the jaw bone and has divided the ear, forming a very unsightly wound, one over the right temple, and a dreadful gash on the back of the neck, which slightly scratched the windpipe: a musket ball in the hip, which made its way through my back, slightly grazing the back bone: five sabre cuts on my right arm and hand, three of the fingers broken the hand cut three fourths across, and the wrist bones cut through; three cuts on the left arm, the bone of which has been broken, but is again uniting. One slight wound on the right leg, and two d° [ditto] with one dreadful gash on the left, to say nothing of a cut across the fingers of my left hand, now healed up. I am nevertheless, as I have already said, doing well, and hope to return to England with much important geographical information'.

Laing also informed Warrington that Babani had died and added that 'there are some that look upon his demise as a visitation'.

The next disaster — an outbreak of something like

yellow fever — hit the Timbuktu Mission in June, while they were still in Sidi el Muktar. Jack le Bore, Laing's loyal and invaluable assistant, was among those who died; but Laing, also racked by the disease, once again managed to pull through.

Clapperton had by now seen the Niger (March 1826) and was on his way to Kano.

Timbuktu

It would seem from a conceited letter to Warrington that Laing felt it was his duty to discover Timbuktu: 'I am well aware that if I do not visit it [Timbuktu] the world will ever remain in ignorance of the place, as I make no vainglorious assertion when I say that it will never be visited by a Christian man after me'.

The ragged remnants of the Timbuktu Mission arrived at the 'far famed capital of Central Africa' on 13 August 1826.

For 500 years this enigmatic city had puzzled and eluded Europeans. Did it really exist? Was it a magnificent desert metropolis with streets rich with gold? Rumours had excited the mind and had allowed daydreamers and romantics to let their imagination build a dazzling capital in the dark mysterious interior of Africa.

A bad time to arrive

Gordon Laing became the first European to visit Timbuktu and send home information about the place. But it was a bad time to arrive, as the Tuaregs and Fulani were fighting over the city and in addition both these tribes hated Christians.

Laing spent five weeks in Timbuktu. In a hurried letter he wrote to Warrington: 'In every respect except in size (which does not exceed four miles in circumference) it has completely met my expectations'. Very little else remains of Laing's observations of Timbuktu, but this comment cannot have been truthful as the city was built of mud buildings and looked nothing like the fabulous picture painted in Europe. Laing probably did not want to destroy the illusion; by doing so the public would lose interest in this legendary city, in his feat and in him.

The Sheikh of Timbuktu received Laing warmly as did many of the inhabitants and merchants and the Scotsman, wearing European clothes and claiming to be an emissary of the King of England, wandered around freely taking notes (these never reached

Tripoli). However when he visited the port of Kabara he did so under the cover of night so as to avoid the prowling Tuaregs.

Soon a letter arrived from the Fulani Sultan who had claimed rule over Timbuktu ordering the death or exile from the city of the Christian. The sheikh, not wanting any harm to come to Laing, implored him to leave as soon as possible.

By now Laing was keen to get home and had given up any intention of travelling down to the Niger to its mouth. This would have been too dangerous; going upstream through Fulani-occupied territory was also out of the question, and the route across the desert to Tripoli was too hazardous to attempt a second time. So Laing decided to go to Arawan and then double back southwest to Segu thus making a large detour to avoid the Fulani.

Murder On 22 September Laing, with his servant Bongola, an Arab boy and Mohammed ben Abayd — the man the Sheikh of Timbuktu had assigned to look after him — left Timbuktu with a small caravan bound for Morocco. They seperated from the rest of the party, and at Sahal on the night of 24 September Mohammed ben Abayd, an agent for the Fulani, broke into Laing's tent and slaughtered him and the Arab boy. Bongola escaped and later gave the account of his master's death in Tripoli. The bodies were buried by passers-by and in 1910 they were dug up and reburied in Timbuktu.

Events After
In October 1826 Clapperton arrived in Sokoto, but there he remained until April 1827 when he died of dysentery at the age of 40. He had not discovered the mouth of the Niger nor visited Timbuktu.

It was a tragedy that Laing, the first European to travel from Tripoli to Timbuktu, probably the most difficult route to the desert city, died without having the opportunity to tell the world of his remarkable achievement and that his notes, which would have contained invaluable accounts of life in the Sahara, were lost.

A sordid affair In Tripoli Warrington vehemently accused the French Consul, Baron Rousseau and the Pasha's Minister, Hossane D'Ghies, of having somehow obtained Laing's records and that in fact D'Ghies had been behind his son-in-law's murder. Treachery between England and France was not unknown; the two nations were vying for supremecy in North and West Africa and both wanted to gain as much information as possible about this area and Timbuktu.

How much truth there was in Warrington's allegations is debatable, but certainly the whole affair was sordid and embarrassing. Rousseau fled to America; D'Ghies eventually went to London to plead his innocence, which he did successfully — though many disbelieved him.

There are still hopes that Laing's records will one day turn up somewhere.

And Events Before

In the 15th C it is thought that a Florentine and later a Portuguese merchant reached Timbuktu. In 1670 Paul Imbert, a Frenchman, was taken as a slave to Timbuktu where he died without sending information home about the city. In 1811, Robert Adams, an American, visited the city as a slave and managed to return to England to tell his tale; but his adventure was not believed and was officially discredited. Both Imbert and Adams were sailors who were shipwrecked off the north coast of Africa. Because of a lack of documentary evidence in support of these earlier claims, Laing has been honoured as the first explorer to reach Timbuktu.

Was Laing the first?

RENE CAILLIE: THE FIRST EUROPEAN TO RETURN ALIVE FROM TIMBUKTU

Rene Caillie, son of a baker, was born in France in 1800. At a young age he became fascinated by exploration, as his memoirs later revealed: 'I ceased to join in the sports and amusements of my comrades; I shut myself up on Sundays to read all the books of travel that I was able to procure'. His attention became focused on Africa; 'the map of Africa, in which I scarcely saw any but countries marked as desert or unknown, excited my attention more than any other'.

At the age of 16 he took a boat to Senegal. But after unsuccessful attempts to penetrate the interior he was forced to return to France due to illness and **Caillie goes** shortage of money. In 1824 Caillie was back in Africa. **native** He went native and lived with the Moors: by adopting their customs and learning Arabic, he hoped to pass as an Arab and therefore travel in the interior without fears of the taunts and attacks which had plagued Mungo Park. He called himself Abd Allahi which means 'Slave of God'.

After nine months Caillie returned to St Louis, Senegal, and then moved down the coast to Freetown, Sierra Leone, where he found work in an indigo factory. Nobody showed interest in his proposal to go to Timbuktu. Undeterred he saved 2000 francs — 'this treasure seemed to me to be sufficient to carry me all over the world' — and in March 1827 he set off alone from Freetown bound for Timbuktu.

Dead or alive

Before his departure Caillie had heard that the Geographical Society of Paris had offered a prize amounting to around 10,000 francs to the first person to reach Timbuktu and return. 'I said to myself: Dead or alive, it shall be mine, and my sister shall receive it'. A passion to succeed for his crippled sister Celeste to whom he was devoted combined with 'visions of glory, and patriotism' were further incentives to spur the already determined Rene Caillie onto his goal.

Having converted his savings into gold, silver and various knickknacks which he could barter, Caillie — unbeknown to anybody — headed to the Rio Nunez, a journey which took him nine days from Freetown. Here, about half way between the River Sierra Leone and River Gambia, nobody would recognise him. Disguised as an Arab he claimed that he was an Egyptian and that Bonaparte's forces had captured him when he was young and taken him to France. His master had brought him to Senegal and later granted him his freedom. He now was on his way home to Egypt. This story accounted for any holes in Caillie's knowledge of Arab customs and language and also his alleged descent explained his features and swarthy, light brown complexion.

The 'Egyptian' Heads East

People were continually leaving from Rio Nunez for the interior and Caillie soon joined a small group heading for Timbuktu. On the day of departure they passed the graves of Major Peddie and members of the ill-fated expedition who had died 11 years before in their attempt to reach the mouth of the Niger. Caillie remembered: 'I was seized with an involuntary shudder at the thought that the same fate perhaps awaited me'. They continued eastwards for several weeks; sometimes the locals, particularly the Fulani, were suspicious of the Frenchman's 'Arab' origins. But he managed to convince the dubious with his story, occasionally to the extent that they would hold this 'Arab' in awe and insist on rubbing his legs to relieve his tiredness.

Caillie had to be particularly cautious when he took notes; one of his guides, Lamfia, kept a sharp eye on him, but so as to prevent detection the Frenchman put a piece of paper on a page of his open Koran and pretended to recite passages as he wrote.

The Battle Against Illness

On 11 June Caillie reached the River Niger at Kouroussa, having walked the whole distance from Rio Nunez. Suffering from fever, the tremendous heat and general tiredness, he plodded on downstream to Kankan and then southeast to a village called Time, where his worsening condition finally got the better of him and he collapsed. An old Negro woman took care of him, but as his foot was sore and swollen he decided not to travel with any of the caravans until after the rains. Caillie only narrowly survived the wet season; for a month severe illness confined him to his damp hut.

The Frenchman, normally reticent about his hardships, wrote the following about an attack of scurvy he suffered: 'I soon experienced all the horror of that dreadful disease. The roof of my mouth became quite bare, a part of the bone exfoliated and fell away, and my teeth seemed ready to fall out of their sockets. I feared my brain would be affected by the agonising pains I felt in my head, and I was more **Praying for death** than a fortnight without sleep. ... Alone, in the interior of a wild country, stretched on damp ground, with no pillow but the leather bag which contained my luggage, with no medicine ... I was soon reduced to a skeleton ... One thought alone absorbed my mind — that of Death. I wished for it, and prayed for it to God.'

At the beginning of January 1828 Caillie joined a small party heading for Djenne. The rains were over and he had recovered sufficiently to travel. Caillie was greatly indebted to the kind woman who had looked after him for over five months, and without whom he would certainly have died.

By Pirogue from Djenne to Kabara

Two months after his departure he arrived at Djenne. Ironically he became a guest of the Moors and was befriended by the town's sheikh who arranged his passage to Timbuktu.

Caillie spent less than a fortnight in Djenne; he was impressed with this wealthy bustling market town, though he deplored the selling of human beings. On 23 March he boarded a 30-metre pirogue which was carrying food and slaves to Timbuktu. The voyage proved to be far from a pleasure ride. The master of the boat treated the strange 'Arab' passenger like one of the slaves and made him suffer their poor diet and sleeping conditions. After a week Caillie became sick; he was allocated a place in a cabin but there was not even room to stretch his legs. At a rate of 3 kms an hour they slowly headed northeast towards the desert.

The country through which this stretch of the Niger ran did not impress Caillie — 'Here the immense monotonous plains on all sides fatigues the eye of the traveller'. They were now entering Tuareg territory. These desert nomads wandered along the banks of the river on their camels and demanded taxes from the boats' masters. On such occasions Caillie had to remain below deck for fear that if the Tuaregs saw him they may think he was a Moor — therefore wealthy — and consequently demand more tribute. As it was, they seemed to have exacted whatever they wanted, whenever they wanted.

Tuareg extortions

After about four weeks the boat eventually arrived at Kabara and Caillie, who had been hiding from the Tuaregs below deck, wrote: 'About one o'clock pm we arrived at the port of Cabra [Kabara], and I was informed that I might quit my prison ... The river forms a large marshy island, which must be flooded during the inundations. Across these immense marshes is discovered the village or little town of Cabra, situated on a small hill ... A little canal leads to this village; but small boats only can enter the port. If the canal were cleared of the grass and nenuphars which choke the passage, vessels of twenty-five tons burthen might go up it in all seasons'.

Caillie had to transfer to a small canoe which took him to Kabara. Today the situation is much the same, but on a larger scale: the canal now cleared of the various grasses can support the large steamers, like the *Kankou Moussa*, during the high water months; however during the dry season passengers have to disembark onto a pirogue and then travel up the canal to Kabara.

Nobody took any notice of Caillie, as they believed him to be a Moor. That night he spent in Kabara and the following morning slaves of the influential Sidi Abdallahi Chebir took the 'Egyptian' to see their master in Timbuktu, who had already been informed that this stranger was a friend of the Sheikh of Djenne.

A Mass of Ill-looking Houses Built of Earth
By sunset on 20 April 1828 Caillie had fulfilled his dreams: 'We arrived safely at Timbuctoo, just as the sun was touching the horizon ... On entering this mysterious city, which is an object of curiosity and research to civilised nations of Europeans, I experienced an indescribable satisfaction ... With what gratitude did I return thanks to Heaven, for the happy result that attended my enterprise'.

Having thanked God profusely Caillie continued: 'This duty being ended I looked around and found that the sight before me did not answer my expectations. I had formed a totally different idea of the grandeur and wealth of Timbuctoo.' All he could see was 'a mass of ill looking houses built of earth'. The next day he 'took a turn round the city', but if the Frenchman had hoped that his first impressions of the celebrated Timbuktu were false, and that his 2400-km journey (two-thirds of it on foot) would in fact be rewarded with a splendid metropolis, then sadly he was to be disappointed once again on his second viewing.

The 'Egyptian' guest was treated with kindness and to his request to stay in Timbuktu a fortnight his host replied 'You may remain here longer than a fortnight, if you please. You will gratify me by so doing; you shall want for nothing'. People were sympathetic towards him because he claimed that he had been a slave of the Christians. But he feared that his true identity might be discovered: 'I could not repress a feeling of apprehension, lest, should I be discovered, I may be doomed to a fate more horrible than death — slavery'. And about Timbuktu Caillie concluded: 'In a word, everything had a dull appearance'.

What struck Caillie — as it did other early visitors to the city — was that Timbuktu was 'created solely by the wants of commerce, and destitute of every resource except that what its accidental position as a place of exchange affords'. Timbuktu was a market place in the desert, a meeting place for middlemen.

The Tuaregs had virtual control of Timbuktu; though they did not actually live in the city, they bullied the inhabitants into paying tribute and threatened that they would sever trading links if monies were not forthcoming. 'The house of my host Sidi', Caillie wrote 'was constantly infested with Tooariks and Arabs. These people visit Timbuctoo for the sole purpose of extorting from the inhabitants what they call presents, but what might be more properly called forced contributions'.

With all these people around Caillie had little opportunity to write; however, after a few days he was given a house of his own near where Laing had lived. Here in privacy he managed to make notes on the architecture, the local tribes, the slave trade and other aspects of Timbuktu.

The Desert Crossing

Two weeks after his arrival in Timbuktu, Caillie joined a caravan heading north. Sidi Abdallahi tried to persuade him to stay longer, but the young Frenchman was eager to push on and on 4 May, laden with presents from his generous host, he departed from Timbuktu. A few days later they passed the place where Laing had been murdered and soon after they reached Arawan, which like Timbuktu was an important desert market and meeting point. Caillie had to wait here for the caravan to assemble before the desert crossing. He hated Arawan: 'I never saw such a dull place'. He was abused by people who suspected he was a Christian; the water was warm and brackish and hot, violent sandstorms blew. 'I was unable to comprehend,' Caillie concluded, 'how the mere love of gain could induce these people to live for twelve or fifteen years in such a dreadful country'.

On 19 May the caravan, consisting of 1400 camels carrying mainly gold, ivory, gum, ostrich feathers and cloth left Arawan. A short distance on were the only wells for over 320 kms. Everybody seemed apprehensive about the prospective crossing. 'A gloom hung on all faces ... A boundless horizon already expanded before us, and we could distinguish nothing but an immense plain of shining sand, and over it burning sky. At this sight the camels uttered long moans, the slaves became sullen and silent, and, with their eyes towards heaven, they appeared to be tortured with regret for loss of their country'. Only Caillie, 'radiant with hope and joy' was excited about entering the desert and becoming the first European to cross the vast expanse via this route.

Once they were in this harsh wilderness the optimistic Frenchman quickly lost the smile on his face. He was soon struck by excruciating pains of thirst. 'I thought of nothing but water — rivers, streams, rivulets, were the only ideas that presented themselves to my mind during this burning fever'. After a week of agonising travel the caravan reached the Telig wells which were half a day's journey east of the Taudeni salt mines. So desperate was Caillie to drink that he thrust his head amongst the camels and with them eagerly slurped up the brackish warm water. The worst stretch of the crossing was over; from now on the wells were more frequent.

But the conditions were still perilous, as the skeletons along the route testified. Caillie's thirst was rarely satisfied, his stomach was revolted by boiled rice and camel flesh; mirages taunted him; jibes from fellow travellers — one of them wanted to sell him as a slave — added to his misery and the sandstorms and the intense heat did not alleviate his horrible situation.

Homecoming

Towards the end of June the caravan gradually moved out of the desert into semi arid scrubland, and a month later they had reached 'the beautiful and majestic palm trees of the country of Tafilet'. The villages, pastures and groves of trees were proof that the desert now lay behind them.

From the town of Ghourland in Tafilet Caillie headed north over the Atlas mountains to Fez, which he reached on 12 August 1828. Weak and in a poor condition he hired a guide and mule and headed west to Meknes and then on to Rabat and finally Tangier. Caillie had travelled 4500 kms across Africa.

In Tangier he met the French representative and related his remarkable story. That night at the consulate he threw off his disguise for the first time in 18 months and 'after returning thanks to Almighty God, I lay down upon a good bed, rejoicing in my escape from the society of men debased by ignorance and fanaticism... I believed myself to be in a dream and asked if it was true that I might soon be restored to my country, or whether this enchanting hope was but a delusion'. Caillie did not have to wait long; his host arranged for a boat to pick him up and take him to France. On 28 September, Caillie, suffering from fever, set sail for Toulon. Ten days later he set foot on his native soil.

'I believed myself to be in a dream'

Honour and controversy

Rene Caillie, the first European to reach Timbuktu and return home alive, received the award of 10,000 francs plus a pension of 6000 francs and he was made a Chevalier of the Legion of Honour. But controversy surrounded his heroic achievement. Some disbelieved he had ever reached Timbuktu, others criticised him for changing his religion. This hurt Caillie and in the concluding paragraph of his *Travels Through Central Africa to Timbuctoo* he wrote: 'I must confess that these unjust attacks have affected me more sensibly than all the hardships, fatigues, and privations which I have encountered in the interior of Africa'.

In 1830 Caillie married and bought a farm in Mauzé near where his crippled sister lived. After a few years he was longing to go back to Africa; he tried to get support, but none was forthcoming. On 17 May 1838 the Frenchman who had bluffed the fanatical Arabs with his disguise and survived some of the harshest conditions on earth, died of consumption aged 38. His dream of returning to Africa was never fulfilled.

HEINRICH BARTH: THE THIRD EUROPEAN TO REACH TIMBUKTU

In 1849 James Richardson, who had already spent time in the Sahara, asked the Foreign Secretary, Lord Palmerston, to sponsor an expedition into the interior. The purpose of the mission was to study how slavery could be abolished and to try and raise the Africans up to the level of European civilisation. Palmerston agreed to provide aid, so long as a recognised geographer joined the party. Heinrich Barth, a former Berlin University student, was eventually selected and many believe that he became the greatest and most professional of the 19th C African explorers. He had excellent credentials. Born in Hamburg in 1821, he was strong in mind and body, healthy, 196 cms tall, and fluent in German, English, French, Italian and Arabic. He was very well read, was an Egyptologist and he had travelled in North Africa before. He was also extremely meticulous — as is evident from his long and detailed *Travels in North and Central Africa*.

Perhaps the greatest of the 19th C explorers

Despite being just the man they were looking for, the British made Barth contribute £200 to his own expenses; the German's condition was that his role only required him to explore the middle Niger and Benin area.

A young German lecturer, Dr Adolf Overweg, was the third member of the expedition.

The Expedition Gathers

Barth and Overweg arrived in Tripoli around the middle of January 1850; Richardson, accompanied by his wife, joined them six weeks later. Their host there was Frederick Warrington, the British Consul, whose father had helped Clapperton, Laing and other adventurers. At the beginning of April the party headed south to Murzuk, the capital of Fezzan, and having stayed there a month they pushed on to Ghat.

The characters of the three explorers were very different and during the course of the journey an element of friction built up between them. Richardson, the most senior in age and position, was rather self righteous and, to the impatient young Barth, he seemed coddled and cautious. Overweg played second fiddle to Barth.

On one occasion just before they reached Ghat, Barth, irritated that nobody would accompany him up a particularly desolate hill, set off by himself 'determined ... to visit the mountain at any cost'. Overweg and a guide tried to catch up with him, but exhausted and parched with thirst they were forced to return to camp. Barth, who had got lost, later wrote about the incident in his journal: 'Having lain down for an hour or two, after it became quite dark I arose from the ground, and, looking around me, descried to my great joy a large fire SW down the valley, and, hoping that it might be that of my companions, I fired a pistol, as the only means of communicating with them, and listened as the sound rolled along, feeling sure that it would reach their ears; but no answer was returned. All remained silent ... I fired a second time — yet no answer. I lay down in resignation, committing my life to the care of the Merciful One ... Restless and in a high fever, I tossed about on the ground, looking with anxiety and fear for the dawn of the next day ... The sun that I had half longed for, half looked forward to with terror, at last rose. My condition, as the heat went on increasing, became more dreadful, and I crawled around, changing every moment my position, in order to enjoy the little shade afforded by the leafless branches of the tree. About noon there was, of course, scarcely a spot of shade left — only enough for my head — and I suffered greatly from the pangs of thirst, although I sucked a little of my blood till I became senseless, and fell into a sort of delirium'.

Thirst and near-death

By chance a passing Tuareg found the unconscious Barth and returned him to his camp. Richardson, amazed that his colleague had not died, wrote: 'Twenty eight hours without water in the desert! Our people could scarcely credit that he was alive; for their saying is that no one can live more than twelve hours when lost in the desert during the heats of summer'.

Renounce Christianity or Die

From Ghat the expedition pushed south. Along the way they were attacked by nomads, and at first it seemed that the three Christians would be slaughtered because they refused to renounce their religion. Barth wrote: 'Our own people [guides and servants] were so firmly convinced that, as we stoutly refused to change our religion, though only for a day or two, we should immediately suffer death ... We were sitting silently in the tent, with the inspiring consciousness of going to our fate in a manner worthy alike of our religion and of the nation in whose name we were travelling among these barbarous tribes, when Mr Richardson interrupted the silence which prevailed with these words: "Let us talk a little. We must die; what is the use of sitting so mute?" For some minutes death seemed really to hover over our heads, but the awful moment passed by ... when ... the benevolent and kind hearted Sliman rushed into our tent, and with a most sincere sympathy stammered out the few words, "You are not to die"'.

Though they escaped death their baggages were plundered.

By the end of September 1850 they had reached Tintellust and from here it was agreed that Barth alone should visit Agadez which lay some 200 kms to the southwest. He set off on 4 October and six days later, disguised as a Tuareg, he arrived at the famous Saharan oasis. On 5 November Barth was back in Tinteggana Valley, just south of Tintellust, where he met up with Richardson and Overweg — who it seems were rather jealous of his enlightening Agadez journey.

The expedition headed south and eventually with the desert behind them the three explorers split up once again. Richardson wrote: 'We took leave one of the other with some emotion, for in Central Africa three travellers who part and take divergent routes can scarcely count on all meeting together again'. Richardson had reason to doubt whether he would be a part of a further rendezvous: 'The fatigue is killing', he had already written in his journal, 'I must save my strength. I am very weak'. Barth had commented, 'He [Richardson] was quite incapable of bearing the heat of the sun, for which reason he always carried an umbrella, instead of accustoming himself to it by degrees'.

Richardson's umbrella

It was the early part of January 1851 when Richardson travelled to Zinder, Overweg to Maradi and the Hausa kingdom of Gobir, and Barth to Tasawa — 'the first place of Negroland proper' he came across — and Kano. The idea was that they would all meet up again at Kukawa in Lake Chad in April. Barth was impressed by the artisans and trade of Kano and after staying here five weeks he set off for Lake Chad.

The Deaths of Richardson and Overweg

Enroute he heard the sad news that Richardson had died between Zinder and Kukawa. He noted: 'My way of looking at things was not quite the same as that of my late companion, and we therefore had little differences; but I esteemed him highly for the deep sympathy which he felt for the native African, and deeply lamented his death'.

Barth arrived at Kukawa on 2 April but it was not until May that Overweg, completely exhausted and tormented by fever, turned up. Barth himself in good health, was rather irratated by his countryman's frail condition. He decided to push south and explore the upper reaches of the River Benin, while Overweg stayed behind and surveyed the shores of Lake Chad from the boat, the *Lord Palmerston*, which they had carried across the desert for this purpose.

The two men gathered a lot of information over the following 16 months. Barth's work — which included charting the upper reaches of the River Benue — was particularly impressive and set a precedent which has hardly been matched by modern experts in north and central Nigerian field studies. Among his many adventures there was one gruesome tale of how he joined a slave raid (so as to get first-hand information on this horrific trade — which was after all the original purpose of the mission). Over 500 slaves were rounded up and 'not less than 170 full grown men

Barth joins a slave raid

were mercilessly slaughtered in cold blood, the greater part of them allowed to bleed to death, a leg having been severed from the body'.

By mid-August 1852 the two German explorers were reunited in Kukawa. Overweg became sicker than ever before, and then one day he became delirious, jumping up repeatedly in a raging fit of madness and rushing against trees and into the fire. He died shortly after; he was 29 years old.

In Sight of the River

Barth was now alone but he still felt strong and was confident that he would make more discoveries and return home safely. After Richardson's death he had received orders from Palmerston to go to Timbuktu instead of attempting a journey to East Africa. With this in mind Barth headed west to Say, just below Niamey, on the River Niger.

He recorded: *'Sunday, June 19th*. We were now close to the Niger; and I was justified in indulging in the hope that I might the next day behold with my own eyes that great river of Western Africa, which has caused such intense curiosity in Europe, and the upper part of the large eastern branch of which I myself discovered.

'Monday, June 20th. Elated with such feelings, I set out the next morning, at an early hour; and after a march of a little less than two hours, through a rocky wilderness covered with dense bushes, I obtained the first sight of the river, and in less than an hour more, during which I was in constant sight of this noble spectacle, I reached the place of embarkation, opposite the town of Say.

Noble spectacle   'In a noble unbroken stream, though here, where it has become contracted, only about 700 yards broad, hemmed in on this side by a rocky bank of from twenty to thirty feet in elevation, the great river of Western Africa (whose name, under whatever form it may appear, whether Dhiúlibá, Máyo, Eghírrëu, I'sa, Kwára, or Báki-n-rúwa, means nothing but "the river", and which therefore may well continue to be called the Niger) was gliding along, in a NNE and SSW direction, with a moderate current of about three miles an hour. On the flatter shore opposite, a large town [Say] was spreading out, the low rampart and huts of which were picturesquely overtopped by numbers of slender dum palms'.

Perilous Months in Timbuktu

Instead of taking a boat up river to Timbuktu Barth decided to cross the Niger and travel overland via Hombori to Kabara. His greatest obstacle was the floods, but he slowly plodded on and after recrossing the river he reached Kabara on 7 September 1853.

Disguising himself as an Arab, once in Timbuktu Barth came under the guardian wing of Sheikh El Backay. The German, the third explorer to reach this city, stayed here and in the surrounding countryside eight perilous months. It was not long before his Christian identity was revealed and from that time his life was constantly at risk; many, in particular the fanatical Fulani who claimed rights to the city, wanted him killed, and it was only El Backay's protection which prevented them from fulfilling their wish. For his own safety Barth stayed inside his house and when necessary displayed his small arsenal of pistols so as to frighten off potential assailants.

Even so, pressure to get rid of him increased and El Backay thought it wise if the two of them moved out to his family encampment, which lay about 16 kms northeast of Timbuktu. Whenever he thought it safe Barth would visit the city, and though he spent longer in Timbuktu than Laing or Caillie his freedom of movement was not as great as that of his two predecessors. All the same he gathered a lot of information about the city and managed to quote extensively from the famous *Tarikh* (the historical records of Timbuktu which he had had access to earlier in his journey). The following is an extract from his account of the city; surprisingly little has changed since his day.

Timbuktu little changed since Barth's day

'The circumference of the city at the present time I reckon at a little more than two miles and a half; but it may approach closely to three miles, taking into account some of the projecting angles. Although of only small size, Timbuktu may well be called a city — medína — in comparison with the frail dwelling-places all over Negroland. At present it is not walled. Its former wall, which seems never to have been of great magnitude, and was rather more of the nature of a rampart, was destroyed by the Fúlbe [Fulani] on their first entering the place in the beginning of the year 1826. The town is laid out partly in rectangular, partly in winding streets, or, as they are called here,

PLAN OF TIMBU'KTU.

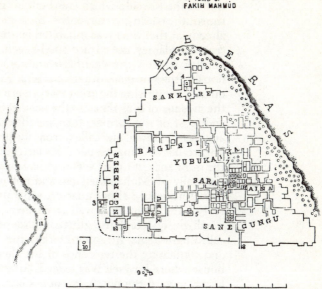

100 200 300 400 500 600 700 800 900 1000 1100 1200 1300 1400 1500 1600 yards.

1. House of the Sheikh A'hmed el Bakáy, with another house belonging to the same close by, and having in front of it a small square, where he has established a "msíd," or place of prayer for his pupils, several of whom pass the night here.
2. House belonging likewise to the sheikh, where I myself was lodged, the ground-plan of which I have given above.
3. Great mosque, "Gíngere (Jíngeré, or Zángeré) bér, Jám'a el kebíra," begun by Mansa Músa, King of Melle, A.D. 1327, and forming, for many centuries, the centre of the Mohammedan quarter.
4. Mosque Sankoré, in the quarter Sánkoré, which is generally regarded as the oldest quarter of the town. The mosque has five naves, and is 120 feet long by 80 feet wide.
5. Mosque Sidi Yáhia, much smaller than the two other large mosques.
6. Great market-place, or Yúbu.
7. Butchers' market, where in former times the palace, or "M'a-duk," or M'a-dugu, is said to have been situated.   8. Gate leading to Kábara.
9. Well, surrounded by a small plantation of date-trees.
10. Another well, with a small garden belonging to Mohammed el 'Aish.
11. Spot in a shallow valley, up to which point small boats ascended from the Niger, in the winter 1853–4.

"tijeráten", which are not paved, but for the greater part consist of hard sand and gravel, and some of them have a sort of gutter in the middle. Besides the large and the small market there are few open areas, except a small square in front of the mosque of Yáhia, called Túmbutu-bóttema…

'The only remarkable public buildings in the town are the three large mosques: the Jíngeré-bér, built by Mansa Músa; the mosque of Sánkoré, built at an early period at the expense of a wealthy woman; and the

211

mosque Sídi Yáhia, built at the expense of a kádhi of the town... Of the royal palace, or M'a-dugu, wherein the kings of Songhay used to reside occasionally, as well as the Kasbah, which was built in later times, in the southeastern quarter, or the "Sane-gungu," which already at that time was inhabited by the merchants from Ghadámes, not a trace is to be seen. Besides this quarter, which is the wealthiest, and contains the best houses, there are six other quarters, viz, Yúbu, the quarter comprising the great market-place (yúbu) and the mosque of Sídi Yáhia, to the west of Sane-gungu; and west of the former, forming the southwestern angle of the town, and called, from the great mosque, Jíngeré-bér or Zángeré-bér. This latter quarter, from the most ancient times, seems to have been inhabited especially by Mohammedans, and not unlikely may have formed a distinct quarter, separated from the rest of the town by a wall of its own. Toward the north, the quarter Sane-gungu is bordered by the one called Sara-káina, meaning literally the "little town" and containing the residence of the sheikh, and the house where I myself was lodged. Attached to Sara-káina, toward the north, is Yúbu-káina, the quarter containing the "little market," which is especially used as a butchers' market. Bordering both on Jíngeré-bér and Yúbu-káina is the quarter Bagíndi, occupying the lowest situation in the town, and stated by the inhabitants to have been flooded entirely in the great inundation which took place in 1640. From this depression in the ground, the quarter of Sán-koré, which forms the northernmost angle of the city, rises to a considerable elevation in such a manner that the mosque of Sán-koré, which seems to occupy its ancient site and level, is at present situated in a deep hollow — an appearance which seems to prove that this elevation of the ground is caused by the accumulation of rubbish, in consequence of the repeated ruin which seems to have befallen this quarter pre-eminently, as being the chief stronghold of the native Songhay. The slope which this quarter forms toward the northeastern end in some spots exceeds eighty feet.

'The whole number of the settled inhabitants of the town amounts to about 13,000, while the floating population during the months of the greatest traffic and intercourse, especially from November to

January, may amount on an average to 5000, and under favorable circumstances to as many as 10,000.'

The politics of Timbuktu were complicated and though most people wanted the Christian to leave (as the months drew on Barth became more frustrated, depressed and desperately keen to be on his way) it actually proved quite difficult for the explorer to get permission to start his journey. In addition he suffered from recurring bouts of illness and the fact that from 'a sanitary point of view Timbuktu is no wise to be reckoned among the more favoured places of these regions', did not help matters.

Farewells

On 17 May 1853 Barth was eventually able to depart. Accompanied by El Backay he travelled along the north and east bank of the River Niger as far as Gao. As it was the dry season it would have been difficult or impossible to travel even by a small boat; this gave Barth an opportunity to write a thorough account of the river at low water.

The German was irritated by the party's leisurely pace, but it seems that this leg of the journey was quite pleasant and punctuated by several lighthearted incidents, like the occasion when he was visited by the daughter of a local chief: 'She was one of the finest women that I saw in this country ... Her features were remarkable for their soft expression and regularity, but her person rather inclined to corpulency, which is highly esteemed by the Tawarek [Tuareg]. Seeing that I took an interest in her, she half-jokingly proposed that I should marry her; and I declared myself ready to take her with me if one of my rather weak camels should be found able to support her weight. As a mark of distinction I presented her with a looking-glass, which I was accustomed to give to the most handsome woman in an encampment, the rest receiving nothing but needles'.

A fine woman though inclined to corpulency

On 20 June they reached Gao and stayed in this former Songhai capital for just short of a month. Here Barth bid an emotional farewell to his faithful friend El Backay: 'This was the day [9 July] when I had to separate from the person whom, among all the people with whom I had come in contact in the course of my long journey, I esteemed the most highly, and whom, in all but his dilatory habits and phlegmatic indifference, I had found a most excellent and trustworthy man'.

The Homeward Journey

Barth is 'found'

Barth hurried onto Sakoto and then Kano. At the beginning of December he was on his way to Kukawa when 'I saw advancing towards me a person of strange aspect — a young man of very fair complexion, dressed in a tobe like the one I wore myself'. This 'person of strange aspect' was Edward Vogel, who had been sent by the Foreign Office to replace Richardson and look for Barth — who most people believed was already dead. He was the first white man Barth had encountered since the death of Overweg over two years before.

When he arrived in Kukawa, Barth found that his bags, which he had left here on his southward trip, had been plundered of their valuable articles. Consequently he had to wait until funds arrived before recrossing the desert to Tripoli. In May 1855 he finally embarked on the last leg of his journey and 'turned my back with great satisfaction upon those countries where I had spent five full years in incessant toil and exercise'.

It took Barth four months to cross the Sahara; he stayed in Tripoli only four days and on 6 September 1855 he was back in London. Barth had spent almost five and a half years in Africa and during that time he had travelled 16,000 kms.

Final Years

Popular with Arabs and Africans

Barth had been popular among the Arabs and Africans and it is interesting that a later adventurer, Emile Hourste, pretended that he was the great explorer's nephew and therefore 'was able to emerge safely from every situation'.

Barth justifiably received recognition and many important honours, including the Order of Bath from Queen Victoria. However he did not get popular acclaim, possibly because of the rather heavy style of

...less so with the British

his book, or possibly because he was German — albeit a representative of the British. He fell out with various institutions, such as the Royal Geographical Society, and returned to Germany where he was made President of the Berlin Geographical Society and a professor at Berlin University. But he became a frustrated recluse, dissatisfied with those around him, and eager to travel again (he tried to get money for a polar expedition, but without success). His spell in Africa had aged him and in 1865 Heinrich Barth died aged 44 years.

INDEX

In the index that follows, present-day places that are in the countries through which the route described in this Guide passes are identified as being in Nigeria (Na), Niger (N), Mali (M), Senegal (S) or Gambia (G). Places not in these countries, eg Tripoli, places of past importance, eg Songhai Empire, and areas or rivers which fall into more than one country, eg the River Niger, are not identified by country.

Note that the Arab prefixes *el* and *al* have not been taken into account for the purpose of alphabetisation.

NOTES

NOTES

NOTES

NOTES